THE FALSE INSPECTOR DEW

Secret

'The first impression... ...
Mauretania in the yea...
the Atlantic.... Lov...
setting ... so thorou...
fingertips a dozen facts to choose from at
any instant. Secret No. 1 of the charge that
powers his book.

Secret No. 2

Lovesey has devised a series of turn-around
surprises (who's murdered whom on this
racing liner, who's the detective even?) and
with each turn you get a new view of events
that fires your curiosity anew. . . . Secret
No. 2.

THE COMBINED RESULT IS THE SORT
OF BOOK THAT OUGHT TO BE A
BESTSELLER AND DESERVES TO BE.'

H. R. F. Keating, *The Times*

THE FALSE INSPECTOR DEW

Peter Lovesey

THE SHERIDAN
BOOK COMPANY

This edition published in 1994 by
The Sheridan Book Company

First published in Great Britain in 1982 by Macmillan London

Arrow paperback edition 1983
Random House, 20 Vauxhall Bridge Road, London SW1V 2SA

Mysterious Press edition 1988

Printed and bound in Great Britain by
Cox & Wyman Ltd, Reading, Berkshire

ISBN 1-85501-605-2

'Apart from the Jack the Ripper case,
I was never associated with what is
described as an unsolved murder.'

ex-Chief Inspector Walter Dew
I Caught Crippen (Blackie & Son, 1938)

FOREWORD

Sixty years have passed and no-one has explained the mystery of the false Inspector Dew.

It was confidently thought that the only scrap of evidence had been destroyed, shredded on the orders of the Commissioner of the Metropolitan Police. But Scotland Yard was unaware of the existence of another file. It was in the Cunard Company archives. It contained the statements of the captain and certain officers of the *Mauretania*. And it contained the crucial wireless message drafted by the captain and transmitted to the Cunard office at 9.30pm on 9 September, 1921, and telegraphed to Scotland Yard for information.

This reconstruction of the salient events begins the following morning, when the Commissioner picked the message off his desk.

PART ONE

The Tramp

SS MAURETANIA. 9 SEPT 1921.
REFERENCE SUSPICIOUS DEATH ON BOARD HAVE
INVITED CHIEF INSPECTOR DEW OF SCOTLAND
YARD TO INVESTIGATE.
A. H. ROSTRON, CAPTAIN.

Chief Inspector Dew. The Commissioner remembered Dew.
He was the man who had pulled in Dr Crippen. That was back
in 1910. He was damned sure Dew had quit the force the same
year.

He picked up a pencil. Under the message he wrote:

What's this tomfoolery? Comedians are your department.

Smiling to himself, he addressed it to his deputy.

The Deputy Commissioner was at Waterloo that day with
Charlie Chaplin. Two hundred constables with arms linked
were standing in support. Chaplin had come back to London
after nine years in America. He had gone there as a member of
the Karno troupe of music hall comedians. He was returning as
one of the world's most famous men. Thousands had gathered at
the station.

When the train steamed in, the Deputy Commissioner and his
senior men raced towards the compartment reserved for
Chaplin. They seized him like a prisoner and hustled him along
the platform. Beyond the barrier where the crowd was waiting,
the blue line stood firm. Chaplin was funneled into a waiting
limousine. Few people saw him.

The Deputy Commissioner in a police car drove ahead
towards the Ritz Hotel. In Piccadilly it was like Armistice Day
again. They took the back way through St James's into
Arlington Street.

Chaplin and a cousin sat white-faced in the Lanchester, the
doors locked and the windows up. Grinning faces pressed
against the glass. The cars inched forward. More police
materialised. Chaplin was ordered out. They had reached the
Ritz side entrance. He refused to use it. He was home in
triumph. As a lowly music hall performer, he. had often
dreamed of staying at the Ritz. The crowd had come to see him
take his place among the rich and famous, the little tramp
among the toffs. He announced that he would enter at the front.

The cars edged into Piccadilly. Chaplin got out and stood

waving on the running-board. The people surged towards him. The Deputy Commissioner was in despair. By some amazing gift of character or training, Chaplin controlled his public. He made a simple speech. They listened solemnly. They cheered. They let him go inside. But they would not disperse. A double line of traffic stood from Hyde Park Corner to Piccadilly Circus. Chaplin was in the Regal Suite. He had the windows opened. He gathered the carnations from a vase and threw them to the crowd. It was hours before the police could be withdrawn.

Late that night, the Deputy Commissioner came back to Scotland Yard. He had to clear his desk. He was hungry and his feet ached. He went swiftly through his correspondence. He read the wireless message and the Commissioner's droll comment: *Comedians are your department.* He did not smile.

Walter Dew was vivid in his memory. It was his opinion that Dew was not a great detective, despite his reputation. He had been careless over evidence. He had been far too tender-hearted. He had betrayed a lot of sympathy for the murderer Crippen. He had been lucky to convict him and he knew it. On the day that the appeal was lost, Walter Dew had left the force. He was only in his forties at the time. The Deputy Commissioner had never seen a man so glad to take his pension. Dew had gone to live in Worthing, on the coast. It was strange that he should turn up on an ocean liner, offering to assist with an investigation.

But Dew was an enigma. And at sea, the captain's word was law. It would be interesting to see if Chief Inspector Dew was equal to his legend.

What could Scotland Yard do now, except take note?

The Deputy Commissioner ticked the message, tossed it in a tray, dismissed it from his mind and went to find a taxi.

Next day a clerk consigned the message to a box-file.

The man who would become the false Inspector Dew was called Baranov. His life had been unexceptional until 7 May, 1915, when he was unwittingly involved in one of the notorious incidents of the first world war.

The water off the southern coast of Ireland was dead calm, and a pure, pellucid green. Reflected sunlight shimmered on the huge hull of the Cunard liner *Lusitania*, steaming towards the port of Queenstown with nearly two thousand passengers and crew and a secret cargo of two hundred and twenty tons of ammunition and sixty-six tons of the explosive pyroxylin. She had been instructed to divert into Queenstown following reports of a German U-boat in the channel ahead.

At 2.10pm the lookout in the crow's-nest saw a clear white track cleaving the water on the starboard side. From its line and speed it could only be the trail of bubbles of compressed air emitted by the driving motor of a torpedo. It was certain to hit the ship. He shouted to the bridge.

Captain William Turner had taken lunch on the bridge as usual. He was a veteran of the days of sail, with no liking for the social life aboard a modern passenger liner. On the previous evening he had steeled himself to join the first class passengers for dinner. After it, in the smoking room, they had staged a veritable inquisition. They had a spokesman called Baranov, a veteran music hall performer who was travelling back to England with his son. Baranov senior had his leg in plaster. His manner was aggressive. He had demanded to be told why the cabin stewards had blacked out the portholes, why the lifeboats had been swung out on their davits and why the officers were stopping passengers from lighting their cigars on deck. Captain Turner had explained that these were routine precautions in a war zone. This had not appeared to reassure Baranov.

The torpedo struck the *Lusitania* slightly forward of the bridge. A mass of water, smoke and wreckage blocked the captain's view. He shouted to the quartermaster to close all watertight doors that were not already secured. He checked the instruments for evidence of fire or flood below. The ship was listing fifteen degrees.

A second, heavier explosion rocked the *Lusitania*. It was not another torpedo. It was the secret cargo destroying her from within. Captain Turner gave the order to lower the boats, and then was horrified to feel a coolness on his face through the smoke and dust. Incredibly, the ship was still under way. So long as she was moving, the lifeboats could not be safely lowered.

Third Engineer George Little heard the captain order full speed astern to halt the onward movement of the ship. He felt sick with fear. The last inspection of the valves in the low pressure turbine had revealed a defect. The captain had been warned that full speed astern could cause a dangerous feedback of steam. Little had no choice. He obeyed the order. There was an immediate blowback, fracturing a main steam pipe. Stunned and frightened, Little reacted by throwing the engine room controls back to full steam ahead. The blowback had reduced the head of steam, but the *Lusitania* still made way steadily.

Lunch is never hurried on an ocean liner, and many first class passengers were in the white and gold Louis Seize dining saloon when the torpedo struck. Walter Baranov was with his crippled father at a table near the entrance staircase. He led the movement to the deck to see what had happened. The foredeck was already under water and it was obvious that the ship would sink. He forced his way back to his father. Baranov senior was an acrobat. Touring in America, he had fallen from the highwire and sustained a compound fracture of the leg. The son, an army dentist, had been granted leave to help him back to England. The father's crutches slowed them. They were the last to leave the saloon.

On the boat deck things were happening that would haunt the dreams of survivors for their remaining lives. The listing of the ship had swung the starboard lifeboats out of reach, so there was a rush to occupy the lifeboats on the port side. When Staff Captain Anderson, the officer responsible, assembled his men at their stations, the eleven conventional lifeboats and the thirteen collapsibles underneath them were crammed with frightened passengers, up to eighty in each. As a precaution against a dangerous inward swing, each boat was fitted with a chain that linked the inboard gunwale to the edge of the deck. Third Officer Albert Bestic asked for help to swing the first boat outwards, over the ship's side. It weighed almost five tons when unladen; the human cargo was as heavy again.

As the volunteers began to push, someone released the chain.

The boat lurched inwards over the helpless volunteers and crashed onto the people sitting below it in the collapsible. The wreckage of two lifeboats and a hundred screaming injured slid forward with the tilt of the ship and smashed against the superstructure of the bridge.

Within seconds the carnage was repeated with the next boat. Even as officers screamed at passengers to climb out, three more lifeboats hit the deck and careered into the bloody heap of splintered wood and bodies.

Cabin stewardess Katherine Barton was below on B Deck checking that the first class passengers were all alerted. Many of the doors stood open. The richest passenger on board, Alfred Vanderbilt, had vacated number 8, and the theatre producer, Carl Frohman, was out of 10, but there was a sound from 12, the stateroom of Mrs Delia Hawkman, a New York socialite. Stewardess Barton looked in and saw someone at the dressing table. It was not Mrs Hawkman. It was a stocky young man in a dark suit. He was in the act of filling his pockets from an open jewel case. Stewardess Barton challenged him. The looter turned and swung the jewel case at her head.

In the same corridor, cabin steward Hamilton was checking the odd-numbered staterooms, unaware of what had happened. He heard a door slam and saw a young man he did not recognize come towards him. Hamilton reminded the young man to take a life jacket, but he pushed past without a word and sprinted towards the companionway. Hamilton resumed his check. He reached the end and realised that stewardess Barton had stopped checking the other side. He went back and found the door of stateroom 12 was locked. She was inside on the floor, insensible, blood running from her mouth and nose. Both Hamilton and Barton were among the survivors.

On the boat deck, Staff Captain Anderson had succeeded in persuading sufficient passengers to vacate a lifeboat to manhandle it over the rails. As it was lowered to the level of the promenade deck below, more people tried to climb aboard. Those inside had to fight them off with oars. Someone in the boat shouted upwards to the crewmen to lower away. Something went wrong. The fall supporting the stern of the lifeboat gave way. The boat upended, pitching everyone into the sea. It swung a moment there, and then the bow fall broke. The five-ton lifeboat plunged onto the people in the water.

Three more lifeboats splintered on the projecting rivets of the *Lusitania*'s port flank. They broke up and sank.

Staff Captain Anderson was one of the *Lusitania*'s dead.

Isaac Lehmann, a New Yorker, had collected a revolver from his stateroom. He went to a lifeboat that had not been launched. It was packed with passengers. A seaman stood, axe in hand, waiting to cut the falls as the deck sank to the level of the sea. Lehmann insisted that the boat was launched without delay. He drew his gun and threatened to shoot to kill. The seaman freed the snubbing chain and the boat plunged onto the collapsible below it and slid, like the others, down the slope of the deck. Some thirty people were crushed to death. Lehmann survived.

A number of passengers and crew declined to join the scramble for the lifeboats. Alfred Vanderbilt and Mr and Mrs Carl Frohman were seen in the entrance hall tying life jackets to the basketwork cots in which several babies had been sleeping in the nursery after lunch. Vanderbilt, the Frohmans and the infants in the cots were drowned.

Some fifteen minutes after the first explosion, the bow of the *Lusitania* struck the granite ocean floor. The stern pivoted high above the water, the propellors still revolving. Hundreds were still aboard. Some worked hopelessly to free more lifeboats. Others waited calmly to step into the waves as the stern settled. Among them were Walter Baranov and his crippled father. They kept afloat until they were helped aboard a lifeboat.

A boiler burst. One of the four huge funnels heeled over in a cloud of steam and sparks. Seconds later, the ship itself was gone. Its captain, William Turner, remained clinging to the navigation bridge until the water swept him clear. He was one of the survivors. As he arrived for the subsequent Board of Trade inquiry, he was handed a white feather.

In all, the survivors from the *Lusitania* numbered 764. Many of these had fallen or jumped or stepped into the water and climbed aboard the half-dozen lifeboats successfully launched from the starboard side. Others stayed afloat by clinging to wreckage. One officer and his mother climbed aboard the grand piano from the main lounge.

1201 lives were lost. For days after, bodies were found on the Irish beaches. The search was furthered by rewards from the Cunard Company and the relatives. £1 was offered for each body found; £2 for each American; £1000 for Alfred Vanderbilt.

PART TWO

Limelight

The next stage in the making of the false Inspector started in the spring of 1921.

In the dental chair, Alma Webster focused on Mr Baranov's right hand and ignored the probe he was holding. She studied the crop of fine, fair hairs on his fingers and followed their course along the back of his hand as far as the shirtcuff. On his wrist they sprouted more thickly and wildly.

She loved him to distraction.

This was the third appointment in a course of treatment that would last at least six weeks. 'Not that you need be concerned about the state of your teeth,' Mr Baranov had explained. 'For a young lady of – what are you? – twenty-four? – they are in fine condition. A cavity here and there, that's all. No extractions will be necessary. I believe in conserving teeth, Miss Webster, not removing them. I work slowly, and I make no apology for that. It will encroach on your valuable time, but you have my word that you will not be disappointed with the result.'

Alma did not begrudge a moment of her valuable time. Her dislike of dental treatment had practically evaporated when she had first stepped into the surgery in Eaton Place. It was furnished like a room in the Winter Palace, with a glittering chandelier, a log fire blazing in a massive brick and brass hearth, gilt-framed portraits of wild Cossacks on black hunters, a golden Afghan carpet and leather armchairs made for people the size of Chaliapin. There was an aroma of Balkan cigarettes. Mr Baranov had been writing at an ebony desk. He had risen at once, smiled, and given a slight bow. As their eyes had met, Alma had felt a pricking under her skin, the kindling of something strange.

She had not corrected Mr Baranov about her age. She was twenty-eight.

At fifteen she had discovered the romantic novels of Ouida. They had become her most treasured possessions. She had been amazed to find how much she had in common with Vere Herbert, the heroine of *Moths*. She, too, had a passion for books and scenery. She, too, was quite unconscious of her own great beauty. She, too, had a feckless mother who scarcely knew her. And she saw with startling clarity that there were only two sorts of men in the world – paragons like the brilliant, vulnerable tenor, Corréze, and brutes like Prince Zouroff, intent on having their unspeakable way with hapless girls. It had taken writing of great force to challenge Ouida in Alma's affection, but eventually Ethel M. Dell succeeded with the climax of *The Way of an Eagle*, when Nick proposed to Muriel on a mountain peak and a meteor fell from Heaven.

That was before the war. The war had changed everything. She had stopped reading novels. She had taken a job. Like the women working in munitions factories, she had cut her hair. She had had it bobbed. She was not herself employed in a munitions factory, because there were none within a bus-ride of her home. She had dealt with correspondence to the *Richmond and Twickenham Times*. When she had got home after having her hair bobbed, she had looked in the mirror and discovered that her face had changed. It was no longer beautiful. It was heroic. She had deep-set eyes with long, dark lids capable of seeing the worst of the world with compassion. Her nose, she noticed, was a fraction too long in profile, but as she no longer tossed her head or turned shyly away from the opposite sex, it did not matter in the least. Her mouth had stopped looking like a cupid's bow. It was small and resolute. Her complexion was pale and her neck and ears were unadorned. She lived alone in a white, three-storied house on Richmond Hill that had once belonged to her Aunt Laura. At night she knitted socks and balaclava helmets for the men on the Front.

When the Armistice came, it was difficult for Alma to adapt. She had learned how to conduct herself in a country at war. She was not impoverished, and she really did not need to work. She resigned her job at the newspaper. But soon she took a part-time job, three days a week, in a flower-shop next to the railway station. It made her feel useful again. It gave her opportunities to comfort the bereaved when they came in to order wreaths and sprays. She told them her man had not returned from France. She also liked the flower shop because gentlemen with spats and walking sticks called there to buy buttonholes. She started wearing a little rouge. She looked so pale among the roses.

It was Mrs Maxwell, the manageress, who had recommended Mr Baranov when Alma had complained of toothache. There were several dentists in Richmond, but Mrs Maxwell was not able to recommend them with any confidence. Mrs Maxwell could not understand why so many modern girls were not more discriminating in their choice of dentists. If one pearl in a necklace were damaged, you wouldn't go to a jeweller in Richmond High Street to have it replaced. You would go to London, to Bond Street or Regent Street. How much more precious than pearls were one's own teeth?

Mr Baranov had made a strong impression on Alma from the beginning. He was totally unlike the young men who had always peopled her dreams. He was not a young man at all. The youngest she could make him was forty-five. His hair and moustache were flecked with silver. His eyelids had formed into folds where the skin overlapped. His joys and tribulations could be traced in the fine lines at the edges of his eyes and mouth. There glinted in his pale blue eyes a look of deep serenity. He was supremely happy in his work.

At that first appointment he had ushered Alma into one of the armchairs. With a few courteous questions he elicited her dental history. He spoke about his fees. She hardly listened. She was listening to the music of his voice. It was as slow and resonant as a prelude by Rachmaninov.

She was spellbound. She sat demurely with her white-gloved hands folded over her crocodile-skin handbag, imagining what might happen if she fainted with excitement when he asked her to stand up. Would he be quick enough to catch her? Would he grasp her in his arms and carry her to the settee? And as she lay swooning with her head against his chest, would she hear the pounding of his heart?

'Are you ready, Miss Webster?'

'Ready?'

'For the inspection. Of course, if you are feeling nervous, we can talk a little longer.'

'Oh, no. I'm quite ready, thank you.'

'Excellent. Let us see what there is to be done.'

On cue the crimson velvet curtain behind Mr Baranov's desk was drawn aside by the nurse, an oriental woman of uncertain age and unlovely features, immaculately groomed and wearing a pale blue uniform. From her solemn manner it appeared that she was neither wife nor mistress to Mr Baranov.

Behind the curtain was a dental chair on a square of black marble. Above and around it was an array of dental machinery and adjustable lights. There was a steel trolley covered with a pale blue cloth. Mr Baranov extended his hand towards the

19

chair and gave a reassuring smile. The pale blue cloth was a cape that was put over Alma as she sat in the chair. The trolley of instruments was no longer in her view. Nor was the nurse. There was only Mr Baranov, now in a white linen jacket. He came close and stood looking at her face in an approving way. She returned his gaze without blushing. She was not embarrassed. She knew about sex. She had read Marie Stopes.

'If you please.'

Alma looked steadily into his eyes.

Mr Baranov pointed to her mouth.

'Oh, yes.'

As he inserted the probe with his left hand, something gleamed in the electric light. It was a gold wedding ring. Alma gave a jerk.

'That didn't hurt, I hope?'

'No.'

'You're quite all right?'

'Perfectly.'

In the movement he had rubbed some rouge from Alma's cheek. There was now a smear of pink on the knuckle above the ring.

She kept calm. Probably his wife was dead, gunned down by the Bolsheviks. Or perhaps her frail health had not been equal to the long journey into exile after the Revolution. Poor soul. And poor Mr Baranov, alone with his grief in a foreign land.

Alma knew about grief. She, too, had lived with it for years. On Easter Monday, 1914, when she was twenty, she had gone with her best friend Eileen to walk among the daffodils in Kew Gardens. They wore white hats with huge soft brims that flounced as they moved. They ignored the rain clouds overhead. When the first heavy spots pierced their cotton frocks they were on the west side of the lake, far from the buildings and glass-houses. With mock shrieks of panic they ran through the down-pour to the shelter of a yew-tree. They looked at each other and started giggling. Their new hats drooped like sou'westers.

Suddenly their laughter froze. Someone had politely cleared his throat. He was a young man in a flat cap and tweeds who had been standing on the other side of the tree. He was carrying a large umbrella. He was as handsome as the Prince of Wales. He raised his cap and said his name was Arthur. He offered to escort them to the gate if they did not object to squeezing together under his umbrella. Giggling again, each of them took one of his arms.

It was still raining when they reached the Victoria Gate. Arthur insisted on treating them to toasted teacakes at the Maids of Honour across the road. They sat in the window-seat while the rain streamed down the leaded panes outside. Arthur told them he was down from Peterhouse, Cambridge, for the Easter vacation. He was bored at home, so most afternoons he came to Kew. As he mentioned this, his hand touched Alma's. For a moment she felt the pressure of his fingers. Her pulse raced.

That night Alma hardly slept at all. In the morning she put on her pale pink suit and white silk stockings and took the bus to Kew. She stood under the yew tree. She waited there two hours. She searched the Gardens for Arthur until the bell rang. She was desolate. She went again on Friday. It rained, and he was not there. Her clothes were ruined. In the bus, she wept silently.

When she got home she took a bath. She lay in the warm water despairing of romance, convinced that she was singled out by fate to be deprived of the blissful companionship of young men. The water cooled and she got out and put on a dressing gown. The doorbell rang. It was her friend Eileen, to see if she was coming to choir practice. She said she was too tired from walking at Kew.

For self-esteem, and to gratify Eileen's curiosity, Alma invented a story. It owed a certain amount to Ethel M. Dell. She said Arthur had secretly engaged to meet her under the yew. When she had got there, he was nowhere in sight. Then she had heard him call her name, softly, above her head. He was sitting in the fork of the tree. He had jumped down without another word and snatched her into his arms and kissed her with savage passion. First she had frozen in his grasp, then her blood had quickened and she had summoned more strength than she knew she possessed and forced him away. She had not run away. She had faced him, her lips burning, her bosom heaving, and shamed him with her eyes. Hot-faced, he had told her that her beauty had overwhelmed him. He had never before committed such a lapse of decorum, and he apologised, but he could give no undertaking that it would not happen again, so uncontrollable was his passion for her. His honesty had surprised Alma. Behind the brute force of his action and the candour of his words she had felt the vitality of the man encompassing her. She had relented to the extent of allowing him to walk beside her to the teashop. There he had asked her to be his guest at the Cambridge May Ball. As if mesmerised by his smouldering eyes, she had agreed to go.

To give substance to the fantasy, she persuaded Eileen to go with her to Gosling's next afternoon to choose material for a ball gown. It relieved her despair unimaginably.

She kept up the pretence. At the end of May, she related her account of the Ball to Eileen. Arthur had behaved impeccably until the small hours on a punt below Magdalene Bridge when he had brushed her cheek with his lips and in a whisper asked her to marry him. Impulsively she had drawn him to her and given her tremulous lips to his. She had almost forgotten to say yes. It was to be a secret engagement until Christmas, when Arthur's parents would be back from the Amazon, where they were missionaries.

Alma surprised herself with her brilliance in fabricating the details. Already she had thought ahead to explain why there would be no engagement ring at Christmas. Arthur's parents would disappear in the jungle. Arthur would lead the rescue party, and be stricken by an incurable tropical disease. Or he might be felled by a poisoned arrow.

Real events provided Alma with a more enthralling plot. In August of that year, Germany invaded Belgium and the next day Britain entered the war. Across the country, thousands upon thousands of young men enlisted. Undergraduates at the universities abandoned their studies to fight for King and Country. There was no doubt in Alma's mind that Arthur was among them. In September she told Eileen she had received a letter from France. He had obtained a commission in the Royal Fusiliers. She realised that she could end the deception as soon as she liked by saying he was one of the fallen, but she was unwilling to do it. She wanted to be one of the brave women praying for their men to be spared. She was knitting balaclavas for the Red Cross Society and she told the local committee that she would be content if *someone's* husband or lover in the trenches was comforted. When one of them asked, she answered without hesitation that the man she had promised to marry was out there.

So as the war progressed, Arthur acquired a service record of distinction. He served in the trenches for two years. Alma awarded him the Military Cross for his gallantry at Neuve Chapelle. Towards the end of 1916 she attached him to the Royal Flying Corps. He was given a flight to command and he led scores of daring raids over Germany. One of the Red Cross ladies whose brother worked for Handley-Page asked which machine Arthur flew. Alma replied that he never mentioned such things in the letters. He wrote passionately about their few, precious days together in England before the war. He thought only of coming home and getting married.

Alma looked forward to the Armistice as keenly as anyone, and when it came she realised that Arthur was still alive. Eileen was thrilled for them both. She wanted to know how soon they would name the day. Alma gave the matter some thought. She said there might be some delay. Arthur was in hospital. He had caught the influenza that had become an epidemic in Europe. In his letter he had described it as a mild case, but damnably inconvenient.

When Eileen saw Alma next, she was wearing black. She was incredibly brave.

She really mourned the loss of Arthur in a way no-one could understand. There was a void in her life. People were kind. They urged her to go out more. A new age had dawned. Pleasures were taken in public. Cinemas, dance halls and night clubs were opening everywhere. Alma was still young, but she felt as if she belonged in another era. She was not ready for the twenties. She was unimpressed by young men.

'A little wider, please,' said Mr Baranov. 'Tell me if this hurts.'

She was certain it would not. Mr Baranov was a marvellous dentist. He would be a marvellous lover.

'Some of my patients ask me to put them to sleep – with chloroform, you know – but I try to convince them that they will feel no pain this way.'

Mr Baranov belonged to the more dignified world of the pre-war years. You would not see him at a public dance. His setting was the private dinner party, where his conversation must have sparkled like the cut glass. Everything he said seemed brilliant for being spoken by that sonorous voice. For a Russian, he had mastered the language amazingly well. You would not have known he was a foreigner. Alma supposed he had received the education of an aristocrat, probably from an English tutor.

'There's a dentist in the Strand,' said Mr Baranov. 'An American. He specialises in crown, bar and bridge work. He advertises every week in *The Stage*, the journal for theatrical performers. In his advertisement this fellow actually provides a list of his most illustrious patients, the actors and actresses who have passed through his surgery. Presumably he does it with their permission, so I don't object to that. I wouldn't do it myself, of course. I promise you that you won't find your name in the papers next week. What I *do* find objectionable in his advertisements – and others like them – is the slogan *American Painless Dentistry*, as if in some mysterious way the Americans are the only people capable of treating their patients without causing them pain. I'll tell you the secret of American Painless Dentistry. It's good, old-fashioned chloroform, Miss Webster. Personally, I use it only as a last resort. If you take care, you can operate without causing pain. Would you rinse your mouth, please?'

A tumbler of water was put into Alma's hand, and the nurse held out a porcelain bowl.

'Let's take another look,' said Mr Baranov.

She believed him. He was incapable of hurting her. She could feel the slight pressure of his thigh and stomach against her right arm as he leaned forward to examine her mouth. She tried not to tense the arm. But sooner or later she would have to find some way of signalling to him that he was the most adorable man she had ever met.

'Mind you, some of the things that are perpetrated in the name of dentistry are indefensible. I remember reading something before the war about that doctor in Holloway who murdered his wife. Crippen. I don't suppose you remember. You must have been in pigtails at the time. It created quite a sensation because when the police called at the house – there was a gossip among the neighbours, I think – Dr Crippen and his – if you'll pardon the expression – mistress took fright and booked a passage to Canada. The young lady, Ethel something or other, dressed up as a boy and Crippen shaved off his moustache and went without his glasses to pose as her father. The disguise couldn't have been too convincing, because the captain of the ship spotted who they were on the first day at sea. He sent back a message on the wireless and Scotland Yard sent a man on a faster ship to arrest them at the end of the voyage. Inspector Dew. Rinse out, please.'

Mr Baranov adjusted the light while the nurse mixed some paste for the filling. He came close again.

'Nearly done. I expect you are wondering what Dr Crippen has to do with the dental profession. Well, before the murder, he was in partnership with a young fellow-American. They called themselves the Yale Tooth Specialists. Crippen was a medical man if he was anything at all, so he looked after the business side of things and helped occasionally, and Ethel was the nurse. Now this is the point of the story. Ethel suffered from head-aches. Neuralgia. They decided the pain was caused by her teeth, so they extracted them. Twenty-one teeth at one sitting. The poor girl was no older than you are now. Criminal. I wish I could remember the girl's surname. It was something rather exotic.'

Alma tried to say "Le Neve" without moving her mouth.

'Yes, Miss Webster. I know it's a little uncomfortable. Just bear with me a few minutes more.'

She remembered the Crippen case. The papers had been full of it for weeks. It was in 1910, when she was seventeen, and reading Ethel M. Dell. She had been deeply affected by it. She had felt nothing but pity for the two fugitives pacing the deck of that poky little steamer in their pathetic disguises for ten days, while thanks to a sharp-eyed ship's captain and the miracle of wireless every Tom, Dick and Harry who could read a news-paper knew that Inspector Dew would be waiting with the handcuffs in Toronto. She had wept for them when the news of the arrest came through. She had tried to decide whether she, too, could have faced that moment with dignity. Love, and love alone, must have fortified them.

'There.' Mr Baranov removed the instruments from her mouth. 'Try not to use that side of your mouth this evening. Nurse will arrange the next appointment. Is there anything the matter?'

'I was going to say that the name of the woman was Le Neve, Ethel Le Neve.'

'So it was. You do have an excellent memory.'

'Here in England, it was in all the newspapers.'

'Oh, I remember that.'

'You were in England in 1910?'

'And all my life,' said Mr Baranov with a smile.

'But . . .'

'You thought I was Russian, did you? It's a reasonable assumption, and you aren't the first to make it. My father's name was Henry Brown. He worked the halls as a tight-rope walker.' He gave a rapid mime, with arms outstretched. 'The Great Baranov.'

Alma was stunned. 'So you are English?'

'I was christened Walter Brown. I say, you do look pale.'

'Your father called himself Baranov for the music halls?'

'And I adopted it for my signboard. In this work, it's no handicap to have a foreign-sounding name. The English don't believe they're getting a decent dentist if he has a name like Walter Brown.'

She was speechless.

'You're frowning,' he said. 'It's quite legal, you know. For my father it was simply a stage-name, but I decided to get it done by deed poll. I was about to get married, and my wife-to-be was strongly in favour, being on the stage herself. Lydia Baranov – not a bad name for an actress, is it? Perhaps you've heard of her. She's quite well known in the theatre.'

His wife was alive.

Alma swayed slightly. She had to get out of this place. She turned away from him and crossed the room. Tears were blurring her vision. The nurse held the door open and put an appointment card into Alma's hand.

Out in the street she tore it in half and dropped the pieces down the nearest drain.

Another young woman featured in the case. Her name was Poppy Duke.

Lord's Day Observance operated in reverse for Poppy. She rested for six days and worked on the Sabbath. Her place of work was the Petticoat Lane market. She was eighteen, bright-eyed, with a smile that teased and natural golden hair in tight, fine curls. She was a brilliant thief. She had slim hands with long fingers that could slip a wallet from its owner's pocket as she bumped against him and said, 'Do you mind?' She could unfasten a handbag and the purse inside and remove the paper money in one continuous movement imperceptible to the owner or the stallholder trying to extract it more legitimately. She was tolerated in the market because it was said that she was a sort of modern Robin Hood. She robbed only the visitors who came to look rather than to buy. And she employed up to half a dozen children as stalls and stickmen, and paid them generously.

This morning she had hardly started when she spotted a perfect quarry, a youngish man in a smart suit and a trilby, with an officer's trenchcoat draped round his shoulders like a cape. He had stopped at a stall selling tea and caused some annoyance by producing a pound note. He claimed he had no change.

'Well, you have now, duck,' said the woman on the stall as she dropped a quantity of small coins into his hand. 'Are you going to count them?' She handed him the mug of tea.

He was still holding his wallet. He stuffed it into the outer pocket of his trenchcoat and took the tea.

Poppy moved in. She wasn't leaving this to some beginner in the trade. She stood as if waiting in the queue. With her left hand she flicked up the pocket-flap and felt for the wallet.

To her horror, a hand gripped hers inside the pocket. She could not remove it. The man turned and grinned. He still held the tea in his right hand. It was his left, drawn across his front and through the division in the coat lining, that was holding hers.

He said, 'Well, Poppy, I'd say that was like taking sweets from a baby.'

She said, 'I got me hand caught.'

'You certainly did, and I don't intend to let it go. If you don't want trouble keep it there and hold yourself against me. I've got a taxi waiting up the street.'

'Are you taking me in? Give us a chance, mate.'

'Just walk, Poppy.'

She obeyed. She was afraid that her small boy accomplices might try to stall them and get caught as well. Alone, she couldn't get done for much.

When they reached the taxi in Whitechapel High Street, he released her hand. She was expecting him to handcuff her, but he didn't. She said, 'Here, are you the law, or what?'

He pushed her firmly into the cab and sat beside her.

'Poppy darling,' he said with another grin, 'it's your birthday.'

'What the hell do you mean? Where are you taking me?'

'To choose a present, sweetheart.'

'I don't know what sort of girl you take me for, mister.'

'Calm down. I'm just taking you for a ride, aren't I?'

They drove through the City and Holborn to Oxford Street. Poppy glared at her companion, trying to fathom who he was. She hadn't seen him in the Lane before this morning. He was dressed like a gent, which he obviously was not.

The taxi turned left into Bond Street and stopped.

'What are we doing here?' demanded Poppy.

'Get out, and I'll show you. But don't embarrass me, will you? It's a very nobby area.'

He steered Poppy, wide-eyed towards a dress-shop she had only ever read about in magazines. 'Choose one,' he told her, 'for a party.'

'Hold on a mo – what do you really want?'

'I'll tell you, Poppy,' he said, as they both stared into the window. 'I was told that you're the smartest dip in London and I want to hire your services for an evening. It's a party, so you need to have a dress. What do you think of the black number over there with silver sequins? If you enlist with me, you get a decent uniform. And you keep it. Right?'

In her large house on Putney Hill, Lydia Baranov was using the telephone. She had been using it ever since she got back from her audition. She was shouting into it. She told whoever it was on the line that he was incompetent. She said she failed to understand why a simple matter created such monumental difficulties.

Downstairs in the hall, the front door opened and Walter came in. Sylvia, the housemaid, was waiting as usual to take his hat, coat and umbrella.

The tirade on the telephone continued. Walter glanced upstairs. He looked at Sylvia and raised his eyebrows questioningly. Sylvia shook her head. Walter made a grimace. He went into the drawing room, poured himself a whisky and downed it in a gulp.

When he got upstairs, Lydia was saying that her time was too precious to waste talking to idiot clerks. She said she would expect a call from the manager in the morning, not before ten and no later than eleven. She hung up the phone.

'And what sort of day did *you* have?' she asked in a way that brushed his answer aside before he made it.

'Extremely frustrating,' he said with emphasis. 'I take a very poor view of people who waste my time. Two broken appointments, without a word of explanation. You'd think people would have the common courtesy to notify the surgery. I suppose I can expect no better from Lady Burke. She's notoriously absent-minded. She'll probably come in tomorrow in a state of high agitation. But the second patient, Miss Webster, has her wits about her and really ought to know better. We've given her the same time on the same day for the last three weeks. It's not as if she suffered any pain. I find it inexplicable.'

'If you've finished,' said Lydia, 'perhaps you would like to know what happened to *me*.' With her dramatic training, she knew all about up-staging. This morning she had been to an audition for a minor part in *The Gay Lord Quex* at the Richmond Theatre. She was thirty-four. She had not appeared on the West End stage since 1914.

'I gather it was disappointing,' said Walter.

'Disappointing? It was ridiculous. A joke.' If a casting director had seen Lydia like this, she would have been assured of major roles for the rest of her career. Outrage transformed her. Her usually pale skin was feverishly pink. The black curls danced with each swift movement of her head. Her nostrils flared and her brown eyes blazed with gypsy passion. 'The director's mad. I couldn't possibly work with him. It would finish my career. The man has no idea what the play is about. He doesn't understand Pinero.'

'Who got the part?'

'Some little trollop with six weeks' experience in revue. They said I could understudy. You know what that means? Selling chocolates in the interval. I told them I was in *The Second Mrs Tanqueray*.'

'What did they say about that?'

'They said this was comedy. They said my experience was unsuitable. I agreed with them. I said they had made it crystal clear that the sort of experience they were looking for was what one learned in Mr Cochran's chorus line, and I was glad to say I hadn't sunk to that.'

'Quite right.'

'With that, I left the theatre. I was so incensed that I left my book of notices there.'

'Perhaps they'll look at it and realise what a mistake they've made.'

'Small chance of that. Anyway, the play is cast now. I wouldn't take the leading role if they offered it. I have my pride. But I will need my notices.'

'Of course you will.'

'Walter, darling.'

'Yes, my dear?'

'Would you collect them for me?'

'I don't have time tomorrow. I have a full day of appointments.'

'Go tonight, then.'

There was a moment of silence between them.

'It won't take more than an hour,' said Lydia. 'I'll ask cook to keep your meal warm.' She kissed him lightly. 'You know I couldn't bear to lose my notices.'

He collected his hat and coat from Sylvia.

From the window, Lydia watched him go down the hill to get a taxi at the station. His patients might be in awe of him, but at home he did exactly as she asked. It was out of gratitude.

Without her money and farsightedness he would still be hawking his ludicrous mind-reading act round the shabby music halls of the provinces. She alone had persuaded him that he was totally unsuited to the stage. She had pointed out the potential profits in dentistry and as a token of her confidence she had married him. She had paid for his apprenticeship at Reading as a dental mechanic and his three years at the Dental Hospital at Newcastle-upon-Tyne. Walter had never been so happy in his life. He had found his vocation. They rarely saw each other, because she was in *The Second Mrs Tanqueray*. Acting exhausted and fulfilled her.

Their marriage had continued as a part-time occupation until Walter passed his final examination in 1914 and became a dental surgeon. He came down to London for the graduation ceremony. Lydia took him to lunch at Frascati's. Noises kept coming from the kitchen. The waiter asked if they had heard the news. Mr Lloyd George had made a statement in the Commons. The country was at war with Germany. Unmarried men below the age of thirty were urged to volunteer for service. Walter was married. He was thirty-nine. He called at the recruiting office in the Strand. For the next four years he pulled soldiers' teeth for King and Country in the north of Scotland.

Lydia had a less distinguished war. There were not so many good productions to audition for. Most able-bodied actors had enlisted. She was in *The Harbour Lights* at Woolwich with a leading man so decrepit that when he knelt before her to declare his love she had to help him to get upright again.

By 1917 she was so discouraged that she took a rest from the boards. She passed the time reading her notices from pre-war days in the big house she had inherited from her father on Putney Hill. She was sexually frustrated. She formed a secret passion for the bearded man on the tea counter in Fortnum and Mason. It never came to anything. Life in Britain was made harder by the German U-boats. There were shortages of food. There was talk of rationing. Hoarding was made a criminal offence. Lydia's housemaid was a gossip. When the house was searched, the police found 68 packets of Fortnum and Mason tea. All but a few were confiscated. Lydia was fined £10 with £7 costs. Her name was printed in the newspapers. It was the first notice she had ever received from *The Times*.

Walter climbed into the first cab on the rank. In less than

twenty minutes he was paying the driver outside the Richmond Theatre. It was a few minutes after seven. The theatre was quiet. Evening performances started at 8.30, so that people could dress and dine first. The current show was a revue. Lydia had been right; music hall was dying. Mind-reading had gone out with animal acts and Dan Leno.

He told the girl in the booking-office what he wanted. She sent him to the dress circle bar. There was a crowd inside. Cigar smoke lay on the air. The postured hands and clipped, projecting voices told him these were professionals, the director and the new, elated cast of *The Gay Lord Quex*.

Walter bought a dry sherry and stood near the main group. From the conversation he learned that the man they called Jasper was the director. Jasper had his hand on the shoulder of a pretty, red-haired girl who trilled with laughter at almost everything he said. She had one of the new, backless dresses. She looked ten years younger than Lydia.

He waited for a break in the conversation. Jasper asked the girl if she would have another martini. He turned to the bar to order it. Walter introduced himself.

'Enchanting name, my dear,' said Jasper, 'but I don't believe I know you.'

'Lydia, my wife, auditioned for you this afternoon.'

'The same again, George,' Jasper called to the barman.

'She didn't get the part.'

'My dear, auditions are quite hateful for all concerned. I'm sure mistakes are made from time to time, but we never conduct post mortems. It just isn't done.'

'She left her book of notices with you.'

'Oh, I see. Heavens, I wonder what we did with it.'

The girl with the backless dress turned. 'It's over there, darling. I was reading it. I'll say one thing – she's a lot more experienced than yours truly.'

'I wouldn't say that, Blanche,' commented a voice heavy with innuendo.

'Some people have minds like sewers,' Blanche said worldwearily.

'There's your drink,' Jasper said curtly. He took Walter's arm and crossed the room with him to the table where the book was. 'Lydia auditioned well. She's a professional, Mr Baranov. You have a talented wife. If it had been left to me alone —'

Walter interrupted without seeming to raise his voice. 'I have worked in the theatre. I have listened to hypocrisy like that since I was three years old. If you really have a scrap of interest in my wife's career, do her the credit of telling me the truth.'

The rebuke was the more telling for being so reasonably expressed.

The bar was suddenly quiet. Someone called across the room, 'Is everything all right, Jasper?'

'Yes, perfectly,' said Jasper. To Walter, he said, 'If you really want to know, she's too mature for these young girl roles, and she isn't ready to play dowagers and matrons.' To soften the remark he added, 'Not for a long time.'

Walter said nothing. He picked up the scrapbook.

'It's always a difficult phase in an actress's career, 'Jasper went on. 'Possibly if she could be persuaded to go into some other sphere of production, it would be all to the good. With her experience, she must know a lot about make-up. Costume, if she's any good with a needle and thread.'

Walter gave him a disbelieving look. 'Where can I get a taxi?'

'At this time, by the station. Right outside the theatre, then right again. Thank her for coming in, won't you?'

Walter went downstairs and followed the directions. At the station, he got into a cab. As they moved off, his eye was caught by something. He tapped the driver's shoulder.

'Would you stop a moment? The flower shop. I want to buy some flowers for my wife.'

'You'd better be quick, mate. I'm obstructing the rank.'

In the florist's, he glanced over the bunches in their pots.

The shop assistant came from the back. 'Good evening, sir. Can I . . . Oh.' She stopped, staring at him.

'Yes, please. I, er . . . Why, it's Miss Webster, isn't it?'

Alma answered in a whisper, 'Yes.'

'Walter Baranov, your dentist. Remember? You missed your appointment today. Did you realise?'

She was pink with embarrassment. She said nothing.

He was clearly embarrassed too. 'I'm so sorry. It sounds as if I'm checking up. Just seeing you like this, quite by chance, I was taken by surprise.'

'Oh.' She had a stem in her hand. She was snapping it into small pieces.

'You see, my wife had an audition today at the Richmond

Theatre. She's an actress.'

'Yes. You told me.'

He was still holding Lydia's book. 'She left this behind. All her notices. Very precious. I came to collect it.'

Outside, the taxi-driver sounded his horn.

'I wanted some roses,' said Walter. 'A dozen, I think.'

'Yes. Any particular colour?' She crossed the shop to the vases. There were several shades of red and pink roses, as well as yellow and white. 'They are all three shillings a dozen.'

He put the book on the counter and felt in his pocket for the money. 'It doesn't matter. The pink.'

'I could make a mixed bunch.'

The horn sounded again.

'If you please.'

'Would you like to pick them out?'

He stood beside her and selected a dozen of various colours. She wrapped them. He handed her the money. 'Thank you. I must hurry, I'm afraid. I have a taxi waiting.' He raised his hat. 'I hope to see you again, Miss Webster.'

He had left the shop and the taxi had pulled away before Alma noticed the scrapbook left on the counter.

To locate another lady in the story, the setting moves to Paris.

Wherever Marjorie Livingstone Cordell found herself on a Friday evening, she liked to have a hot bath, preferably Turkish, followed by a full body massage. As a reviver, it beat strong coffee, liver salts, cocktails and walking in the park, all of which she had tried. She was proud of her reputation for vitality. She enlivened any party, and she was invited to plenty. Her age was a secret, but she was into her third marriage and she had a daughter of twenty-two. The nice thing about the Friday massage was that she relaxed completely. In New York City, where she lived, she had a marvellous little man from the Bronx with hands like velvet, and he knew more about her private hopes and fears than any of her husbands.

This evening she was on the table in the massage parlour of the Paris Carlton, where she was staying with Livy, her third. They were vacationing in Europe this year because her daughter Barbara had just completed a course in fine art at the Sorbonne, and they were going to travel back with her to New York. She communicated this in simple English to the Algerian who was easing the tension in her shoulders. He was quite good-looking, with sleek hair and a pencil-thin moustache, only there was garlick on his breath. She turned her face the other way.

'Would you do my ankles now?' she asked, wiggling a foot in case he didn't understand. 'I'm really grateful to the Good Lord for supplying me with such beautiful ankles. Would you believe that each of my three husbands was attracted to my ankles first? Regular massage keeps them slender – my ankles, I mean. Good – that's terrific. Livy – that's short for Livingstone – he's my third – a wonderful guy – no Douglas Fairbanks, I grant you, but quite good-looking in his way – Livy sometimes asks me to let him massage my ankles, but I don't allow it. I say that's a job for a professional. Hm. You're pretty good. What's your name?'

'Alain, madame.'

'Well, Alain, it's my opinion that a woman ought to take care of her body. She never knows when she's under observation. I'll tell you something that happened to me four years ago in the Biltmore Hotel in New York. I was caught in the elevator with seven men, all strangers. Really caught, I mean. It was stuck between the second and the third floors for almost an hour. I was petrified, but, do you know, Alain, that was how I met Livy. You think I'm going to tell you he was one of the guys in the elevator, don't you? Well, he wasn't. He was on the second floor watching when the maintenance men finally got the sliding doors open. The car was way above their heads, so all that he could see of me was my ankles, and he couldn't take his eyes off them. Isn't that romantic?'

'*Charmant*, madame.'

'We got married the same year, and I still catch him sneaking looks at my ankles when he thinks I won't notice. We're devoted to each other. I just wish my daughter Barbara was as fortunate as I am. She's beautiful, I mean really pretty, with my white skin and classical features and the most amazing chestnut hair, only she scares men. She's so severe. She majored in mathematics and all she would talk about was coefficients and things like that. We sent her over here for a year to broaden her education at the Sorbonne, thinking maybe the Parisians would teach her some other things. Well, she's crazy about Greeks now.'

'Greeks, madame?'

'Of the fifth century B.C. She spent this afternoon showing Livy and me around the Louvre. Okay, it's a change from logarithms, so we went. I had just a small hope that there might be some young professor there who was the real attraction. I was wrong. It was strictly antique objects. Well, there are some very fine Greek statues in the Louvre. Manhood unadorned and large as life. Larger, here and there. I said to Livy this may not be a bad thing. But do you know, Alain, my daughter Barbara led us right through the rooms with the statues without stopping once. She didn't even turn her head. She wanted to show us the Greek vases. Vases! She adores them. I was so depressed I just collapsed onto a bench.'

'It's not so bad, madame.'

'What do you mean?'

'You didn't look at the vases?'

'I told you I was bushed.'

'On the vases, madame, many little men.' Alain indicated the size with finger and thumb. 'No clothes. Maybe Barbara start with little men.'

'Oh.' Mrs Cordell considered the suggestion. She began to giggle. 'Little men. I like that.'

'I am not so big myself, madame.'

She laughed. 'I don't care what size he is, but my daughter's husband has got to be rich.'

5

When Walter got back to Putney, his dinner was not fit to eat. Cook said she would make him a salad.

Lydia had heard them talking about it. 'You took your time,' she remarked as he came into the drawing room.

'I thought you would like these.' He handed her the roses.

She was agreeably surprised. While he was out, she had been thinking about leaving him for good. 'Where did you get them, Walter?' It was the nearest she could get to thanking him.

'I didn't take them from a neighbour's garden.'

She handed them back. 'Ask Sylvia to find a vase for them. Did they give you my book?'

'Yes.'

But it wasn't tucked under his arm, and as she asked him she saw his free hand tighten suddenly. 'Who did you see?'

'The director. He was still there in the bar.'

'That doesn't surprise me. He reeked of gin this afternoon.'

'He said you were very good, my dear.'

'Hypocrite. They always say that.'

'He paid you a very nice compliment.'

'Hm.' She set her mouth contemptuously.

Walter said, 'I'll give these to Sylvia.'

'What was that, then?'

'What was what, dear?'

'The compliment.'

'Oh. He said you were a real professional.'

'A fat lot he would know about that!'

'That wasn't all he said.'

'What else, then?'

'I'll just find Sylvia.' He had crossed into the hall. 'Would you like them in your room? They might look rather good on the stairs in the majolica jardinière.'

'Leave it to Sylvia. Put them on the table in the hall and come and tell me exactly what Jasper said.'

He called back from the passage to the kitchen, 'Would you like a glass of Burgundy? I might enjoy it with the salad.'

She made a sound of irritation. The wretched man was so evasive on occasions. She could not be sure whether he really had something interesting to impart, or whether he was covering up about the book. He did this sort of thing deliberately. He knew the force of the theatre in her life. She craved it like a drug. It was painful parading herself for auditions in the provinces, but she went on doing it because she could not stop.

For as long as she could remember – she had actually been born backstage in one of the six theatres her father had owned – everything that mattered to her had been connected with the stage. Before she was twenty she had met Pinero, Barrie and Shaw. She had played at the Adelphi. Sir Herbert Tree had told her that in a year or two she would have the power to enslave a West End audience. Yet she had seen the danger of a life devoted wholly to the theatre. It was vital to her character and her art to keep a link with the real world outside. She had married Walter and financed his dental training with part of the legacy her father had left her. Walter was her hedge against unreality. What could be more down to earth than a husband who pulled teeth?

He came back into the drawing room with his salad on a tray and two glasses of wine. He handed one to her ceremoniously. He sat opposite her in the tall armchair her father had used for saying family prayers. She twitched her skirt impatiently.

'My dear,' said Walter, 'I have something rather important to discuss with you.'

The sign on the flower shop door said "closed". The blinds were down. The till was cleared and the money put away in the safe. Alma was performing her last duty of the day, assembling the bouquet that a fortunate bride would carry into church next morning. Her mind was so full of Walter Baranov that she had almost forgotten it. Her unsteady fingers snapped the head off a carnation as she wired it. She reached for another.

She was more excited than nervous. He had taken her completely by surprise, simply walking into the shop like that. It was as amazing and romantic as the arrival of Everard Monck at the desert encampment during Stella's unhappy honeymoon in *The Lamp in the Desert*. What Walter had said may not have amounted to much, but the fact that he had come had told her all she needed to know. He cared enough to have found out where she worked.

He must have gone to extraordinary trouble. She had not mentioned the flower shop to him before. She had not made any reference to it on the form she had filled in for the nurse. Walter – she had already discarded his surname in her thoughts – had located the address and he had come to find her: after one missed appointment. He could not have told her more clearly that he desired her. He was a married man, and it made no difference. He wanted her more than his wife.

She was flattered and intrigued and aroused. She was gripped by the sort of recklessness that was so often the making or undoing of women in books. She had always promised herself that in a situation like this she would take her chance with destiny. She would be spirited, vivacious, zestful, exuberant – all those dazzling adjectives that were applied to heroines.

But she had not performed too well at the start. She had been tongue-tied when he had come into the shop. She needed to cultivate confidence. She was secure in the knowledge that she was paramount in Walter's life, so there was no reason to behave like a nervous schoolgirl. She would resist the wild impulse to go looking for his house tonight with the scrapbook he had so conspicuously left on the counter. She would wait till her lunch hour tomorrow and take it to the surgery.

Tonight she was going to take it home and look at it.

Lydia sipped her Burgundy and let Walter hold the stage. She seldom gave him the opportunity. It was hardly likely that a man who spent his days investigating open mouths would learn anything of consequence to pass on. This evening was exceptional. She listened closely.

'Of course you and I know the state of the modern theatre,' he said, liberally sprinkling the salt over his salad. 'It doesn't need a puffed-up provincial director to tell us that talent hardly matters at all these days. Just think what you've come up against at auditions in the last few months: bribery, nepotism, the old school tie, politics and sexual trafficking. I sometimes ask myself if you wouldn't be wiser to employ your marvellous experience in some other area of production – at least until sanity returns to the theatre. Curiously enough, Jasper made the same suggestion.'

'That I should try something different?' said Lydia in a calm voice.

'Well, yes. It's worth considering, I feel.'

She smiled. 'Darling, I have reached the same conclusion. It's no use going on with this. It makes a mockery of my life in the theatre. It has a terrible effect on my nerves and my digestion. In the end it will undermine our marriage. You are absolutely right. I shall not attend another audition in the English theatre. I am going to America.'

Walter stopped eating. 'America?'

'You do sound surprised.'

'Are you serious, my dear?'

'Totally. I am going to offer my talent to the cinema.'

'Good Lord.'

'It *is* another area of production.' She was pleased by the effect of her announcement. Walter was white.

'It wasn't quite what I had in mind.'

'Think it over. The only films of any quality are being made in America. And it's obvious, isn't it, that the cinema is short of actresses of my experience. Look at Mary Pickford. What has she ever done in the theatre? The Gish sisters. Theda Bara. They are known to millions, Walter, and what do they know about the art of acting?'

'I rather think that acting in the theatre isn't quite the same thing. Bernhardt isn't much of a success in films.'

'Bernhardt is an old woman.'

'But film is such a different form of art, Lydia. There's no sound. Your voice expresses so much in the theatre. It would be such a loss.'

She had expected him to try to thwart her. He would not succeed. 'I shall make more use of gesture and expression. My mind is made up, Walter. You heard me on the telephone this evening. The house is going up for sale. I've already made enquiries about booking a passage. I want to leave as soon as possible.'

The tray shook as he put it aside. 'What about me? What about my practice?'

'Didn't I make it clear? I want you to come with me. We can sell the practice and start a new one in Hollywood. There must be plenty of cinema actors wanting their teeth improved. The cameras come in so close.'

He got up and stood by the window, looking out. He was clearly very shocked.

Lydia could sympathise. She had suffered shocks enough at auditions. Walter had led a sheltered life of late. He had settled into a comfortable routine. The life of a dentist might seem unutterably boring to most people, but Walter enjoyed it. He was making a success of it. He didn't have the income yet to justify the Eaton Square surgery, but there was the prospect of full financial independence in a year or so. Giving it up for America would be a sacrifice.

He was very transparent. He turned and said that he had read that life was dangerous in California. He described the violence between rival film companies. He talked of hired thugs, and shootings, and studios behind high fences, patrolled by armed guards with dogs.

Lydia was unperturbed. She said she was sure the companies looked after their leading players.

Walter got more earnest. He recalled the efforts he had made to build his practice. He said it would be madness to abandon his distinguished patients and his handsome surgery.

Lydia said that if it meant so much to him he had better stay behind and let her face the perils of California alone. Noticing a certain look in his eye, she added that he would have to manage without her money.

He switched the subject back to her career. He said he had a duty to point out that her reputation on the English stage was beyond dispute, but it was unlikely to have reached America.

Lydia smiled. 'My dear,' she murmured, 'I'm afraid you're misinformed. It's time that I confessed to you that I've been holding something back. It happens that I have an associate in Hollywood. His name is not unknown in the cinema. Mr Charlie Chaplin.'

'Chaplin? You know Charlie Chaplin?'

'From before the war, when he was with the Karno Troupe. Charlie and I were on the same bill at the Streatham Empire. That was when Papa was owner of the Empire, before I became a serious actress. I was in a song and dance group called the Yankee Doodle Girls and Charlie was the comic drunk in *Mumming Birds*. He must have been about eighteen, no more, and he had an eye for the girls. He used to watch us from the wings. He looked so funny standing there with eyes like saucers and that red nose and his white tie and tails that we used to giggle. One night I laughed so much, I slipped and hit the boards with an almighty bump. My friend Hetty Kelly winked at Charlie and he fell hopelessly in love with her. She was only fifteen and he proposed to her. Oh, yes, I knew Charlie very well. I've got a cutting in my book to prove it. Go and get it. I'll show you.'

Walter looked round for the wine. 'Would you like some more? He was very good in *Shoulder Arms*. I saw it up in Scotland. Did you ever see it?'

She put her hand over her glass. 'First, I would like to show you the notice in my book.'

He said, 'My father was in America, remember. That was when he had his accident. I wonder if he met Chaplin.'

'Walter, tell me what has happened to my book.'

He cleared his throat. 'I'm not entirely sure that I can. I collected it all right, but when I came in I didn't have it with me.'

'What do you mean – you've lost it?'

'Left it somewhere. In the taxi, I suppose. I'm fearfully sorry, my dear.'

She got up from her chair. She despised him. In a quiet voice she said, 'That book was the most precious thing I owned. No amount of money can replace it.'

She ran from the room. In the hall she picked up the roses he had bought and flung them on the floor. She ran upstairs to her room and locked the door. She collapsed on the bed and wept.

Later, she smoked a cigarette. She heard cook leave the house by the tradesman's gate. She heard Sylvia go up to her room in the attic.

There was a soft tapping on her door. Walter's voice said, 'Are you awake, Lydia?'

She did not answer. She had nothing to say to him.

She heard him turn the handle and find that the door was locked.

'Lydia, my dear, it's me.'

She said flatly, 'Go away.'

'I just remembered where I left the book. I saw the roses and remembered. It was in the florist's where I bought them. I put the book on the counter when I chose the colours. I had a taxi waiting outside and he was sounding his horn. In my hurry I left the book in the shop. I can get it back tomorrow. The shop is next to Richmond Station. Lydia, do you hear? I'll collect it in the morning.'

'No you won't.'

'What?'

'I wouldn't trust you again. I'll go myself, and it had better be there.'

'But the girl in the shop doesn't know you.'

'Idiot. The book is full of pictures of me.'

There was a pause. 'About the other thing,' he said. 'America, I mean. Let's talk again when we have both had a chance to think the matter over.'

'There's nothing to talk about. I've made my mind up. I'm going, Walter. You can do what you like.'

8

Poppy shared a flock mattress with her sister Rose – all the sisters were named after flowers – in the family's rooms above the dairy in Chicksand Street. Rose was seven. She liked to wake at first light and go downstairs to see the milkmen harnessing their horses to the carts. This was Poppy's opportunity to stretch her arms and legs and roll into the centre. She would sink into a deeper sleep, secure from Rose's lively knees and elbows. She usually slept until eleven, except on Sundays. She had no conscience about sleeping late. She kept the family clothed and fed from her takings in the Lane.

This Monday morning she was startled and annoyed to be disturbed from sleep by Rose, pulling at the blanket. It was not much after nine o'clock.

'Pop, wake up.'

'Leave off, or I'll murder you.'

'Man downstairs wants you.'

'What man?' She sat up, swearing, and shuffled to the stairs and looked down. 'Him!' She jerked back out of sight and started nervously fastening the buttons of the shirt she wore at nights. 'Strewth.'

'What's he want?' asked Rose, interested.

'Tell him I won't be long.' She went to find her clothes. She had practically forgotten her adventure of the day before. The stranger who had trapped her in the market had warned her with mysterious threats to say nothing of their "business". She had so far dismissed it from her mind that she had got three parts drunk on stout that night and felt like death this morning. She had decided anyway that the bloke was strange. She had probably had a narrow escape.

Yet he hadn't tried anything. And here he was this morning, just as he had promised, to take her to that nobby dress shop.

She shouted after Rose, 'Make him some tea.' Then she took off the shirt and considered what to wear.

When she got down, he was sitting in father's chair. He was quite good-looking, with wide blue eyes and slicked-down, honey-coloured hair. She didn't mind him taking stock of her. She had put on a crepe-marocain dress supposed to have been worn in the Savoy. She had bought it secondhand in the market and made some adjustments. She was clever with a needle and thread. The blues had faded rather, but it fitted better now.

'What are you wearing under that?'

He *was* strange after all. She gave him one of her withering looks and poured herself some tea.

'I only mention it,' he explained, 'because you'll have to take off the dress to be measured.'

She hadn't considered that. She went back to her room and found some underclothes.

As they left the house, Poppy was disappointed to find no taxi waiting. It was round the corner, in the next street. She laughed, and he asked her what was funny. She chanted a rhyme she had learned in the streets about "that demmed elusive Pimpernel".

He didn't seem amused. He said, 'My name is Jack.'

The taxi took them only a short way and stopped. Poppy looked out. At the same moment, Jack put something into her hand. It was a bar of lavender soap. They were outside the public baths in Aldgate High Street. 'Blooming cheek!' she said. But she thought of that elegant dress shop and said she wouldn't be long.

When they finally got to Bond Street, she was grateful for Jack's forethought. After the gratification of having bolts of fine materials unrolled before her while she sat in a beautiful gilt chair to make the selection, she was taken to be measured. Without Jack looking on, she expected the assistants to treat her differently, but they still called her madam and helped her out of her dress and put it on a padded hanger as if it were the latest thing from Paris. It took three of them to measure her. One was there to provide conversation in the form of compliments on Poppy's looks and figure; another used the tape measure; and the third wrote down the measurements. Poppy said little. She had chosen a gold crepe de chine that made her throat ache with anticipation. The dressmaker asked her to come for a fitting on Wednesday afternoon.

On Friday it was finished. For once the assistants spoke the truth: madam looked exquisite.

'Now,' said Jack when they had left the shop with the dress wrapped in white tissue in a black and silver box, 'we will choose some shoes and stockings. Then I will take you to my flat.'

Poppy was young, but she was not simple. She knew what a man meant if he invited you home. She had suspected all along that this was behind Jack's generosity. Still, she thought as she walked at his side along Regent Street with the box under her arm, it was a gratifying way to go. No one could say she was cheap.

And he was quite a handsome fellow.

He took her to a Georgian terrace with a view across Hyde Park. The walls were papered white and silver. There were Chinese lacquer cabinets and oriental rugs. There was a woman standing by the fireplace with a King Charles spaniel in her arms. She was in a dress of pleated silk with a posy of parma violets on her left shoulder. She was elegant.

'Poppy, this is Kate,' Jack said, and he was grinning as he added, 'My adoring wife.'

'So you're the fingersmith,' said Kate in a voice that fell short of her appearance. 'You don't look a bit like one.'

'That's why she's the best,' said Jack. He had a decanter in his hand. 'What do you like with your gin, Poppy?'

'I take it neat, thank you.'

'You can't do that, my dear,' said Kate firmly. 'Let her try it with tonic, Jack.'

Poppy took the glass and it made her sneeze. 'I'll never pass as upper class, if that's what you are hoping,' she told them.

'You'll be perfect as you are,' said Jack, and to Kate he added, 'She looks divine in the dress.'

Kate asked to see it, so they unwrapped it and Poppy held it against herself.

'It's very bold,' Kate commented. 'Did you choose it yourself, dear?'

Poppy decided to ignore the question. She felt waves of jealousy from Kate, but she could understand the reason for them. She put the dress back in its box and said, 'Aren't you going to tell me what you want me for?'

'I'll show you,' answered Jack. 'Choose one.' Apparently from nowhere, a pack of playing cards opened into a perfect fan shape in his right hand.

Poppy took a card. 'Do I tell you what it is?'

He nodded.

'Seven of hearts.'

He squared the pack and cut it. 'Put it back now.'

She watched him cover the card with part of the pack. He cut it several times. 'Now can you find your card?'

'Is it the top one?'

He shook his head.

'He's taken you in,' said Kate. 'It isn't there.'

Poppy took the pack and searched for the seven of hearts. She went slowly through the cards. It was not among them.

'That's a marvellous trick! So you're a conjurer.'

'No.' He picked up the cards and fanned them again. 'Choose any one you like.'

She found that she had picked the seven of hearts. 'Blimey!'

'You should have watched his left hand,' said Kate in a bored voice. 'He palmed it.'

Jack said, 'Watch.' He dealt two hands of five onto a glass-topped table. 'Look at yours.'

She had the eight, nine, ten, jack and queen of clubs.

'I just dealt you a straight flush,' he said. 'What would you stake on that, Poppy? Your new dress? Better not. Mine's a royal.' He turned over the ace, king, queen, jack and ten of diamonds. 'No, I'm not a conjurer. I know a few tricks, yes, but I don't do them to amuse. I make my living playing cards, and so does Kate. It's money for jam when you can work the pack.'

'Oh, no,' said Poppy in embarrassment.

'What's the matter?'

'You bought me that dress because you want some help?'

'Well, yes.'

'Jack, you picked the wrong girl. I can't play cards to save my blooming life.'

9

In the morning there was a violent incident in the florist's next to Richmond Station. A woman in a jade green velvet hat and a black coat with beaver trimming entered the shop a few minutes after it had opened. Alma was selecting blooms for the window. She recognized Lydia Baranov from her photographs. The face had lost the girlish softness of Trilby at the Theatre Royal, Windsor, and the fragility of Dora Vane in *The Harbour Lights*, but it still had an elegance of shape, a confidence of expression, emphatically theatrical.

In bed the night before, Alma had slowly turned the pages of the scrapbook. If she had hoped to find some portrait of Walter as a younger man, on his wedding day, or in a soldier's uniform, she was disappointed. It was exclusively a record of Lydia's life in the theatre, most of it pre-war. She had brought it back this morning in a canvas shopping-bag, covered with a knitted scarf in case of rain. It was hanging on the trellis behind her.

Alma was used to being treated as a menial by customers, particularly women. To them she was a shopgirl. She expected them to sniff the flowers and ask how much they cost without a glance in her direction. She expected them to tap their gloved fingers on the counter when another customer was being served. She expected them to pick over the bunches they had chosen and insist that certain blooms were replaced with fresher ones. But she was unprepared for Lydia Baranov.

It was firmly in Alma's mind that she was going to the surgery at lunchtime with the scrapbook. She was going to hand it personally to Walter.

So when Lydia swept in and demanded her book, Alma hesitated.

'Which book do you mean, madam?'

'Don't you dare be insolent to me.'

'I'm sorry, madam, but I don't recall meeting you before.'

Lydia said as if she were speaking to an imbecile, 'My husband Mr Baranov left it here yesterday evening.'

Alma knew she would have to hand it over. She turned to get it. She realised with disquiet that she would have to explain what it was doing in her shopping-bag. She was about to say that she had put it there this morning with the aim of delivering it to Mr Baranov's surgery, when Lydia grasped her by the arm.

'What have you got there? What on earth is my book doing in that shopping-bag?'

Without waiting for an answer, she wrenched the bag from Alma, snatched out the scrapbook and flung the bag and scarf across the shop. They hit a vase of gladioli in the window and tipped it over. Water streamed across the floor. Lydia paid no attention to it. She grabbed at Alma as she came round the counter to pick up the vase. She gripped the collar of her blouse and forced her against the counter.

'It's obvious what you've been up to. You took my book home last night to look at it. That's a violation, an invasion of my privacy. It was a vile, disgusting thing to do.' She slapped Alma hard across the face.

When Mrs Maxwell, the owner of the shop, arrived at 10.15, the vase of gladioli was replaced on its pedestal in the window. The floor had been wiped over with a cloth. She complimented Alma. A few minutes' work with a cloth and bucket in the morning freshened the shop for the rest of the day. It was always worth the effort. Mrs Maxwell looked at Alma and saw that her cheek was pink. She decided that the girl was blushing. It had long been a maxim of Mrs Maxwell's that a word of praise was the best bonus an employer could award.

Alma was saying nothing. She was determined not to mention the incident with Lydia Baranov. She had suffered humiliation and assault, but she did not need sympathy. A short time after Lydia had slapped her face and left the shop with her scrapbook held to her chest, Alma had felt a sensation that was not unpleasant. The blood had risen to her cheek to fill the capillaries. The stinging was subdued by a stimulating glow. Alma had concluded that Lydia was a desperate woman who had lost her husband's love.

When things were quiet in the shop, Alma was expected to assemble sprays and wreaths in the room at the back. Towards lunchtime she was wiring sprigs of holly into a funeral cross when she overheard a voice she knew. Walter Baranov was speaking to Mrs Maxwell in the front of the shop.

Alma waited breathlessly.

Mrs Maxwell looked round the door and told Alma that a gentleman had asked to see her about a personal matter. There was a note of censure in her voice. She said Alma had better take an early lunch.

It was hardly credible that a few minutes later she was strolling in the sunshine on Richmond Green with Walter. She kept snatching glances at familiar things to be sure that it was true: the pigeons on the cricket square, the line of elms, the green dome of the theatre, the alleyways between the tall Georgian buildings.

There was strong concern in Walter's voice. The strain showed in the taut muscles of his cheeks and neck and the way his usually square shoulders were slightly hunched. Yet he remained dignified, the more attractive to Alma for taking on this burden of apologising for an offence that was not his own. 'I came as soon as I could,' he told her. 'Lydia – my wife – spoke to me on the telephone at the surgery. She said she struck you. Is that right?'

She answered as calmly as she could, 'I think she was very upset. She saw her scrapbook in my bag. She must have assumed I had taken it home to look at it.'

'I know, I know – but she should never have slapped your face.' He turned towards her and almost touched her arm with his left hand in a gesture of concern. 'Are you all right?'

'Perfectly. I was more shocked than hurt – embarrassed, really.'

'She didn't damage your clothes? I believe there was water spilt.'

'There wasn't any damage, and I haven't mentioned it to anyone.'

'That's more than we have a right to expect. Miss Webster, I don't know how to thank you enough.'

With the sudden recklessness of a true woman of spirit, she said, 'You could call me Alma.'

He half-turned and their eyes met for a moment. He looked startled, jolted out of his prepared demeanour. He was definitely intrigued. As if to restore the proper conventions he quickly brought his hands together. 'Look here ... Alma ... I want to explain how this ghastly thing could have happened. It's the very least I can do.'

'There's no need.'

'I insist. You must do me the honour of dining with me. Is tomorrow night convenient? I believe there's a good French restaurant on the Hill. It should be quiet. We can talk in confidence there.'

Her heart raced madly, yet she managed to accept with dignity. She told him her address and he promised to call for her. His eyes were shining now and his bearing seemed more jaunty. He raised his hat and strode away in the direction of the station.

Alma continued walking across the Green, yielding at last to that quivering excitement, that unutterable joy that she had only ever known before as the printed words on a page. What marvellous compensation for a slapped face! She had an invitation to dinner with the man she loved. The fact that he was married simply added to her triumph. She had done nothing underhand. Whatever followed was the price Lydia would pay for her breach of decorum.

Humming softly, she walked back to the hairdresser's in Duke Street and made an appointment. When she got back to the shop and Mrs Maxwell remarked that she disapproved of her assistants receiving gentlemen friends at the shop, Alma replied evenly that it was most unlikely to occur again.

10

Walter came to the house at 7.30 next evening. Alma had asked the housemaid Bridget to stay late enough to admit him. At her dressing table she heard the voices downstairs. She dabbed her neck with essence of stephanotis. She stood up and smoothed the line of her tawny yellow crepe charmeuse gown. She fingered her necklace of dark amber beads. She was ready. It was the most momentous evening of her life, and she was calm and in control. Such serenity in a woman would surely be a revelation to Walter.

She put her cape around her shoulders and went downstairs to greet him. Bridget had poured him a pale dry sherry. He was studiously formal. He took a step towards Alma and bowed his head and called her Miss Webster. The pale blue of his eyes was a shade deeper this evening. In the white tie of evening dress he could have been a concert pianist or a diplomat. A ruby was inset in each of his gold cufflinks.

He had reserved a table in the Black Grape, only fifty yards down the Hill. She passed it every morning when the shutters were down. Sometimes in the evening when she returned from work there were candles alight at the tables and she could see silver salt and pepper pots and red napkins shaped like water lilies. She had never been inside.

They were shown to a corner position and the table was pulled out for them to take their places. As the waiter pushed it back, covering their knees, Alma had the extravagant thought that it was not unlike being tucked into bed. They were handed menus. She understood the French, but she let Walter take her through it. He asked the waiter his name and then instructed him to tell the chef that Miss Alma Webster and Mr Walter Baranov were dining in the restaurant that evening.

'They don't know me here,' Alma whispered as the waiter left with the order.

'They will in future,' Walter said without lowering his voice. 'They don't know me either, but they feel that they should do, and that makes the difference between first class service and mere sufferance. Now, Alma, I must thank you for your tact and consideration.'

She frowned slightly. 'I'm not sure what you mean.'

He looked quite severe as he said, 'Don't you dare deny,

young lady, that you could easily have read the menu for yourself.'

Alma blushed like a guilty child. She liked his masterful manner. It was straight out of *The Way of an Eagle*. 'How did you guess?'

'I didn't guess, my dear. I watched your eyes. Before the war I earned a meagre living as a mind-reader in the music halls. Nine-tenths of the act was trickery, but you can train yourself to learn certain things by observation. For example, did you know that someone has been talking about us?'

'Oh?'

A waiter had appeared and was speaking from behind her. 'Compliments of the manager, Mr Baranov. He would like to offer you and the lady a glass of champagne.'

'Which we are happy to accept,' said Walter. 'Do thank him, won't you?' To Alma, he said, 'You see?'

'I'm very impressed.'

'I was about to tell you that by studying people's eyes and watching the way they react and noting whether they anticipate remarks, I can find out things they didn't mean to tell me.'

She laughed. 'I shall have to be more careful.'

'You needn't worry. I don't learn very much, or by now I would have made a fortune playing poker.'

'How did you become a mind-reader?'

'It was because I had no sense of balance. I couldn't walk a tightrope like my father. I couldn't ride a monocycle or juggle or throw knives into a board. You see, the way of life in the halls more or less dictates that the children of performers get before the footlights. There's precious little chance to learn anything else. I was a magician's plant when I was eight years old.'

'A plant?'

Walter's eyes twinkled. 'Not a geranium. A plant is an assistant posing as a member of the audience. It isn't easy for a small boy to sit still with a rabbit and two doves secreted under his jacket. I stuck it for a couple of years until I was old enough to get taken on by a mind-reader. I was still a plant.'

'But still not a geranium?' put in Alma.

'More of a forget-me-not, I suppose,' said Walter, returning her smile. 'It was more congenial work, and I learned enough about it to start an act of my own when I was seventeen. Walter Baranov, Clairvoyant and Mind-Reader Extraordinary.'

'It sounds very impressive.'

'I wish the act had been equal to the billing. I have to confess, Alma, that I was never very good on the stage. Something happened to me when I got in front of audiences. Not stage-fright – rather the reverse, in fact. I got over-confident, and things went wrong. Instead of speaking my patter, I extemporised, and nine times out of ten I made a hash of the mechanical things essential to the performance. The best performers are the ones who shake like jellies before they go on. I was never like that.'

'I'm sure it wasn't half so bad as you describe it.'

'My dear, it was grotesque. I carried on for years, but only thanks to the generosity of music hall managers doing favours for my father. That was how I first met Lydia. Her father owned the Streatham Empire, you know. Lydia was between engagements as an actress, and to amuse herself she joined the act as my assistant. Within a week she transformed it. What success we had then!' Walter's eyes were shining. He shook his head, smiling at the memory.

Alma felt a spasm of jealousy, and suppressed it. 'How exactly did she change the act?'

'She said it needed drama, so she sat among the audience and pretended to be sceptical of my powers. She announced that I was a fake. You should have heard the audience cheering when she left her seat and marched up the gangway to the stage to expose my trickery. And when my first attempt at clairvoyance was a failure, they stood up and applauded Lydia. Then there was utter silence as the next test worked. Such drama! Lydia's reactions were magnificent, worthy of melodrama at its best. While she was saucer-eyed with disbelief, I kept my mind on the performance, and finished it in style. At the end they cheered me to the echo.'

'And you married Lydia.'

He snapped out of his reverie. 'There was more to it than that.'

Alma waited, not wishing to seem as inquisitive as she felt.

'I played at the Empire for a week with Lydia and then we parted,' said Walter. 'She had other work in the legitimate theatre. So I returned to my less-than-brilliant mind-reading without her. It was quite depressing, but I had to scrape a living, and I knew no other. Then Lydia's father died and left her a considerable fortune, four theatres and two music halls. She was very busy as an actress, and management was all too much for her, yet she took it on gamely. She remembered me and engaged me at the Canterbury.' He laughed. 'I must have been terrible. She persuaded me to give it up and marry her. She financed my training as a dentist. She said the world needed dentists more than mind-readers.'

Alma could not contain herself. 'Excuse me for saying this, but you make your marriage sound like a business arrangement.'

He sprinkled pepper on his fillet of veal. 'Yes, that's what it is.'

There was silence between them. Alma dared not press him further, yet her mind was racing ahead.

At last he said, 'Perhaps you think I married her for her money.'

'Of course not.' She blushed deeply. 'I'm sure you love each other.'

'Love? I often wonder what is meant by love.'

'It's a kind of magic, isn't it? It's a power that overwhelms one.'

'I was never very good at magic,' Walter said.

'I'm sure it's unmistakable when it occurs.'

'Then I rather think that I was never in love with Lydia.'

She could not be certain from his beaming smile whether he was being candid with her. 'She's a beautiful woman,' Alma said. 'And she has great vitality.'

'You're extremely generous, considering that she attacked you.'

'To be fair, she had the right to take offence. She saw the scrapbook in my bag. She thought I must have taken it home to look at it.' Alma paused. 'She was right. I thought there might be something in it about you.'

He either missed or ignored her admission. 'Lydia has been under great strain for a long time,' he said. 'She has not been given a leading role since 1914. She attends auditions, but the parts are given to younger actresses of less experience. It makes me feel guilty.'

'Why is that?'

'You see, while her career has languished, mine has steadily improved. She got me started, paid for all my training, bought my equipment and set me up in Eaton Place. She still pays the rent for the surgery. It's a lot of money.'

'You mustn't blame yourself for being a success,' Alma said impetuously. 'You justified her confidence. She must have wanted you to be successful.'

'Yes, I'm sure she did.' His voice was generous, even tender.

Alma remembered her determination to remain serene. 'Then why feel guilty?'

Walter turned and looked at her. 'You're very kind. I haven't properly explained why she attacked you in the shop. The night before, we had an argument. That's not unusual. She has a lot of disappointments, and she relieves her feelings by breathing fire and fury on me. I can usually take it, but on this occasion she came out with something so astonishing that I was quite unequal to it. She said she is completely disillusioned with the English theatre, so she is going to America to become a cinema actress.'

Alma's heart pounded. 'Is she serious?'

'Completely, I'm afraid. She's already made enquiries at the shipping office. She once worked with Charlie Chaplin. He has a company in America called United Artists, with Mary Pickford and Douglas Fairbanks. Lydia is confident that Chaplin will remember her and launch her on a cinema career.'

'What an extraordinary idea! What about you? What are you expected to do?'

He gave a shrug. 'She hasn't given it a thought. She's intoxicated by the prospect of America. For Lydia, it's the end of seven years of heartbreak. She just assumes that I'll go with her.'

'But you have the practice.'

'I'm supposed to sell it and start another in America.'

'American Painless Dentistry.'

He gave her a surprised look. 'Did I tell you about that? Yes, I shudder at the prospect.'

'Have you told her?'

'I tried. She seems indifferent whether I go with her or remain. We were separated before, by dental school, and then the war. Ours has never been a conventional marriage. But you see, I owe everything to Lydia. In return, I've always tried to give her my support, if it's only a sympathetic ear. This time, I could only listen in amazement. Worse, I'd lost her precious book of notices. I remembered later where it was, but by this time Lydia

57

had gone upstairs in a towering rage. I'm afraid it all crashed down on you in the morning.'

Alma smiled. 'So you're to blame?'

'Yes, indeed.'

They talked of other things: the flower shops, gardens, favourite walks. The waiter cleared the table. They ate cheese and biscuits and drank coffee. Walter paid the bill and gave a generous tip. The manager came forward with a red rose for Alma. She took it graciously and exchanged a secret smile with Walter. Outside she confirmed that her shop supplied them to the restaurant.

He escorted her for the short distance to her house. At the gate she thanked him. She said she hoped he wouldn't be leaving soon for America. He asked why, and she reminded him light-heartedly that her dental treatment wasn't finished. He gave her a warm smile. The numerous little creases round his eyes shaped into their own signal of appreciation. He said it had done him good to pass an evening without histrionics. As for America, he had not decided yet.

While Walter had been speaking, Alma had regarded him steadily. The evening had taught her much more about him. His calm exterior was deceiving. He was in turmoil. The circumstances of his life had trapped him since he was a child, yet he had suffered them with quiet resignation. To satisfy his father, he had given his youth to the music hall, to which he was temperamentally unsuited. His marriage was devoid of love, but he had endured it for the opportunity of a new career. Now his frustrated and embittered wife proposed to destroy his livelihood, his peace of mind, his self-respect. He desperately needed help.

Alma loved him more tenaciously than ever. Before long she would have to let him know. But this was not the time.

For the present it had to be enough that he exercised his powers as a mind-reader to arrange to meet her again.

'That walk that you described,' he said, '– the one to the heronry in Richmond Park. I'm rather tempted to try it on Sunday. What was the name of the plantation, Alma?'

'Sidmouth.' She was discreet enough to hesitate before she added, 'I could show you if you like. What time will you be going?'

He could have named any time of the day or night. Alma would be there.

11

At the Paris Carlton on fine days in the summer months, break-fast was served on the terrace. The warmth of the sun, the gentle movement of air and the aroma of coffee could be guaranteed to kindle romantic thoughts in Marjorie Livingstone Cordell. This morning there was an extra impulse.

'Livy, my darling,' she announced as she joined her husband at one of the white metal tables, 'I have just learned something really sensational.'

Livingstone Cordell had not come to terms with breakfasts in Paris. Fresh bread rolls gave him indigestion if he ate enough of them to satisfy his appetite. Yet when he ordered grapefruit segments and a cooked breakfast it was so slow in coming that it limited his capacity for lunch. Without looking up at his wife he said, 'While you're still on your feet, would you ask that god-damned waiter what happened to my bacon and kidneys? I gave the order all of twenty minutes ago.'

Mrs Livingstone Cordell waved at the waiter and pointed urgently towards her husband. Livy was not the sort of man who got quick service from French waiters. He looked too comfort-able in his chair. He was short and overweight and he wore a cheap linen jacket that he had bought years back in Chicago. His hair was fairish, with patches of grey that gave him a commonplace pepper-and-salt look. His eyebrows were so colourless and meagre that it was difficult for him to look any-thing but docile. French waiters and the world at large – with the exception of Marjorie Livingstone Cordell – remained unaware that he had the most amazing and outrageous tattoos on unseen areas of his body.

The waiter returned a nod that could have meant anything. Mrs Livingstone Cordell sat down.

'Don't you want to hear my news, Livy?'

'They have a sale on at the Galeries Lafayette.'

'Do they?' She studied his small grey eyes in case he knew something she did not. 'You incorrigible man! You're kidding, aren't you? My news is totally reliable. Listen to this. I just went to Reception to fix another massage and by sheer good fortune I happened to notice the bellhops wheeling in some luggage. Four or five enormous trunks and some smaller stuff. You know me, Livy: I just couldn't resist a little peek at the label. You're not going to believe this: they belong to Mr Paul Westerfield II!'

'Oh, yea.' Livy went silent for a moment. 'What the hell do you suppose they are doing with my bacon and kidneys?'

'Paul Westerfield II, honey.'

'I never heard of the guy.'

'He only happens to be one of the most eligible young men in New York. His father is the millionaire architect who designed those beautiful frame houses just across the Hudson from us in New Jersey.' Mrs Livingstone Cordell shut her eyes and sighed. 'It must be providential, young Paul putting up here at this time, when our Barbara has finished her studies and is free to show him over Paris. She knows the city. This is her big break, Livy. If you were twenty-four years old and on your first trip to Paris, wouldn't you be glad of a sweet American girl to show you around?'

Livy shook his head. 'Forget it. You can bet your life this guy hasn't come to Paris to see the Louvre with a special lecture on the Ancient Greeks. Besides, we're moving on to England at the end of the week. I have it on good authority that you can actually get served with a breakfast at the Savoy Hotel.'

Mrs Livingstone Cordell pressed her lips into a pout and emitted a moan audible only to herself. Livy was so insensitive to the things that mattered to women. She could forgive him plenty when she thought of his tattoos, but she wished he would sometimes pay attention to what she was saying.

'Looks like Barbara has been working on the problem,' Livy remarked.

'What do you mean?'

'Take a look to your right.'

'Oh my God!' whispered Mrs Livingstone Cordell.

Her daughter Barbara was crossing the terrace to their table hand in hand with a very tall, very slim, very intelligent-looking young man in a cream-coloured three-piece. Beside him in her brown hobble skirt Barbara looked positively dowdy, but her eyes were shining more brightly than her mother had ever seen. 'Mommy and Livy,' she said, 'I want you to meet my college friend, Paul Westerfield. What do you think – I just met Paul in the lobby. We were in the same math class at college. Isn't that incredible?'

'You already know Mr Westerfield? said Mrs Livingstone Cordell, barely able to voice her words.

'Don't mind my mother,' said Barbara to Paul Westerfield. "She thinks any guy under fifty who comes within half a mile of me is a possible husband. She doesn't know that I'd rather drop dead than walk out with one of you monsters from the math class. This is Livy. He's my stepfather, my second actually.'

'What are you doing in Paris, Paul?' asked Livy.

'A little sight-seeing, I thought,' said Paul. 'I'm on my way to London to interview Dr Bertrand Russell about the book he wrote with A. N. Whitehead.'

'*Principia Mathematica*,' said Barbara.

'And I thought I might as well stop off in Paris to meet some of the professors of math at the Sorbonne.'

'Barbara can introduce you to plenty of professors,' chipped in Mrs Livingstone Cordell.

'Mommy, I was studying art, if you remember. Paul needs no introduction from me. He's known thoughout the world for his papers on permutations and the binomial theorem. I was just the coed who used to sit behind him in class and tell him when he had holes in his socks.'

Paul Westerfield laughed and cleared his throat and blushed all at the same time.

'Well, that's it,' said Barbara. 'Those are my parents. Don't let us hold you up. It was a real nice surprise to bump into you like that.'

'It was mutual,' said Paul. 'Goodbye, folks.' He walked rapidly away.

'Anyone got any ideas how we should spend the day?' asked Barbara brightly.

12

Alma was convinced that she could persuade Walter not to go with his wife Lydia to America. She was confident that he was going to fall in love with her. She had learned from the novels of Ethel M. Dell that true love will surmount any obstacle. She was not discouraged by the difference in their ages. She had no conscience about Walter being married. He had not married Lydia for love. If Lydia abandoned him to go to America, he was entitled to accept another's love. He would turn to Alma, and to such happiness as he had never known. It would be the highest plane of love, two minds in harmony. When he kissed her, she would hear the music of the spheres.

She conceded that it was probably too soon to expect the music of the spheres on Sunday, in their walk to the heronry in Richmond Park, but it was not impossible. As they strolled leisurely along the quiet footpaths, they would exchange more confidences about their lives. Gradually they would discover things in common, the hopes and fears and likes and dislikes that chance had given them to share.

But the walk was disappointing. Walter made no attempt at intimate conversation. He talked about the care of teeth. He described the structure of a tooth, as if Alma's deepest wish was to know the difference between canines and incisors. He recommended brushing teeth at least twice daily. He enumerated substances to use. He explained why precipitated chalk was good and camphorated chalk was bad, because it cracked the enamel. He warned her not to use an acid mouth wash or an iron tonic, unless it was in the form of pills.

It may have been that he intended to impress her with his expert knowledge, but he did not. Alma felt neglected. She had not come to Richmond Park for this. While he talked on, she tried to explain it to herself. Perhaps he was struggling with his conscience, drawing back from the familiarity that could lead to a liaison. Perhaps he could not trust his inner passion.

Alma said little. It was not possible to bring him round to personal matters.

Yet at the end of the walk when they got back to the Richmond Gate, he said in the same discursive tone of voice he had used all afternoon, 'What a boring companion I have been. Did you know that you can walk right down to the river through the Terrace Gardens? Let's hire a boat for an hour, and I promise not to mention teeth.'

She took his arm as they walked down the steep incline.

His manner altered. The air was cooler near the water, so he took off his jacket and put it round her shoulders.

He was not very expert with the oars. He splashed her several times and apologised profusely. Alma laughed. She was so happy to be noticed that she said it didn't matter, and meant it.

'The last time I was in a boat,' he explained, 'must have been six years ago, and then there were seventy others to share the rowing, so I didn't get much practice.'

'Seventy in a rowing-boat?' said Alma, laughing. 'Whatever were you doing?'

He smiled too. 'Trying to stay alive. Really, it was no laughing-matter. We were survivors from the *Lusitania*.'

'The ship that was torpedoed? You were on the *Lusitania*?'

'With my father,' answered Walter. 'I had compassionate leave to help him back from America.'

'The Great Baranov.'

'Once Great, I'm afraid. By 1915 he was too old to be touring in vaudeville. He fell from the highwire and broke his leg. He had tremendous spirit. The night before we sank, he led a protest to the captain because the passengers weren't being told the reason for certain obvious precautions against U-boats. Poor old Dad – he was always spoiling for a fight. Not like me – I take the line of least resistance.'

'Was he drowned?'

'No. He survived. He had plaster up to his hip and we were in the water over an hour. Eventually one of the lifeboats picked us up.'

'You must have kept him afloat. You're braver than you care to say. You saved your father's life.'

'Yes – but I sometimes wish I hadn't. He was a cripple. He could never work again. Six months after that he hanged himself. He used a length of the wire he used to walk on.'

'Walter, what a dreadful thing!'

'Yes.' He looked down. 'It was tragic.'

Neither of them spoke again for several minutes. Walter rowed slowly in the direction of Twickenham until they reached a stretch where an island divided the stream. On the narrower side an overhanging willow formed a natural arch.

'The place to get my breath back,' said Walter as he steered the skiff towards an iron ring set into the bank. He tied up and shipped the oars. 'Is there room on the cushion for one more?'

She felt a flutter of excitement, the more exquisite for coming after such a disappointing afternoon. She smiled shyly and said, 'Of course there is.' As she made room, she told him, 'You'd better have your jacket back. You'll soon get cold.'

Clutching the willow branches, Walter moved along the boat and sat beside her. 'I'm warm. Just feel my hand.'

She was suddenly aware that the next few moments could uplift her from near-despair into ecstasy. She held his hand with both of hers, feeling its broadness, stroking her fingertips over the fine covering of hair. She did not let go. She said, 'Those people in the lifeboat must have been glad to have had you there.'

'Why?'

'To turn to for support and confidence. You radiate such calm, whatever you may feel inside yourself. It gives strength to others.'

'Does it strengthen you?' he asked in mild surprise.

She looked steadily into his eyes. 'Immensely. It makes me more confident every second.'

He frowned slightly, as if uncertain where this was leading, but he was smiling, too. 'Confident of what?'

She hesitated. She had not imagined in her daydreams of this moment that she would need to indicate in words that she was ready to be kissed. She said impulsively, 'Confident that if I close my eyes, I will not be disappointed.' As soon as she had said it, she shut her eyes, more from shock at her boldness than anything else. There flashed through her mind the mortifying thought that he might still draw back. It was so vivid and appalling that she tugged on his hand and swayed towards him.

Their faces bumped. She felt the rasp of his moustache. She kept her eyes shut tight.

She heard him say, 'Oh, dear. Have I hurt you?'

She opened her eyes. 'No – but I feel so ridiculous.' She was on the point of tears.

He appeared to understand. 'Don't be. There's no need. We surprised each other, that's all. Put your head back and relax. Keep still now. Keep absolutely still.'

She obeyed as if she were in the dental chair.

Walter moved his face close and their lips touched lightly for a second. It was the first time any man had kissed her on the mouth. She heard no music in her head and no meteors flashed across her vision, but she was exquisitely content.

'And now,' Walter said, 'I think I had better row us back.'

Before he left her, she said she would like to cook him a supper in return for the dinner he had given her. He accepted, but not for that evening. He promised to come on Tuesday, two days later.

Alone that evening, she went over and over the memory of that kiss under the willow. What had it meant to him? Had he tried to deny himself the pleasure that a married man ought not to give or take except with his wife? Had his placid manner covered a ferment of guilt and passion? Or had he kissed her out of sympathy, to save her from embarrassment?

She remembered Trevor Mordaunt, the imperturbable hero of *The Rocks of Valpré*. He was like Walter, hiding his emotions, exuding strength through his aloofness, but true and dependable and generous. Strangely, Alma had not warmed to Trevor when she had read the book, but he seemed more attractive now.

13

There was no kissing on Tuesday. There was conversation, earnest, serious conversation. And as they talked, Alma realised that this was more binding than a kiss, because Walter was involving her in the crisis of his marriage. He told her that Lydia was still serious about going to America.

'She refuses to discuss it,' Walter said. 'She's making the arrangements hour by hour. She's written to Chaplin to tell him she's coming. She's been showing people over the house – it's already up for sale, you know. She's giving ornaments away to friends and neighbours because she doesn't want to take them with her. And she's buying heaps of clothes for the voyage over.'

'Has she booked the passage yet?'

'It's to be booked as soon as she has a buyer for the house. From what she tells me, there are two offers with the agent.' He paused. 'And what is more, she has told me I must put the practice up for sale.'

Alma turned from the sideboard where she was about to serve the meal. 'Walter, that's ridiculous. Does she still assume that you'll give up all that you have worked for?'

'She does,' said Walter.

Alma thought she had detected a note of resignation in his voice. 'You wouldn't consider the idea – would you?' she asked, unable to disguise the anxiety she felt. She tried to busy herself with the dishes.

He answered bleakly, 'I fear I'm in no position to refuse. Believe me, Alma, I've agonized over this. Without Lydia's money I can't possibly keep up the surgery. The fees I charge wouldn't pay the rent and keep me alive. In a few years, possibly, but not yet.'

'Can't you buy a less expensive practice?'

'I have no capital to speak of. It's out of the question.'

She was stunned. He was going to leave her. She fought back her tears. 'But the whole idea of going to America makes no sense.'

He nodded. 'I know, my dear. It's quixotic. She's risking everything we have.'

And he had capitulated to her! Why wasn't he prepared to fight? He *had* to be persuaded that something could be done.

'Walter, you told me the other evening that you married

Lydia as a business arrangement.'

'That's right.' He added caustically, 'And now I'm going to pay for it.'

'Can't you convince her that it would make better business sense if you kept up the surgery here so that she has something to return to if her hopes don't materialise in America?'

'My dear, when you say it, it sounds eminently reasonable, but Lydia refuses to consider the possibility of failure.'

Alma would not give in. 'Perhaps she would agree to go alone if you offered to join her later. There must be so much to attend to with the selling of the house and your practice.'

Walter said that there was a solicitor who would arrange all that. Alma persisted. They talked so intensely that the Ragout of Duck was eaten and the plates removed before Walter praised Alma's cooking. He was still doubtful of making any impression on Lydia, but he agreed to suggest he should remain in England while she was getting known in Hollywood.

He promised to meet Alma on the Green on Friday at lunch-time to let her know what Lydia had said.

'This is a difficult time,' he said as he put on his hat. 'I really shouldn't burden you with my problems.'

'I want to share them,' said Alma simply.

After he had gone, she found one of his cigar-stubs in an ashtray. That night she put a match to it in her bedroom and imagined he was there.

At some stage of the night there crept into her mind a possible solution. It was extravagant and dangerous, a last resort. Surely in the morning it would seem outrageous. But while she gave it thought, and plotted stage by stage, it seemed to gain in plausibility.

14

The news from Walter on Friday was worse than she had feared. The house was under offer. Lydia had booked a first class passage for two on the *Mauretania*, sailing from Southampton in fifteen days' time.

'For two?' said Alma. 'She still believes you're going with her?'

He looked away towards the elms on the far side of the Green.

Alma gripped his sleeve. 'Walter, what have you told her?'

He put his left hand gently over hers. It was shaking. 'My dear, you have been very sweet to me.'

'You're going, aren't you?'

He nodded. 'I can't do otherwise. Her solicitors are taking care of everything, even the selling of my practice.'

'But it belongs to you.'

'I may have built it up, but legally it's Lydia's. I signed papers when she paid for my equipment. She owns me.'

'No.' She buried her face in his jacket and hugged him. She sobbed convulsively.

That afternoon Alma did not return to the flower shop, and Walter telephoned the surgery to cancel his appointments. They walked along the towpath to Twickenham. In Marble Hill Park they found a quiet place beside an uprooted tree. Walter sat against the trunk and cradled Alma's head and shoulders. They talked for a long time. He admitted that the trip to America was almost certain to end in fiasco. Lydia would not be wanted by Chaplin or anyone in Hollywood. Her money would not last long there. Walter would find it difficult to set up a dental practice. Lydia would be angry and embittered.

'But she won't listen to reason,' he told Alma. 'She treats everything I say as an attack on her artistry. She says she won't be deprived of her destiny.'

'Then she's going, whether you are with her or not.'

'Yes.'

Alma was fighting for the man she loved. The fight was not with Lydia, who cared only about her career. She was pitted against Walter's fatalism. She had to convince him that he had a choice of his own. 'When you talked about your father committing suicide so soon after you were saved from the *Lusitania*, you seemed to be saying that it was a waste.'

'So it was. He might as well have drowned.'

'Aren't you throwing your own life away if you go to America?'

'My dear, I couldn't survive here without work, without a place to live.'

'You could live with me.'

'What?' For a moment that look of surprise bordering on panic flitted into his eyes. 'Oh, no – I couldn't do that.'

She regarded him as steadily as she could considering what she had decided to tell him. 'Walter, I love you.'

His grip on her arm tightened. He closed his eyes. 'I feared that this was so.'

'Feared?'

'My dear, I have been selfish. I took advantage of your kindness to get sympathy. You have helped me to face up to my problems. But it must stop at that. We both know why – don't we?'

Alma had often sighed and shed tears over scenes like this in books, but now that it was happening to her she felt more bullheaded than romantic. She sat up and faced Walter and said, 'I don't expect you to say that you love me. I am twenty-eight years old and I have no experience of men. But I know what I am suggesting. I will not let you be destroyed by that fanatical woman.'

He shook his head. 'It would destroy you, Alma. Believe me, I am overwhelmed by what you say, but I am still a married man nearly twenty years your senior with no money of my own. Imagine the scandal it would create.'

'I *have* imagined it,' Alma said vehemently, 'and I'm indifferent to it. People who don't know the facts of the matter only betray themselves by gossiping. Please understand that I am serious.'

They started back along the towpath, and she pleaded her case all the way to Richmond Bridge and up the Hill to her house. Walter gently, but adamantly, refused to be persuaded. At the gate she asked him in.

'No,' he said softly. 'We must part now, with dignity.'

She saw that his eyes had moistened, and she could only guess at the thoughts of this unhappy, undemonstrative man.

She said, hardly believing it, 'Shan't I see you again?'

He shook his head. Then he kissed her.

69

She pressed her lips against his, trying to hold the kiss for ever. He put his hands on her face and gently pushed her away.

Alma said, 'I believe I could murder that woman.'

Walter frowned slightly and looked at her and the frown receded and was replaced by an expression that to Alma seemed very like enlightenment. The frown returned and he shook his head. He said, 'I shall never forget you.'

Alma put out her hand, but he had turned and was already walking fast down the Hill.

Livingstone Cordell and family arrived at the Savoy Hotel in London on Saturday and Marjorie had a massage from a man who called it friction and said he looked after a football team called the Hotspurs. Her skin had never felt so raw, but that night she was dancing to the Savoy Orpheans until they stopped and then she persuaded Livy to take her to the Silver Slipper club in Regent Street, where she was still one-stepping on the glass floor at 3am. As a consequence Livy missed his full English breakfast on Sunday. To mollify him, Marjorie bought tickets for the newest show in town, called *The Co-optimists*.

'I got three seats in the front row of the Royal Circle for next Friday evening,' she announced on Monday.

'Are there chorus girls?'

Marjorie winked at her daughter Barbara, 'I was told there's a tenor called Gideon who has a voice like pure honey.'

'Mommy, I don't want to seem ungrateful, but I'd rather not go, if you don't mind,' said Barbara, twisting the table napkin tightly.

'Is that so? Livy, do you have something to say about that?'

Livy did not look up from the *Daily Mail*. He quite liked the British papers.

'Well, I do,' said Marjorie. 'I'd like to say that the way you're going on, young lady, life's going to pass you by. Your head is stuffed so full of logarithms and old pots that you've got no conversation. Maybe *The Co-optimists* doesn't appeal to you, but if you go and see it at least you can talk about it. I'm sure there are some charming English boys who would like to hear you talk about it, even if you tear it to shreds. I suppose you have something better to do next Friday night.'

'As a matter of fact, I do,' said Barbara.

'And what might that be?'

'A lecture on philosophy by Mr Bertrand Russell.'

'Oh, my God. Have you taken up philosophy now?'

'No. Paul Westerfield has. He invited me along.'

Livy looked over his newspaper and said, 'Nice one, kid.'

Lydia reached for a slice of toast and started to butter it. Without looking up, she said, 'By the way, if you're going to the surgery today, you'd better give that nurse a week's notice. I've sold the practice.' She had kept this piece of news for breakfast on Monday morning to avoid a weekend's bickering. Walter was so insufferably possessive about his tooth-pulling.

'You've what?' His voice was shrill with disbelief.

'Sold the practice, darling. We did discuss it, if you remember. It's gone to a Mr Edwards, Simon Edwards, a charming and attractive man who happens to be the brother-in-law of my friend Maggie. The poor darling has been doing nothing but gold crowns for Jewish tailors in the Mile End Road for the last ten years. He's absolutely thrilled.'

Walter pushed his plate aside. His face was purple. 'I haven't even met this man. He hasn't seen the surgery.'

'Oh, but he has, Walter. I took him there on Friday afternoon. You weren't there. The nurse said you had telephoned to cancel your appointments. Were you feeling ill, or something? Anyway, Simon adores the place and is quite prepared to take it over from next week. The point is that he doesn't need Nurse Tung, or whatever she is called, because he is bringing his own assistant.'

'You don't appear to understand, Lydia. I can't consign my patients to a man I haven't even met.'

'Darling, he's perfectly respectable. He went to Charterhouse, which is more than we can say for you. You'll meet him soon enough. He wants to go through the files with you on Wednesday. He's taking over the lot – the furniture, the dental equipment, even your forceps and things.'

'He can't have my instruments! Damnit, I shall need them in America.'

Lydia chipped at the varnish on one of her fingernails.

'I've used them ever since I trained,' Walter went on, his outrage increasing by the second. 'This won't do, Lydia. It's like depriving a musician of his violin.'

By Walter's standards, this was quite an eruption. Lydia said evenly, 'Not really, darling. I think you ought to know that I have changed my mind about what you will do in America. You won't need your instruments after all, because there is something much more important to be done. I shall need an agent to negotiate my contracts with the film companies. It's obvious that you should do it. I can't entrust my future as a film star to some American I have never met, so the job is yours.'

He stared at her like a trapped animal. He was speechless. He was shaking his head.

'Come now,' Lydia appealed to him, 'this is important to me. You've had years of pleasure finding holes in people's teeth, and now it's time for a change.'

'I don't propose to change,' Walter said in a voice so low it was almost threatening.

Lydia was not used to being defied. She had been about to tell him that he would earn a good commission if he worked for it. Instead she said, 'You have no choice, Walter. You couldn't set up as a dentist in America without money. They don't pull teeth in the street any more.'

'I'll have the money from the sale of the practice. How much is Edwards paying us?'

'That money belongs to me.'

'I built it up. I'm entitled to something back, for God's sake.'

'Not according to my solicitor, darling. Be sensible, Walter. We both have an interest in my future.'

He stood up and shouted, 'What future?' He stormed out of the room and out of the house. The front door slammed.

For a moment Lydia wondered whether Walter *was* the right person to be her agent. Then she reflected that it didn't matter because she only wanted him for window-dressing. Everyone in Hollywood had an agent. Walter would be answering the telephone, but she would decide which offers to accept.

She went upstairs to attend to her face. She was seeing the solicitor this morning. And she would be buying more new clothes for the voyage. She needed at least three full changes for each of the six days at sea.

While she was putting up her hair, the telephone rang. She let Sylvia pick it up. In a moment she was at the bedroom door.

'It's for you, ma'am. A lady.'

'Who is it?'

'She didn't say.'

Lydia said over her shoulder as she went downstairs, 'Really, I don't know what I pay you for.' She picked up the earpiece. 'Lydia Baranov speaking.'

There was a slight hesitation at the other end, then: 'I want to speak to you about your husband.'

'Who are you?' said Lydia.

'Someone who cares what happens to him.'

'What do you mean? You'd better tell me who you are.'

'Never mind that, Mrs Baranov. I want to appeal to you as one woman to another to treat him fairly. He doesn't want to go to America with you. He's happy here. You've treated him generously in the past. I wouldn't ask this if you loved each other, but you know that isn't so. Please be generous again and let him remain in England with the one who does love him.'

'What? I don't know who you are, but I think you must be mad. You're not that nurse of his, are you?' Lydia pressed the instrument harder to her ear. Before she hung it up, she wanted to be certain who this woman was. There was something in the voice that sounded familiar.

'I appeal to you, Mrs Baranov. Let him have his freedom.'

'This is utterly ridiculous.'

'I'm trying to be reasonable, for all our sakes. God knows, I love your husband.'

'He's never mentioned you. Are you claiming to be his lover?'

'If you wish. Would you agree to a divorce?'

Lydia began to laugh. 'My dear, whoever you are, and I've got my suspicions, you've gone a bit too far. I know my husband. He wouldn't know what a mistress is, let alone what to do with one. So own up, and let's both enjoy the joke.'

'It is not a joke. You wouldn't know my name if I told you. You'd better ask Walter. He can decide how much to tell you. But don't under-estimate him, Mrs Baranov. And don't think you've heard the last from me.' The line went dead.

Lydia sat by the telephone for a long interval. She was trembling. She got up and went to the cocktail cabinet and poured herself a brandy. She drank it at a draught.

She said, 'You animal, Walter. You stupid, rampant beast!'

17

Alma said goodnight to Mrs Maxwell and unfastened her umbrella. It was a sudden downpour that might last only a few minutes, but she did not propose to stand in the entrance to the shop a moment longer than was necessary. She wanted to get home and see whether her prayers were answered and a message was waiting on the mat, or the telephone was ringing as she opened the door. Neither was to happen.

She took two steps and her arm was taken and the umbrella snatched from her hand. Without a word, Walter hustled her across the pavement into a taxi and got in beside her. His clothes were saturated. Alma pressed close to him and kissed him on the cheek. It was cold.

She said, 'I thought we wouldn't see each other again.'

'You're getting wet.' He took off his raincoat and hat and let her come close again. This time she kissed him on the lips. She was intensely happy. His hand grasped the back of her neck and loosened her hair. He said, 'I'm supposed to be reprimanding you for telephoning my wife.'

'I had to think of something. Are you angry with me?'

'I ought to be. It's no good, you know. She wouldn't give me a divorce.' He gave a low chuckle. 'But it's a terrible shock to Lydia to be told I have a lover.'

Alma pressed closer to him. 'Am I really your lover?'

'There's a teashop at the foot of the Hill. Shall we stop there?'

The rain had already eased as they got out of the taxi. The shop was full of people escaping the shower, but someone got up to leave. The table was in a quiet position shielded by the coatstand. Walter told Alma that Lydia had renounced her promise to let him practise dentistry in America. She wanted him to act as her agent.

She felt the blood drain from her face. 'Is that because of me?'

He reached across the table and put his hand over hers. 'No, my dear. She announced this over breakfast. And she has sold the practice and I won't get a penny from the proceeds.'

Alma shook her head slowly, but she said nothing. She knew intuitively that Walter was on the point of saying something momentous.

He still held her hand. 'I have decided not to go to America.'

'Walter, my darling!'

'It's ruinous, of course, but I'll manage somehow.'

'We'll manage together.'

'No. I thank you, but I couldn't do that. I couldn't allow myself to subject you to gossip and scandal.'

'I don't care a jot about my reputation. I love you!'

He stared down at his tea.

Alma decided that this was the moment to mention the plan she had conceived as she lay sleepless at home in the small hours of the morning. It would sound outrageous, spoken coldly like this in a public teashop, but when otherwise could she tell him? She pitched her voice low. 'There could be another way.'

'Hm?' He did not look up.

'Once, in the surgery, you talked to me about someone else who was treated unbearably badly by his wife, and who fell in love with another woman who cared deeply and passionately about him.'

He looked up and regarded her innocently. 'I don't seem to recall this.'

'Dr Crippen.'

'Oh.' He gave a jolt.

Before he could stop her, Alma said, 'They were caught because they tried to disguise themselves. They tried to escape across the ocean on a small steamship and the captain was suspicious.'

'Crippen was a murderer.'

Alma brushed that aside. 'You told me Lydia has booked your passages on the *Mauretania*.'

'Yes, but I'm not going now.'

'Just suppose for a moment that you *did* go, not with Lydia, but with me. I would travel as Mrs Baranov. It wouldn't be a difficult part to play, darling. No-one would suspect us, because no-one would know any different. We would be in America in six days and live there for ever as man and wife!'

'But what about Lydia?'

'Chloroform.'

'I think I need a cigar.' He put one in his mouth and broke two matches trying to light it. 'Are you serious about this?'

'Absolutely.'

'I couldn't do it – not even to Lydia.'

'You *can*. You're very brave. You saved your father from drowning.'

He managed to smile. 'It isn't exactly the same thing.'

'Please don't laugh at me. This isn't some absurd idea that just occurred to me. I've been planning it for days. Don't you see? By booking for the voyage already, Lydia has given us the chance to succeed where Dr Crippen and his Ethel failed.'

A voice asked, 'Did you want some more hot water, dears?'

They both looked up at the waitress. Her face showed only the weariness of a long day at work.

'No, thank you,' said Walter. He paid for the teas and they left the shop.

The sun was shining thinly.

'They were caught because Inspector Dew found the remains of Mrs Crippen under the floor in the cellar,' said Walter.

'There is another thing,' said Alma, ignoring Walter's observation as they walked up the Hill together. 'If I take Lydia's place, I can copy her signature. I can write you a cheque for the sale of your practice. I can write any number of cheques. We can live in style and you can be the most successful dentist in America.'

'Using Lydia's money?'

'It would be criminal not to use it, darling,' said Alma, and she squeezed his arm.

'That's clever.' He smiled. 'That really is rather clever.'

'I shall have to use her passport, but that ought to be all right. We're about the same height and we both have brown eyes. She's darker than I am, but you couldn't tell from a photograph. Nobody looks like their passport photograph anyway. And you'll be there to vouch for me.'

'There must be a flaw in this.'

'Darling, there isn't. If we give Lydia the chloroform the night before we sail, none of her friends will miss her. She'll have signed the papers for the solicitor. The bank will have transferred her money to America. We simply step aboard that liner and start our new life together. Our honeymoon.'

Walter looked dazed. He had obviously been staggered by the boldness of the plan. His first reaction had been to reject it, then to look for faults in it. Now he was seriously considering it. Alma could see it in his eyes. He was coming to terms with the necessity of chloroforming Lydia.

He raised more difficulties, but they were details only. He asked what Alma would say to Mrs Maxwell, and what she would do about the house on Richmond Hill. He asked about her family and friends.

From the nature and manner of his questions, it was clear that Walter was prepared to be convinced. Alma told him what she would say to Mrs Maxwell. She told him there were people at the church who would rent the house. She would tell them she was going to winter on the continent. She would tell her closest friends. She had no immediate family. She could be ready in a week.

Walter listened carefully. Then he was silent for a time.

Alma walked beside him up the Hill. She contained herself. She didn't want to rush him into a decision. She wanted him to see the soundness of the plan. She was confident that it would work.

At last he spoke. 'We'll have to think of what to do with her.'

From the way he said it, Alma knew that he had been persuaded.

PART THREE

The Knockout

1

To Alma, the plan to do away with Lydia and escape with Walter to America was more romantic then anything in Ethel M. Dell. It made *The Knave of Diamonds* seem insipid. It was wicked and audacious and it would bind her more strongly to Walter than any ceremony of marriage. Their secret would unite them for ever. They would live in luxury in Manhattan, and Walter would be the finest dentist in New York. They would take trips to Niagara and Nantucket and New Orleans and San Francisco. Mentally she was still touring the United States when Walter, firmly bogged down in England, said, 'We really ought to decide what to do with her.'

'Do with her?'

'Lydia.'

'But we decided, darling.'

'No, I don't mean that. I mean after that. Where shall we put her?'

'Oh.'

They were sitting on a bench in the Richmond Terrace Gardens. It was one of those brilliant September evenings when every detail of the Thames Valley was picked out by the low-angled sun. Filaments of cirrus cloud lay across the sky becoming pinker by the minute.

'Dr Crippen buried his wife in the cellar,' observed Alma.

'And Inspector Dew went down there with a spade.'

'Horrid Inspector Dew.'

Walter gave a shrug. 'Just doing his job.'

'How about the garden?'

He shook his head. 'It's like a bowling green. We have an ex-serviceman to look after it five mornings a week. He was an officer in the Guards. Nothing escapes him.'

'Could you put her in the bath and say she was drowned by accident?'

'It's been tried.'

'It's so maddening!' cried Alma in frustration. 'Everything else works perfectly.'

'It's a practical problem, my dear,' said Walter. 'Getting excited about it isn't any help.'

Alma was actually pleased by this mild reproof. Walter was treating her like a wife already. And his concern to perfect the plan removed any doubts she had that he was determined to see it through. He was as calm and deliberate as if they were discussing a simple extraction in the surgery.

She said, 'If we had a car, we could leave her somewhere.'

'No,' said Walter. 'That won't do. Someone would find her soon enough. Have you heard of Bernard Spilsbury?'

'The pathologist?'

'That fellow doesn't simply name a cause of death; he announces the murderer's size in hats and where he buys his shirts and how he likes his eggs done. We can't afford to leave a body.'

As Alma felt the shock of words like *murderer* and *body*, the thought passed through her mind that Walter was facing the cold reality of their intention more realistically than she had dared as yet. To cover her unease she said flippantly, 'And we can't afford to take her with us.'

He turned and grasped her wrist. 'But we can! That's the answer, Alma. You've got it!'

'I don't see how.'

'We can tip her into the sea. Push her through a porthole after dark. She'll never be found.'

'But how would we get her aboard?'

He laughed. 'She'll walk. It's beautiful. You're a genius!'

'A very confused one at this moment,'

'I'll explain. Forget the other plan and listen to this. I'll tell Lydia that I refuse to go with her to America. She'll fly off the handle and tell me to go to the devil, because nothing will come between her and her wonderful future in films. She'll sell the house, my practice, my equipment, everything, and she'll be on the *Mauretania* on Saturday week. What she won't know is that you and I will also be aboard. I will have booked a passage in the second class under some other name.'

'For both of us?'

'No. You will stow away in my cabin.'

'Walter, I couldn't. I'm sure to be discovered.'

'I'm sure you won't be,' he said flatly. 'Don't forget I've been aboard an ocean liner before. On sailing day about a thousand friends and relatives crowd on board to see the passengers off. It's chaotic. Half an hour before sailing time they send round some boys with gongs to ask the visitors to go ashore, but there are always some who don't, because they know they can leave on the pilot tender or at Cherbourg. My dear, it's perfectly simple to stow away for the first hour or so, and that's all we need. After that you'll have a first-class stateroom of your own. You'll be Mrs Lydia Baranov.'

'Do you mean that you will have . . ?' Alma's voice faltered.

Walter nodded. He began to talk more rapidly as he convinced himself of the possibility of the new plan. 'Obviously it has to be done as soon as possible. I'll go to her stateroom with a bottle of highly concentrated chloroform ready in my pocket. When I knock, she'll be surprised to see me, but she'll admit me straight away. I'll push her face-down on the bed – physically she's no match for me – and chloroform her immediately. When I'm absolutely sure she's dead, I'll put her body somewhere.'

'Her cabin trunk!' said Alma excitedly.

'Perfect. It can wait there until it's dark enough to push her through the porthole. The *Mauretania* sails at noon, you see. Lunch is served at one, and you'll be in the first class dining room telling the steward that you are Mrs Lydia Baranov and you require a table for one. They'll accept it without question.'

'What will you be doing?'

'Sitting in Lydia's stateroom with the "Do Not Disturb" notice on the door. The important thing is what *you* will be doing. You must establish yourself firmly as Lydia in the eyes of the passengers and crew. You can take a leisurely lunch and then talk to some other people over coffee in the lounge. Take a stroll on the promenade deck and see the deck steward to reserve a deckchair on the side facing the sun. Make sure that your name is clearly heard. Do you think you can do it?'

'I'm sure I can.'

'Good. Later in the afternoon, you can come to the stateroom and I'll let you in.'

'Darling, it's going to work!' She kissed his cheek and kept her head resting against his shoulder. 'It's so beautifully simple.'

Walter seemed reluctant to admit success yet. He talked on, refusing to let the rest of the plan speak for itself. 'I'll give you the key to the stateroom, and then you can come and go as you please. But we must stay apart after that. You'll have to go to dinner and come late to bed. By then I will be gone and so will the body. I'll go back to my cabin in the second class and see you five days later in New York. I believe it will work.'

'I'm sure it will, my darling.'

'I venture to say that even our friend Dr Crippen would have seen the merit of a plan like this. No body in the cellar. No ridiculous disguises. And the whole thing paid for by my providential wife, the victim.' The ends of Walter's mouth widened into a modest smile.

'Have you thought of a name to use aboard the *Mauretania*?' Alma asked.

'Not yet. Something simple would be best. Come to think of it, my former name of Brown will do as well as any. I believe I know where I can get a passport made – an old friend of my father's, if he still has a steady hand. I'll look him up tomorrow.'

'Brown doesn't sound like a genuine name,' said Alma.

'But it is my own.'

'Dr Crippen called himself Robinson, and that didn't sound very convincing either.'

'What do you suggest, then?'

'Something short and simple, but uncommon.' She brought her hands together. 'I've got it!'

'Dew,' said Walter.

'Yes! You read my mind!'

'Walter Dew. By courtesy of Scotland Yard.' He began to chuckle. 'I rather like it. Who would be suspicious of a man called Walter Dew?'

He laughed out loud and Alma joined in. Their laughter carried down the terrace. There was a glorious sunset turning everything a deep, romantic red.

2

In her last week in London, Barbara stopped being natural. She turned *chic*. She went to Vasco's and had her amazing chestnut hair bobbed. The sides were set in permanent waves. She put chalk-white powder on her face and painted her lips bright crimson. She bought a moleskin shawl cape and five evening gowns at a store in Knightsbridge. By Friday she had worn them all and bought two more.

The turning-point had been the lecture by Dr Bertrand Russell. Barbara had gone straight from the lecture hall to the hairdresser's. Her mother Marjorie was astounded by the transformation. She had a double brandy and decided it was the best thing that had happened on the trip. She said to Livy that there must be something in philosophy. Livy had a different theory. He said he guessed Paul Westerfield had shown more interest in the lecture than in Barbara.

'If she's going after Paul,' said Marjorie, 'she's playing a very deep game. She has a date this afternoon with a guy named Forbes.'

Forbes took Barbara to a tea dance at the Café de Paris, where she met Arnold, who wore a monocle and was much more entertaining. Arnold treated her to cakes and iced coffee at the Grafton Galleries, where there were pictures covered with tissue paper to spare the blushes of young ladies like herself. A black band played jazz until 2am and Arnold tried to one-step and nudged a woman with his elbow. She spilt her iced coffee down the trousers of her partner and Arnold used the tissue cover from a picture to mop it up. While this was happening a young man called Rex told Barbara that she was the loveliest creature his eyes had ever lighted on.

Rex was very passionate. Over lunch in Claridges next day he threatened suicide if Barbara would not make him happy in the suite he had reserved upstairs. To convince her he took a silver revolver from his pocket and placed it on the table. Barbara kept cool. She was *chic* but she was not available. She picked up the revolver and dropped it in the champagne bucket. Arnold told her later that Rex was famous for producing his revolver in Claridges.

Twice that week Barbara passed Paul Westerfield in the lobby of the Savoy. The first time she was with Forbes and the second time with Arnold. These chance encounters had a positive effect on Paul. On Friday morning he stopped her on the staircase to the dining room. He said her hairstyle was a knockout. He asked her if she had made arrangements for that evening.

Barbara answered that a friend had mentioned something at the Café Royal, but she wasn't too excited by it. This would be her final night in London and she wanted to enjoy it.

'You're leaving tomorrow?' said Paul. 'On the *Mauretania*? How about that? So am I. Let's have fun in London town tonight.'

'What do you suggest?' asked Barbara cautiously. She couldn't take another lecture on philosophy.

'There's a party at the Berkeley. Mainly Americans from the Embassy – the younger crowd, I mean. Some of them are pretty wild, I hear. I was asked to go along. Would you come?'

She smiled and nodded.

Barbara had achieved what she intended. She was attracted to Paul Westerfield despite an inclination to recoil from anyone her mother had set her sights on. She liked the way he looked at her with eyes that valued what she said. She liked the way one eyebrow tilted higher than the other when he was interested. She liked his casual movements as he crossed a room, as economical and deceptive as a cat's. He had power in reserve.

With six days on the *Mauretania* to come, she could be casual too. She was twenty minutes late that evening when she met him in the lobby. She called him by a nickname from their student days. She wanted him to know that she treated millionaires like any other guys.

The party was as wild as Paul had promised. There was unlimited champagne. About a dozen young Americans from the Embassy and as many English friends dined and danced till after midnight, switching partners all the time and clinging to each other with the unrestraint of lovers. When the restaurant closed, the party moved to the coffee-stand at Hyde Park Corner. The taxi-drivers let them take their cups of coffee to the cabs along the rank and sit in there for hours.

Barbara shared Paul with an English girl called Poppy. It didn't seem to matter. He had his arms around them both and kept them entertained with funny stories interspersed with kisses. Poppy laughed a lot. She called herself a proper cockney.

She had tight blonde curls and bright, expressive eyes.

Towards 3am everyone left the taxis and linked hands around a streetlamp. They sang *Knees up, Mother Brown* and *Auld Lang Syne*. Kisses were exchanged all round. They called the taxi-drivers from their shelter and asked to be driven home.

Paul asked Poppy where she lived. Those two and Barbara were already seated in a taxi.

'Chicksand Street,' said Poppy with a giggle. Each few words she spoke were interspersed with laughter. 'You won't have heard of it. I bet the cabby hasn't either. It's down the East End if you want to know.'

'Fine,' said Paul. 'I guess the Savoy is on the way. We can put you down first, Barbara.'

Barbara nodded, but she didn't thank him for the suggestion. She couldn't understand why they could not drop Poppy first, and drive back together to the Savoy. It wasn't as if Poppy was supposed to be his partner for the evening. But she bit back her objection. As she smiled at Poppy she was hoping Paul would be bored to tears by that stupid giggle and that ridiculous accent.

'What about you, Paul?' Poppy enquired, leaning across him to straighten his white tie. 'Where's your hotel, my love?'

'I'm at the Savoy as well.'

Another giggle. 'Strike a light – I didn't know you two were serious.'

'We're on different floors,' said Barbara. 'It's pure coincidence.'

Poppy shook with laughter. 'Oh, yes?'

'Sure,' said Paul. He sounded just a little irritated. He told the driver to take them to the Savoy and then Chicksand Street. Then he turned to Barbara and said, 'There's just no point in taking you all that way when it's so late already. It's an early start tomorrow.'

'Of course,' said Barbara. She tried to be magnanimous by thinking of the five days coming on the *Mauretania*.

As they drove up the Strand, Paul kissed her softly on the lips. He put his hand behind her neck and kissed her harder.

Poppy said, 'Looks as if your time's up, sweethearts.'

The taxi door was opened by the Savoy commissionaire.

Barbara said, 'Thanks, Paul. London was crazy, and I loved it.'

'I guess I'll see you on the boat,' said Paul.

As the taxi drove away, Barbara watched Poppy's hand waving from the small window at the back.

3

'Lydia, the taxi is here.'

'Already? He will have to wait.'

'It is eight o'clock,' said Walter.

'It won't take an hour to get to Waterloo. Why did you call the dratted man so early? The boat train doesn't leave till nine. Are you so eager to see the back of me?' But she spoke without much malice. She had given him the full blast of her fury two days before, when he had coolly told her that he had decided not to come to America. She had thrown a bowl of lentil soup at him. She had thrown the mustard and the cranberry sauce. She had sworn at him in front of Sylvia. Yet after due reflection she began to see it in another light. Walter would have been a burden in America. He was much too dull for Hollywood. He would have cut no ice as her theatrical agent. She would employ an enterprising young American instead.

Of course the prospect of travelling all the way to Hollywood alone was daunting. But she had survived long and tedious journeys before. Actors were forever packing trunks and taking trains to distant places. It would be something to tell the newspapermen when they interviewed her.

As for Walter, that selfish and ungrateful man, he would soon discover what life was like without being featherbedded by a generous and devoted wife. His practice and the surgery in Eaton Place were sold. He had until Monday to move his things out of the house. What he would do for money and accommodation was a mystery, unless he expected his fancy woman to keep him. Some hope of that!

He was at the bedroom door looking in. 'Can I carry anything downstairs, my dear?' Inoffensive to the last. Even with his best suit coated in lentil soup and cranberry sauce the other evening, he had continued to apologise for changing his mind about America.

'You may take my case, if you insist.' The trunks with the bulk of her clothes had been sent ahead on Tuesday, and ought to be on the ship by now. 'Tell him I won't be long.'

She looked round the room, and felt a sudden surge of exhilaration. She was leaving it for ever. What a relief it was to escape from hidebound England, where talent was not valued any longer, to the opportunities of the New World!

Walter was standing at the foot of the stairs as she came down. 'Are you sure you've got your ticket? And your passport?'

'Of course I have.'

'The money?'

'I'm not a child, Walter. When you get a permanent address, be sure to send it to me, care of the Bank of California. But don't be so misguided as to write to me asking for money. You've chosen to be independent and that's the end of it as far as I'm concerned. That's not to say that I shall give you a divorce. I'm not old-fashioned, as you know, but I have no intention of going through all that simply to legitimatize your squalid philanderings with that creature who telephoned me.'

'I've done nothing improper, Lydia, I assure you.' He looked quite shocked at the suggestion.

'Goodbye, Walter.'

'Goodbye.'

'Aren't you even going to wish me *bon voyage*?'

'It didn't occur to me. I'm sorry.'

She walked to the taxi. That was how she would remember Walter, forever saying he was sorry. The handsome, fashionable dentist, idolized by patients, confident and reassuring, was privately a mouse. To the last, she had half-expected, half-hoped that if she goaded him enough he would bare his teeth and bite back, but it was too late now.

4

Livy Cordell liked Southampton Dock. He liked the moment when the boat train steamed into the shed beside the ship, and some guy tugged at the broad leather strap to let down the window and you got the first whiff of salt air laced with the coaldust of the Southern Railway. It brought back the old days when he had made his way in the world, crossing the herring pond more than a dozen times, steerage at first, and then second class as the profits got bigger. This time he was first class. He and his ladies had taken breakfast on the train. It had left at nine, a full hour and a half after the train for third class passengers. No-one talked of steerage any more.

A porter helped them out and humped the luggage onto a truck. Their passports and tickets had been checked on the train. From every side they could hear American voices. For so many it was the end of the vacation in Europe. The *Mauretania* band was on the platform doing its best to restore their spirits with military marches.

Livy took out the embarkation cards. Ahead he spotted a familiar face. 'Say, isn't that young Westerfield?'

'Paul?' said Barbara with undisguised excitement. 'Where?'

'A little way ahead. He's wearing a boater.'

'I can't see.'

'There he goes!' said Marjorie. 'He's left the queue. He's coming this way.'

'Well, isn't that nice?' said Livy. 'Do you think he spotted us?'

Marjorie's voice changed abruptly. 'I don't think so, honey.'

Barbara had turned a bright pink.

Paul Westerfield was with an extremely pretty girl in a gold crepe de chine dress that matched her blonde curls and white hat, but looked out of place on a jetty in mid-morning. She didn't seem at all concerned. She had her white-gloved hand tucked round his arm and she was talking with her face turned towards him, oblivious to everything. But Paul's face registered that he had noticed the Cordells. There was a brief moment of indecision and then he moved towards them. He said something to Poppy and she turned her head and looked at Barbara. The look started as a glassy stare and turned into a radiant smile.

'What a surprise! Hello, Barbara. How's your head this morning?'

'How are you both?' said Barbara in a flat voice. 'Mother, Livy, this is Poppy. We met last night. You already met Paul.'

'Sure,' said Livy. 'Nice to meet you, Poppy.' They shook hands.

Marjorie simply nodded her head and gave an equivocal smile.

'Poppy has come all the way down here to see me off,' said Paul in an obvious attempt to be casual. 'We just heard that visitors have to use a different gangplank.'

'Back there,' said Livy. 'I saw the sign.'

'Thanks. Well . . .' Paul took a step away. 'I guess I'll see you later, folks.'

'Ta-ta!' said Poppy.

As they moved off, Poppy's hand curled round Paul's arm again.

Livy turned to Barbara and said, 'Say, you can just see the hull of the ship through the gap there. When you get on the gangplank, be sure to take a look at the size of her. It's an incredible sight, and you won't get it again till we reach New York.' He knew it was a transparent attempt to distract, but someone had to pick up the conversation for Barbara's sake. He felt quite cut up himself.

'I just want to get on board and have a large gin,' said Marjorie. 'How about you, Barbara?'

Ahead in the queue, Lydia Baranov crossed the gangway and went aboard the *Mauretania*. She had a porter to carry her case. At the purser's desk they checked her embarkation card against the passenger-list.

'You're travelling alone, Mrs Baranov?'

'Yes, my husband had to cancel his passage.'

'That's unfortunate, madam, but I hope you enjoy the crossing, nevertheless.' The assistant purser turned to the line of blue-uniformed bellboys in attendance. 'Stateroom 89 for Mrs Baranov.'

The boy first in line stepped forward and took the key. 'This way, if you please, madam.' With the manner of an old salt the boy headed across the crowded embarkation hall with Lydia and her porter in tow. A touch here and a word there and people obligingly moved aside. As he passed obstacles like sets of golf clubs and terriers on leads the bellboy pointed out the hazards without turning round. He led her into a cherry-wood panelled corridor. Everywhere there were groups of passengers and visitors, talkative, tearful, amorous, agitated and boisterous, while porters, stewards, newsboys and flower sellers passed among them. Lydia stopped to buy a *Daily Mail* and nearly lost the bellboy.

Stateroom 89 was down a flight of stairs at the end of another corridor. The bellboy unlocked the door and Lydia took some money from her purse and tipped the porter. The bellboy pulled aside the curtains.

'So I have two portholes,' said Lydia. 'That will be nice. Which side of the ship are we?'

'Port side, madam. This is D Deck, also known as the Upper Deck. The first class dining saloon is through the door at the end of the corridor and straight ahead. Shall I open one of the portholes?'

'Thank you. What time is it now?'

'About half past eleven, madam. Luncheon is served at one o'clock.'

'I won't bother with lunch. I'll unpack my things and have a quiet hour with the newspaper. Kindly see that I'm not disturbed.' She found a shilling and gave it to the boy.

Left alone, she went to the porthole he had opened and peered out, but all she could see was the tip of one of the cranes on the quayside. The room seemed extraordinarily high in the ship's side. She had not been prepared for the hugeness of the *Mauretania*. She turned from the porthole and saw that her cabin trunk had been brought in and left beside the chest of drawers. That was one worry removed.

All told, it was not a bad place to pass five days in. She inspected the bathroom. It was on the small side, but beautifully finished in white marble. In the main cabin she had the chest of drawers, an armchair, dressing-table, washstand, writing desk and small round table with a vase of fresh roses. The bed felt comfortable enough. The side away from the wall had a wooden board to box the occupant in when the ship was rolling.

There was still half an hour to sailing time.

She was determined not to feel lonely. This was the start of a great adventure. It would be ridiculous to get morbid now. She unlocked the trunk and started to take out the lovely new things she had bought to wear on the voyage.

'You know, this wouldn't be allowed in New York,' Paul told Poppy as they sat together in the smoking room sipping sherrry.

'Ladies in the smoking room?' said Poppy. 'Blimey, I thought *we* was old-fashioned.'

'No. This.' He held up the sherry glass. 'Prohibition. On the way over, we weren't allowed to touch a drop until the ship was past the twelve mile limit. Then you should have seen the rush for the bar.'

Poppy giggled. 'I always thought you Yankees went on British ships because the food was better.'

'Now you know. Imagine five days at sea on a dry ship like the *Leviathan*.' Suddenly Paul's attention was caught by someone on another table. 'What do you know? There's Barbara and her people again.'

This was not good news for Poppy. She had a job to do before she left the ship. She needed Paul to herself. 'Take no notice. They haven't seen us.'

'I could buy them a drink. It was kind of embarrassing seeing them on the pier. Do you want another one, Poppy?'

'I've got a headache. There's too much smoke in here. Let's go up on deck.'

'As you wish. I'll ask Barbara to come along too. Poor kid – who wants to be stuck with their parents?'

Poppy swore to herself as Paul went over to the Cordells. The plan had gone so well up to now. She only wanted a few more minutes with the bloke. After that, Barbara could eat him for lunch if she wanted.

She stood a yard or two back from their table. Barbara's mother was saying, 'Go on, dear. You don't want to stay with us. You young people have much more in common.'

Barbara got to her feet without looking too pleased about it. Paul walked between them.

'Let's go up and see the Verandah Café,' suggested Poppy.

'I thought you weren't feeling so good,' said Paul.

'I'll be all right. There's dancing up there.'

'How do you know?' asked Barbara.

Poppy knew because Jack had told her when they had first talked about this in his handsome house by Hyde Park. Jack knew all there was to know about the *Mauretania*. He had a plan showing every room on every deck. He had a passenger list with Paul Westerfield's name on it. She told them, 'I heard some geezer talking about it.'

The Verandah was modelled on the Orangerie at Hampton Court. Its vast windows and glass roof made it the one public room on the ship without artificial light. There were large potted palms and hanging baskets of bright flowers. There were wicker chairs set at small tables. There was a square of floor where couples were shuffling to the music of a concertina.

'Come on, Paul,' said Poppy. 'Aren't you going to ask one of us to dance?'

'Paul looked uncomfortable, but Barbara said, 'Go on, you two. There isn't much time. I'll just sit here and watch you.' Although she said it with good grace, she still looked as if she wished her mother had not thrust her forward. She could neither walk away nor stay and watch with any dignity. She sat at an empty table on the fringe of the dance square and watched Paul and Poppy expressionlessly.

Poppy let Paul take her slowly round the square. As they turned in one corner she caught a glimpse of slicked-back, honey-coloured hair. Jack was there as arranged, ready for the pick-up. Poppy really did feel ill now, for every step they took was being scrutinised by Barbara. It would be idiotic to try to make the dip while she was there. Poppy knew what was possible in the art of picking pockets. It was always a risk. On this small floor, under Barbara's gimlet eyes, it was futile. She would need to think of something else.

Over the sound of the concertina came a more strident resonance.

'Too bad,' said Paul. 'That's the visitors' gong, I guess.'

Poppy pressed her hips against his and gave an extra wriggle. Paul responded.

'I could stow away.'

'In my cabin, huh?' He grinned.

'Why not? I wouldn't take up much room.'

'They always find stowaways. They'd pretty damn soon find you, Poppy. Curly blonde hairs.'

She gave a sly smile. 'They wouldn't show up like chestnut brown. Why should I leave you to her?'

'Barbara is just a friend from my college days.'

'She doesn't think so. Anyway, what would happen to me if I

.was caught? Would I have to scrub the decks?'

The music stopped. There was a boy in the room now, beating a gong and shouting, 'All ashore that's going ashore!'

This was becoming a nightmare for Poppy. As they turned to walk back to the table, she glanced towards Jack. His face was masklike. She pursed her lips to try to convey her predicament. There was not a glimmer of comprehension from Jack. It was more searing than a blaze of anger.

The concertina player had finished and was taking a bow.

'I'm going to say goodbye right here,' Barbara said to Poppy. 'Paul will want to see you off, and I really must go to my cabin and unpack before lunch. It's been fun, hasn't it? 'Bye, Poppy.'

Poppy was so grateful that she almost kissed her. She watched Barbara leave, and said to Paul, 'Darling, we've still got ten minutes at least. Let's say goodbye in private.'

As they passed Jack's table, she avoided his eyes. But she let him know with a nod that the job was still on.

6

In second class stateroom 377 Alma heard the gong. Her shoulders gave a tremor. She tried to make it seem that she was shifting her position in the chair.

'There's really no need to be nervous,' said Walter in the voice he used with all his patients. It's going to work, I assure you. Nobody questioned my identity when I showed the passport on the boat train. I am Walter Dew. And nobody will think you are anyone else but Mrs Lydia Baranov. They have no reason to question it, my dear.'

'Of course.' She tried to give him a confident smile. 'Mine is the easy part.'

He smiled back, a genuine, easy smile. 'Mine is not difficult. It won't be the first time I've administered chloroform. The only problem with anaesthesia is the danger of harming the patient. In this case it doesn't apply.'

'She won't suffer, will she?'

'Not at all. It will be over very swiftly.'

Ever since that evening on Richmond Terrace when they had thought of this way of making Lydia vanish without trace, Alma had become aware of a change in Walter. He was not so diffident. There was more confidence and more purpose in his manner. He smiled more. The prospect of being free from Lydia had made a different man of him.

She picked up her bag. 'I made these sandwiches for you, as you won't get any lunch.'

'That was thoughtful.' He took the packet and unwrapped it. 'Lettuce and tomato. You couldn't have made a better choice.'

She took out another packet. 'There's chocolate cake as well.'

'My favourite. Did you make it?'

'I needed to occupy my mind. It's silly. I don't know why I'm so nervous when you can keep so calm.'

'It's a matter of training and procedure. I know exactly what I have to do. These are excellent. Would you like one?'

She shook her head. 'It will be difficult enough trying to find an appetite for lunch.'

Walter gave a slight shrug. 'If you can't face a full meal, order something light. Don't let those waiters intimidate you. They are there to serve you, remember, not to spy on you. But you'd better not lose any weight or those new clothes Lydia bought won't fit you.'

Alma managed a smile in gratitude for his attempt to induce her to think beyond the next hour. 'I brought a few things of my own in that bag you carried for me, and there's a needle and thread in case I have to make some adjustments, but I think my size is probably the same as hers.'

'I don't expect your taste is. She always liked flamboyant things. She liked to look theatrical. By the way, my dear – the dress you're wearing is ideal – certain to be noticed.'

Alma thanked him. She had picked out the most colourful day dress she owned, a short-sleeved one in red and white georgette. She had a white straw hat with a red band to match. She said, 'The beads were my leaving present from Mrs Maxwell at the shop.'

'They're most attractive. What reason did you finally give for leaving?'

Alma smiled. 'I said I was going to Paris to learn to paint. She thought it was very rash of me. So did the people who rented the house. They won't be a bit surprised when I don't come back. The bank manager even warned me about white slavers.'

'How did he become an expert?' said Walter with a smile. 'You must have convinced them, Alma.'

Before she could respond, the cabin vibrated to a deafening boom that must have tested every rivet in the ship.

'Ship's whistle,' said Walter. 'Isn't it a marvellous sound to hear?'

'Are we moving?'

'We're about to.'

She got up and put out her arms to him. He held her closely. 'Don't go yet,' she murmured.

'It's all right, he said. 'I can wait for a while yet. I intend to go to her while everyone else is at lunch. She thought she might be prone to seasickness, so I advised her to do without lunch.'

7

It was the duty of the second officer to man the last gangway. The visitors had gone ashore and stood waiting in hundreds along the quay, shouting and waving to the passengers massed at the rails on every deck. The last few shore staff left the ship. The bugle was sounded and the watchkeeping and navigating officers went to their stations. The commander came on to the bridge.

Captain Arthur H. Rostron was a slightly built, clean-shaven man with silver hair. He could have passed as a shopkeeper except that his years at sea had toughened his skin and given his eyes the screwed-up look that comes from years of staring ahead into every kind of weather the elements inflict. He had taken command of the *Mauretania* in 1915. By then his name was a legend in the Cunard Company. One bitterly cold night in 1912, when he was in command of the *Carpathia*, Captain Rostron had received a wireless message from a vessel in distress. Other ships were closer. Arthur Rostron changed course and raced the *Carpathia* for sixty miles to the scene. He coaxed speeds from her that no-one believed possible in those waters perilous with icebergs. He rescued seven hundred survivors from the *Titanic*.

The captain looked down to where the second officer stood at the head of the gangway, craning to catch the signal from the bridge. He raised his hand and lowered it. The time was exactly mid-day. The last gangway was landed. The mooring ropes were slackened fore and aft. The stern tugs stretched the hawsers to their limit and began to tow the *Mauretania* away from the quay. The marine superintendant in his bowler hat supervised the shore gang. They followed the great ship along the quay until the last bow rope was released.

Steadily the tugs hauled the ship out of the Ocean Dock into her swinging ground in the fairway. On the bridge the outward pilot had taken the wheel. The tugs started to swing her. In less than five minutes she was pointing seawards. The tugs cast off.

'Sound the bugle,' ordered Captain Rostron.

The *Mauretania* was under way, first to Cherbourg to pick up more passengers, and then New York.

Under the direction of the master-at-arms, an immediate search was made for stowaways. The searchers looked in the traditional places, the lifeboats, storage chambers, engine rooms, laundry and kitchens. It was a token search to satisfy company regulations. As everyone acknowledged, any stowaway with a modicum of sense would mingle with the passengers at this stage. So Alma, trying to be calm in Walter's stateroom, and Poppy, in the arms of Paul, stayed undetected.

Lydia was still unpacking when she felt the movement of the ship. She went to the porthole. She could no longer see the crane on the quay. She could see white gulls against the blue sky. They were beating their wings in flight, yet they seemed to make no progress until one soared upwards as if it had snapped an invisible thread. It screamed its triumph over the others. Lydia gave a shiver of excitement.

She turned back to the task of emptying her cabin trunk. Some of the dresses would need pressing. She would have to see the steward later. For the present she was content to spend an hour or two in the quiet of her stateroom. She had no reason to stand out on deck watching England slip out of sight. England had not appreciated her. But in five days she intended to be at the rail with the others waiting for the first glimpse of America.

The ship seemed to have stopped for a minute. Now there was another shattering burst of sound from the ship's siren or whatever it was called. The vibration of the engines returned in force. Lydia felt it through her shoes. She was not upset by it, but she decided to sit on the bed while her body got accustomed to the novelty. She disliked the thought of being seasick. Walter had been right. It was a sensible precaution to go without lunch. Poor Walter, so thoughtful, so unadventurous. She reached for the paper and shut him out of her mind.

She need not have worried about the risk of being seasick. She was not seasick. It takes at least an hour before the pitch and roll of a great ship disturbs the equilibrium of the inner ear to that extent.

Lydia had less time than that.

The cold facts may have suggested that Poppy wanted to make a monkey out of Paul Westerfield, but that was not so. She had a job to do, and she did it in the best way she could. She had not been paid to give him sexual favours. She was prepared to allow enough familiarity to smooth the way for the job, and that was all. So when he had taken her back to Chicksand Street in the taxi the previous night, she had presented him with a cup of tea and a kiss on the horsehair settee in the parlour. She had spent what remained of the night upstairs with her sister Rose. At six in the morning when Rose had gone down as usual to look at the milkmen bringing out their horses she had found a strange man asleep in the parlour. She had reported it to Poppy, who had truthfully said that the man was a millionaire who was sleeping in the parlour instead of the Savoy. Poppy had gone back to sleep for an hour. Soon after seven she had put on her crepe de chine dress, tied an apron round her waist and cooked sausages and bacon for two. By eight they had arrived at the Savoy to collect Paul's luggage and by nine they had found themselves seats on the boat train.

If Paul had entertained ideas of seamier scenes in his state-room, he was denied them. Poppy proposed to remove one thing: the wallet from Paul's blazer pocket. She was under instructions to take it and pass it to Jack. One chance had gone. She could not miss another.

She allowed him enough kisses and embraces to allay suspicion. He was no Casanova, but it was not unendurable. Perhaps twenty minutes had passed when his hand discon-nected the first hook and eye at the back of her dress.

She said in a tortured voice, 'Oh my God, I think it's moving.'

'What?' His hand jerked away from the dress.

'The blooming ship – I can feel it. Oh, no, I'm trapped. I never really meant to stow away.'

'Don't worry.'

She sat up on the bed. 'Don't worry, he says!'

'What I mean is that I can pay.'

'Pay what?' demanded Poppy. 'I don't want to go to America. You live there. I don't.'

'You can get off at Cherbourg. We stop there to pick up more passengers.'

'Cherbourg? Where's that, for God's sake?' Jack had told her, of course, in case of emergency, but she was enjoying herself now.

'France. You can stay overnight and be home by tomorrow. I'll pay. I'll give you two hundred dollars.'

'I'll need French money.'

'You go to a *bureau de change*.'

'What's that? I can't speak French.'

'No. Better still, I'll see the purser and get some francs.'

'Paul, I'm frightened.'

'Don't be. I'll fix everything.'

'Can I go to the bathroom?'

'Why, sure. Go right ahead.'

It was like a dream in that bathroom, all spotless white and shining chrome. Much better than a tin bath in the parlour. Poppy pushed the bolt across the door and turned on the taps. She took off her things and tried on the bathrobe that was hanging on the door. She made faces in the mirror. She tried the water with her toes. She dropped the bathrobe on the floor and stepped into the bath. She found that she could lie in there with water up to her chin and her legs stretched out as if in bed.

After a while Paul's voice enquired, 'Are you okay in there, Poppy?'

'I'm all right, darling. How about you?'

'It's just that you've been a long time. I didn't know you were figuring on a bath.'

'I asked you, didn't I? I like a bath whenever I can get one.'

She enjoyed it a few minutes more.

When she unbolted the bathroom door she was fully dressed again. She said to Paul, 'I left the water for you, darling. It's still nice and warm.'

'For me?'

'You want to stop smelling like the Southern Railway, don't you? Them carriages might be comfy, but they always leave a pong. No offence, sweetheart.'

'I had no idea.'

She had him flustered. This was the moment to go to work. She stood against him and put her right hand round his waist inside his blazer. She scratched his back with the tip of a fingernail and said, 'You'd be surprised what you can pick up in them first class carriages.' At the same time, her left hand smoothly lifted the wallet from his inside pocket and dropped it on the bed. She pulled him towards the bathroom. He hadn't noticed a thing. She said, 'Don't be long.' She stepped aside and closed the door after him.

She put the wallet out of sight under the bedspread and waited. She heard him empty the bath and fill it again. She heard him get in. She picked up the wallet and went to the stateroom door and looked out. Jack was at the end of the passageway smoking a cigarette. He waited for a steward to walk by and then he came casually towards her and took the wallet as he passed. Nothing was spoken. Poppy closed the door quietly. But she jumped like a scalded cat a moment later when the bugle sounded for lunch.

'Yes, madam. What name?' asked the chief steward.

'Baranov. Mrs Lydia Baranov.'

The chief steward ran his finger down the list of first class passengers. 'Ah, yes. A table for one, Mrs Baranov?'

'If you please,' answered Alma.

The chief steward snapped his fingers and one of his team stepped forward. 'Number forty-one for Mrs Baranov. Enjoy your meal, madam.'

Alma nodded demurely and followed the man down the steps and along the broad strip of carpet towards the far end of the enormous restaurant, said to be one of the most striking and resplendent public rooms afloat or ashore. It was double-tiered. It was richly panelled with exquisite carvings in the style of the Francois Premier period. Its ornately decorated ceiling was unimaginably high.

She kept Walter's advice firmly in mind: 'Don't be intimidated. Lydia wouldn't. It doesn't matter what gaffes you make so long as you walk in there with your head high and expect to be treated like a lady.' Walter was a tower of strength. He had betrayed no sign of nervousness. He expected her to succeed in this. She could not fail him.

Another steward handed her the menu. It was in several languages. Each dish was more than she could face. She kept calm. She said, 'All I require is a simple salad without meat of any sort. Can you arrange it?'

'Certainly, madam.'

The wine waiter approached her. She waved him away. She

needed a clear head this afternoon.

The salad was put in front of her. She began to eat. She poured herself some water. Her hand shook. Some was spilt. She watched the white tablecloth darken as the liquid saturated the fibres. She had a vivid image of a pad of chloroform. Please God, she thought, let it be over quickly. She covered the wet patch with the jug of water. She forced herself to eat some lettuce. She tried to imagine New York.

A feeling of immense relief came over her. The dreadful tension lifted like a curtain. She glanced at the clock above the chief steward's table. 1.15pm. She was positive that Lydia was dead.

England was reduced to a grey blur between sea and sky astern of the *Mauretania*. A faint arc of steam beyond the Nab Tower marked the progress shorewards of the pilot tender. Captain Rostron in the wheel-house had his glasses trained forward, for the first sight of France. The visibility was good and the Channel calm for late summer. The chief officer and the junior first and third officers stood on duty with the captain. Really there was nothing to detain him on the bridge. He was free to go below for a late lunch with the first class passengers. However, he would not be going.

'Did you know that every passenger liner has three sides?' he said to no-one in particular.

No-one answered.

'Would someone care to name them? How about you, Chief?'

'No, sir. I'm at a loss.'

'Really? I thought I told you last time we crossed. The three sides of a passenger ship, gentlemen, are the port, the starboard and the social. On this ship I take full responsibility for the first two. I look to you and the other officers for some relief from the other.'

'Yes, sir.'

'If the passenger list can be believed, we are in for a smooth crossing. We have no prima donnas, pugilists or politicians. Just the usual complement of millionaires. Be patient with their questions, gentlemen. If they ask you, as they will, about sea serpents, mermaids and the *Mary Celeste*, keep your answers short, truthful and polite. When they raise the matter of icebergs, give them reassurance, not your reminiscences. Tell them the worst hazards on the *Mauretania* are cardsharpers. Tell them that you have no idea how to smuggle the liquor they bought in England through the New York customs. Tell them what you like about me, except that I answer questions.' Captain Rostron paused. 'Any questions?'

The only sound came from the throb of the turbines.

In the hours after lunch, Alma kept rigidly to the plan. She took coffee in the main lounge under the vast domed skylight. She made conversation with a couple from Boston who had been in Europe buying antique furniture. Thirty crates of it were stacked in the hold. She told them she was Lydia Baranov. She took care to articulate her words with clarity. She said she was an actress. The woman said they didn't get much time for the theatre, but it would be a change to have a proper actress in the ship's concert. Alma said she had a contract that prevented her from performing in variety.

She went on deck and promenaded with a woman whose husband was delayed in the smoking room. She took part in the lifeboat drill at three o'clock. She found the deck steward and reserved a chair on the port side. By half past three she estimated that she had spoken to eight people and given her new name to five. At least another ten must have overheard her using it.

The next stage in the plan had to be faced. During lunch she had experienced the utmost difficulty stopping herself from rushing from the restaurant to Lydia's stateroom to be with Walter, no matter what had happened there. Her afternoon alone had altered that. She had disciplined herself to use the time as Walter had suggested, establishing herself as Lydia. The concentration necessary had made great demands. She had tried to banish Walter and the stateroom from her mind. Although the thoughts resurfaced after each encounter with a steward or a passenger, they were more detached. The effort to make contact with other people, unknown, unknowing people, had insulated her from Walter. A kind of trepidation had crept into the space between them. She dreaded knocking on that door.

Stateroom 89 on D Deck.

He had told her several times. She knew exactly where to find it. Her nerves were still so active that she had to consult the passenger list on the board outside the purser's office. Mrs Lydia Baranov . . . 89.

She found the stairs and saw the notice *Staterooms 70 to 90*. A pulse was beating in her forehead. Her hands were icy. She moved slowly up the corridor, counting off the doors. 89. "Do Not Disturb".

She stopped. She looked along the way she had come. She was quite alone. Her mouth was dry. That pulse was throbbing harder than the engines of the ship.

She closed her eyes and tapped her knuckles on the door. Too softly. She tried again. She heard a movement from inside.

The door opened. Walter looked out. He was a changed man. The colour had drained from his face. There were lines of tension across his forehead and at the edges of his mouth. His eyes seemed to have sunk in their sockets.

He said nothing. He simply opened the door and let Alma in.

Her eyes raced over the room. Nothing horrid or disordered was in view. A few of Lydia's things. Hairbrush and comb, scent bottles and vanity bag on the dressing table. Pink slippers by the bed. A newspaper on the floor. Tissue paper from her packing neatly folded on the writing table. The cabin trunk against the wall beside the chest of drawers. It was closed.

The door clicked as Walter pushed it shut.

Alma turned and asked him, 'Is it done? Did you . . ?'

He dipped his head the merest fraction.

At this moment she had planned to fling her arms about his neck and press her face to his. It was to be the turning point in their romance, the moment of liberation. He was free at last. It was like the final chapter of all the novels that had moved her most.

Yet something in her or in Walter held her back. She could not bring herself to touch him. She told herself that he had done this thing for her, that he was brave and cool and resolute, that it confirmed his love as certainly as any ordeal man had undergone in quest of woman. But it had marked him. He was a murderer. Those hands had been in touch with death. Was it possible to love a man and be repelled by him?

He seemed to sense her feeling. He made no move towards her. He asked, 'What did you do? Did you go to lunch? Did you tell people you were Lydia?'

'Of course!' She launched into a copious account of her afternoon. Talking was a release. She found herself imparting confidence by glossing over her attacks of nerves. She felt a duty to restore this shaken man to something like his former self. Anything to suppress the sense of shock that made her shrink from him.

He appeared to listen avidly. He said, 'My dear, I thank you.

108

You have done wonderfully. What time is it now?'

'Almost four. We'll be in Cherbourg in an hour. Then across the ocean to America!'

'I don't think we should stay in here together.'

The panic held her in its grip again. 'I don't think I could be in here alone. Walter, I'm not as brave as you.' She eyed the trunk. 'I couldn't!'

'There's no need. I'll stay. There are things to do. I want to find her personal papers.'

'I suppose one of us has to be here.'

'We can't take risks.'

'You looked so dreadful when I came in. Was it more gruesome than you expected?'

He shook his head. 'Not the way you mean. It wasn't the physical part. You can do it a dozen times in your imagination, you can plan it to the last detail, but the reality is different. Give me time, and I'll get over it.' He extended his hand towards her.

If she could only have taken it! Her own hand went to her throat and fiddled with her necklace. 'Yes,' she said in a low voice, 'we have to come to terms with what we have done. I think I will need time, too.'

He said, 'Time is something we do have, my dear. Why don't you go up on deck and watch us coming in to Cherbourg? The more you're seen, the better. By six we should be under way again, and you'll be wanting to get dressed for dinner. She bought some beautiful new dresses. You'll want to make sure they fit.'

Her eyes went to the trunk again.

He slowly shook his head. 'She unpacked everything.'

'Yes. You are sure they are new?'

'She's never worn them.'

12

Normandy from the sea was a dazzling strip of green with white and grey cottages above blue-pebbled beaches. Cherbourg was a fishing port. It was not built for transatlantic liners. They moored inside the breakwater of the *Grande Rade*, an outer harbour. Two tenders brought the passengers and luggage. The evening sun flashed on the water. The new arrivals waved to the passengers already in occupation.

Paul Westerfield found the Livingstone Cordells at the rail watching the activity from the boat deck. Barbara saw him first.

'Paul! It's really nice to see you again. Are you going to join us?'

She smiled so warmly that it shamed him. 'I'd like to, but I have a problem.'

'What's that?'

Marjorie leaned towards her daughter and murmured, '"*Who's that?*" is the proper question, honey.'

Barbara followed her mother's look to where Poppy was standing some yards away. 'I thought Poppy left the ship at Southampton!'

Paul nodded and tried to cover his embarrassment. 'She was supposed to. Her timing was a little wrong. She's going to be put down here, only I have this problem I mentioned. My billfold has gone.'

'What do you mean, *gone*?' said Marjorie. 'Stolen?'

'No, no, I can't say that. I lost it somewhere. I've been all over looking for it. Barbara, you were with us in the Verandah Café. I thought I kept my jacket on. Poppy thinks I could have taken it off after we stopped dancing. The billfold could have dropped out.'

Barbara shook her head. 'I don't have any recollection that you took it off. But I left before you two. Have you asked the stewards in the Café?'

'Yes, and my cabin steward and the deck stewards. No joy at all.'

'That's too bad!' said Marjorie sympathetically. 'I guess there must be a whole lot of money in there.'

'That wouldn't bother me, only Poppy has to get back to England. It's my fault that she stayed on board.'

'You need money?' said Marjorie without the slightest pause. 'How much do you want? Livy, get out your billfold and give Mr Westerfield whatever he needs.'

Livy knew better than to question his wife. He said, 'Sure,' and started peeling off ten dollar bills.

'Give him ten tens and two hundreds,' ordered Marjorie. 'That should take care of it.'

'I'm really grateful,' said Paul. 'I don't know who else I could have asked.'

'The purser, son,' said Livy. 'He's the guy you see if you need money.'

Marjorie flashed a furious look at Livy and said, 'Only it's a whole lot nicer to go to your friends when you're in a spot of trouble, isn't it, Paul?'

'Absolutely. Thanks, Mr Cordell. I'll make sure you get it back real soon.'

'Forget it,' said Marjorie bounteously. 'Now you had better go and make sure that sweet little English girl knows how to get home.' As Paul left, she added in an aside to Barbara, 'Because we sure as hell don't want to see her again.'

Livy still had his wallet open in his hand. He said, 'Marje, are you going to let me in on what's happening?'

'For heaven's sake, Livy! That boy is Barbara's best hope on the ship.'

'Mother!' said Barbara.

'What I mean is that he's a nice boy, sweetheart. I can tell. Okay, let's admit that Poppy tried to take him over. She was superficially attractive and flirtatious and I can tell you from experience, Barbara, that no man breathing can resist a proposition from a girl like that. They pretty soon find out they made fools of themselves, don't they, Livy? She was nothing. Jetsam – that's the word for her. Just a piece of trash that gets put over the side. Forget her. Paul will, I promise you.'

'So long as he doesn't forget my three hundred bucks,' said Livy.

'I won't chase after him,' said Barbara.

'Of course you won't,' Marjorie agreed. 'He'll be back. After all, he's obligated to us now.'

'I get it,' said Livy.

'Great,' said Marjorie. 'What an agile brain you have, my darling.'

Silence descended on the family for a while. They continued to watch the transfer of passengers from the tender into the ship's side far below them. Further along, the luggage was being lifted from the second tender. It was getting cooler on the boat deck. Not so many people stayed to watch.

'Well, I guess that's it,' said Livy.

'We're not moving from this rail until we see who leaves the ship,' said Marjorie. 'That girl isn't going to make a fool of us a second time.'

Livy shrugged and went back to watching seagulls.

Shortly after, a group of five crossed the gangway to the tender. Four were in the Cunard blue. The fifth was in gold crepe de chine. Poppy turned and waved. The gangway was pulled in. The ropes were loosened fore and aft. The whistle sounded shrilly. The *Mauretania* boomed its answer. The tender chugged away and swung towards the inner harbour. Poppy still waved energetically.

'I'm glad I'm not in her shoes now,' said Barbara.

'Don't go feeling sorry for her,' said Marjorie. 'She's the only woman on that tugboat and if I'm any judge at all, that suits her fine. And it wouldn't surprise me if she has Paul's billfold with her.'

13

The ship had been under way again for nearly an hour when Paul Westerfield got his chance to see the purser. The Cherbourg passengers had all been checked. The coconut matting in the embarkation lobby was being taken up. Stacks of luggage waited to be moved. Paul joined the queue of passengers with queries. When his turn came and he started to explain about his billfold, he had the feeling that the purser recognized him, and it was confirmed.

'You're Mr Westerfield, aren't you, sir?'

'Why, yes. How did you . . ?'

'It's my job to know the passengers, sir. You're travelling with a young lady from England.'

No. She left the ship at Cherbourg. She was seeing me off.'

'I understand. And your wallet has gone. Can I enquire how much it contained?'

'Just over a thousand dollars and my chequebook. Also some photographs, club membership cards and my visiting cards. It's a black leather thing. It has my initials on the front. P.W.'

'Would you wait a moment, sir?' The purser took a key from his pocket and went to a small wall-safe. He could not have been more than thirty-five. He had mastered the art generally practised by elderly English butlers of conveying infinite varieties of meaning through a limited stock of innocuous phrases. It was unwise to press such people. He took Paul's billfold from the safe. 'It was handed in about an hour ago, sir. I had one of my assistants put it away, for safe keeping.'

'I'm deeply obliged to you.'

'I should check the contents if I were you, sir.'

'Sure.' He opened it and counted the money. 'How about that? It's all there. Every last bill. And the chequebook. Say, who was it handed this in? I'd like to thank the guy personally.'

'A Mr Gordon, sir. An English gentleman. His stateroom is situated on A Deck, above us. Number 26.'

'I'll go there right away. I'd like to buy him a couple of drinks. It's good to know there are still honest people about.'

'Yes, sir.'

'Why, yes.' Paul opened the billfold again. 'Thank you, purser.'

'Thank you, sir.'

*

In stateroom 26, Jack Hamilton, alias Jack Gordon, toyed with a deck of playing cards. He cut them into two packs. He put them face down on the bedside table and brought them together, riffling them in the usual way, raising the corners so that the cards intermingled. He brought the packs smoothly together, or almost so. He kept them at a slight angle to each other, and slipped the left pack through the right. He completed the move by putting the left bunch on top of the right. The order of the cards was undisturbed. It was a very neat pull-through.

Jack was the man who had recruited Poppy. He was a boatman. A boatman was a professional gambler who worked the ocean liners. The Atlantic crossing was ideal for a game of cards, or, better still, a series. Scores of boatmen made a living on the liners. Jack had learned the game by observation. He had been on ships before the war. He had seen the boatmen working. In those days they would sit around the smoking room and wait to see which pigeons came for plucking.

Now it was more professional. Nothing was left to chance. They examined the passenger list days before sailing. They selected their mark. They checked his business holdings. They took stock of his real estate. They decided how much to take him for. They used accomplices like Poppy to bait the trap.

There was more to it than that. They studied the crew lists as well. They checked the names of the pursers and the masters-at-arms. They worked all the Atlantic lines, White Star, Cunard, Hamburg-Amerika, North German Lloyd, Transat, Holland America, Canadian Pacific and Pierpont Morgan's half-dozen American lines. If they used the same ship again, it was always after eighteen months or more. Even then, they reckoned never to make the strike at sea. They spent the crossing setting up the victim. They cleaned up in Manhattan, in the mark's hotel. In England they would sometimes play the last game in a compartment of the boat train.

Jack travelled without much luggage. He needed two lounge suits, an evening suit, some reassuring neckties and a range of shirts and underclothes. He carried cigarettes, seed money and his pack of cards. He used the cards only to practise with. All games on board were played with packs bought from the smoking room stewards.

There came the knock he was expecting. He put the cards away in a drawer. He went to the door.

It was the mark. 'Mr Gordon, we haven't met. My name is Westerfield. Paul Westerfield II. I apologise for intruding on you. I just wanted to express my gratitude to you for handing in my billfold.'

'Ah, it was yours then. I hope nothing is missing.'

'Not a cent. Look, Mr Gordon, would you give me the chance to convey my thanks by buying you a couple of drinks?'

'Forget it, Mr Westerfield. There's no need. I appreciate the offer, but I'd rather not.'

'Please. I insist.'

'I'm not really a drinking man. Bar stools give me backache, to be honest.'

'A coffee after dinner, then, with a glass of brandy. We can take it in the lounge.'

'You've tempted me.'

'Good. I'll look out for you. Did I say my name is Paul?'

'Mine is Jack. I'll look forward to it, Paul.'

When the door closed, Jack took out the cards again.

14

In the wardrobe were seven evening gowns, all new. Alma accepted Walter's word that they were new. They had the fresh smell of fabrics that had not been close to flesh. They were made in fine silk and satin and georgette. They were superbly finished. She would have adored them in a dress shop. In Lydia's stateroom she had to brace herself to touch them. At last she picked out one in black georgette with embroidered water lilies.

'This one will do,' she said to Walter. May I go into the bathroom to try it on?'

'Of course you may. This is your stateroom now.'

'Yes.' She tried to sound convincing, but she had not convinced herself. While Lydia's body was contained inside the trunk, the stateroom was a tomb. Everything they did in there defiled it. She was not even sure how she would feel after Walter had pushed the body through the porthole. It had to be done after dark. Then Alma faced the prospect of sleeping there alone. In all their planning she had tried to dismiss that from her mind.

Inside the bathroom she quietly slipped the bolt across the door. She still felt shy of Walter. It was not rational. They were going to live as man and wife. There would be no wedding. If their life together had a starting point it was the moment he had put the pad of chloroform to Lydia's face. Yet she was unwilling to change her clothes in front of him.

It was a loose-fitting dress that seemed to suit her figure. It was sleeveless and cut low at the back. She would not have chosen such a style, but now that she saw herself in the mirror she could not deny that it had elegance and flair. She looked rather pale against the black georgette. She had brought Lydia's vanity bag into the bathroom. She gave her face some rouge. She put on some scent that smelt of violets. She began to feel less morbid. She decided to colour her lips.

'What do you think?'

Walter was in the armchair with the paper. He said, 'Why have you painted your lips that colour?'

'I'm supposed to be Lydia. An actress,' and she added for a touch of the theatre, 'darling.'

'I see.' He looked incapable of smiling.

'I wish you were dining with me.'

'I have a job to do.'

'Will you need help?' she asked, dreading that he would say yes.

'The only help you can give me is to stay away as long as possible. Watch the dancing, visit the library and choose a book, order a late coffee in the lounge. What I have to do cannot be done until everything is quiet.'

'I'll wait until after midnight.'

'That should be late enough. People retire early on the first night. Here's the key. I shall be gone when you let yourself in. And of course so will . . .' He glanced towards the trunk.

'Darling, would you do one thing to relieve my mind? Would you leave the lid open so that I know it is empty?'

'I promise you I will.'

'Shall I see you in the morning?'

He shook his head. 'I think it would be safer not to meet again before New York. They don't like second class passengers straying off limits. The stewards are very quick to notice anything like that. You have been very brave today, and the worst of it is over.'

'I hope so. I feel a lot more sympathy for Dr Crippen and Ethel Le Neve.

'Yes, indeed. But we haven't made the mistakes that they did. I think we ought to forget about Crippen. I'm supposed to be Walter Dew. I feel a lot more comfortable in *his* shoes.'

The bugle sounded for dinner. Walter got up and took a black stole from one of the drawers. 'It might be cold later tonight.' He placed it gently round Alma's shoulders without touching her skin. He seemed to know that she still could not bear to be touched.

She thanked him and said, 'I shall be thinking of you.'

As he opened the door, he whispered, 'Thank you.'

He was still in a state of shock. She wished she had the strength of mind to have kissed him.

She joined the general movement to the dining saloon. The ship's orchestra was playing there among the potted palms. Everyone had dressed for dinner, the men in white ties and stiff collars, the women in a blaze of jewels. At many of the tables people were standing to greet acquaintances or fellow-travellers from previous crossings.

'Excuse me.'

117

Alma looked up, expecting to see the steward. A man she had never seen before was standing by the table. He was tall and thin, with a face that was so marked by weather or whisky or something that she could not have failed to place him. The creases and wrinkles somehow combined to achieve a very disarming smile. His eyes smiled too. He was probably under fifty. He said, 'You *are* the actress, Lydia Baranov?'

Alma froze. She looked up at the amiably interested face like a startled rabbit unable to bolt, fixed in a fatal hypnotic stare.

'I'm so sorry,' said the man. 'Obviously I've made a mistake. I saw the name on the passenger list and thought that's familiar. I'm sure there was a frightfully attractive actress of that name who used to play in Pinero's things before the war. I do apologise.'

'Don't.' By an effort she had not known she could muster, Alma unlocked her voice. 'You are not mistaken. My mind was on other things. I don't expect to be recognized these days.'

'Really?' He looked genuinely surprised. 'Aren't you still on the stage?'

'Not for quite some time, Mr . . .'

'Oh. Finch. John Finch. An absolute nonentity, Miss Baranov. Simply one of the public who likes to visit the theatre. In fact, my friends call me Johnny. Stage door Johnny, d'you see? Look here, I'm probably a dreadful old bore, but I hate to see a lady sitting alone in a restaurant, especially when I know she's one of the loveliest actresses to grace the English stage.'

'I prefer to have a table to myself,' said Alma. 'I'm perfectly happy, thank you.'

The creases re-formed into a look of abject desolation. 'Oh dear. I've said the wrong thing. Stage door Johnny. It's only a name my friends used once in fun. It stuck. The truth is that I'm not that sort of chap at all. Very retiring by nature. I can't tell you what an effort it was to overcome my timidity enough to approach you. Won't you come and sit at my table for this meal only? I believe I'm sharing it with some Americans. I'm sure they would love to meet you.'

Alma had the clear impression that Johnny Finch would not be put off. He would keep coming back whatever she said. After the first shock, she was beginning to sense that he knew very little about Lydia. He was like the velvet-tongued men who used to come into the flower shop and conjure an acquaintance out of the brooches she wore or the way she spoke. She thought she could handle him. She said, 'I will come to your table on one condition, Mr Finch – that we do not talk about the theatre. It's a closed chapter in my life, and a painful one.'

His face lit up. 'Miss Baranov, it will be a privilege to eat with you whatever we find to talk about. My table is over there against the wall.'

'Before we join the others, I ought to mention that Baranov is the name of my husband, not my father,' said Alma as she rose to follow him.

She watched the information sink in. Johnny Finch was not very quick. He said, 'I see,' in a way that showed he did not until after the words were spoken.

Alma felt reassured. She was actually rather relieved to leave her solitary table.

On the other side of the restaurant Paul Westerfield was telling the Livingstone Cordells that his billfold was safe.

'I knew it would turn up,' said Marjorie. 'The kind of people who travel first class are respectful of property. We've never lost a thing in all our trips to Europe.'

'Picked up a few items,' said Livy straight-faced.

'You should be careful what you say,' Marjorie told him. 'People will take you seriously.' She turned back to Paul. 'There's no reason now why you shouldn't enjoy yourself for the rest of the crossing. Will you be staying in here for the dancing? I believe they have an excellent tempo – wouldn't you say, Barbara?'

Barbara gave a small shrug. 'It's all right.'

'Matter of fact, I promised a couple of drinks to the guy who handed in my billfold, so I'll be heading for the lounge,' said Paul. 'I haven't forgotten your money, Mr Cordell.'

'Nor me, son,' said Livy.

'I guess this isn't the place to hand it over.'

'I'm not particular,' said Livy.

Marjorie made a sound of exasperation. 'Livy, this is a public restaurant. Leave it till later. Have you got a table, Mr Westerfield? You know we'd be delighted if you would join us.'

Paul explained that he had a place reserved with some friends of his father. He said it was time that he joined them. He wished the Cordells a good meal and moved rapidly away.

'That's gratitude!' said Marjorie acidly.

'You're crowding the boy,' Livy told her. 'Give him some breathing space. He'll be back.'

'Yes, Mother,' said Barbara. 'Livy's right. I'm getting pretty damn tired of you trying to force Paul to take an interest in me. Why can't you leave us alone?'

Marjorie clicked her teeth. 'I will, if that's what you want. I wasn't doing it for my own amusement, you know.'

There was not much more conversation at their table that evening.

Towards the end of the meal one of the ship's officers got up to announce that it was customary on the first evening at sea to select three chairmen from among the passengers. As most of those present had crossed in the other direction, and many were regular ocean travellers, the choice was swiftly made. They chose the president of the Chase Manhattan Bank as Chairman of the auction pool. The Wimbledon singles champion, Bill Tilden, was persuaded to chair the sports committee. An Italian tenor on his way to the new season at the Met was nominated concert chairman.

'How can he be concert chairman?' asked Johnny Finch. 'He can't speak a word of English. By God, if I were free to make a nomination –'

'You're not,' said Alma quickly. 'You gave your word.'

To give him credit, the loquacious Johnny had been scrupulously fair. He made his living selling motor cars and he had a fund of fascinating stories about his customers. He had a Lanchester 40 in the hold of the *Mauretania*. He was very proud of it. Since he had started with the firm, the Lanchester 40 had outsold the Rolls Royce Silver Ghost. Now he was expanding into the American market.

Alma knew nothing about motor cars, yet she was glad to listen. She laughed at Johnny's stories. She could relax while he entertained the table. She liked the way his wrinkled face exaggerated each emotion as he spoke. She liked to hear him laugh. There were moments over dinner when she practically forgot about the body in her stateroom.

15

Paul ordered two large brandies from the steward. He asked Jack Gordon, 'Do you know the *Mauretania*?

'Not very well. I sail with White Star as a rule. The *Majestic*. German built. It has a solid feel to it.'

'I came over on the *Berengaria*, so I know what you mean. You're a regular traveller, then?'

'Did it sound like that? Only about once a year. I have some people in New York. I like to see them. And I enjoy the crossing.'

'The sports?'

Jack smiled. 'No, I don't enjoy deck tennis. I swim a little sometimes. The Roman pool on the *Majestic* really is worth getting wet for. Unless you're careful on a British ship, it's all sports and games. You get no time to yourself at all.'

The steward brought the brandy. Jack sent him for some cigarettes. He raised his glass. 'Here's to calm water all the way.'

'I've been so busy since I got on board that I haven't given a thought to what the sea is doing,' said Paul. On the principle that the giving of a confidence is a measure of companionship, he told the story of Poppy from start to finish.

'She must have been fun to know,' said Jack. 'One of our cockney sparrows – chirpy and adorable. Pity you had to part. But a chap like you won't be short of female company for long. Nothing can beat an ocean voyage for a short romance.'

Paul laughed. 'Who do you have in mind for me?'

'How about that very attractive young lady I saw you with before dinner?'

'Before dinner?'

'You appeared to be in conversation with her parents in the dining saloon, but you can't tell me you didn't notice the stunning girl with brown hair cut very short whose big dark eyes never left you for a second.'

'Ah, that's Barbara, a sweet girl I know from college days. In fact we went out together a couple of times in London.' Paul stopped. He had noticed from the movement of Jack's eyes that someone was behind him. He turned and felt the brush of soft fabric on his face. The woman was wearing a peacock blue dress with filmy sleeves that swirled gently as she moved her arms. She had extremely fine, black hair gathered in a bun. She was about ten years older than Paul. Her face had the high cheek-bones and narrow brow that preserve beauty indefinitely.

She said in a clear English accent, 'Gentlemen, I hope you will forgive me interrupting your conversation. My name is Katherine Masters and I am trying to speak to everyone about the ship's concert. You see, Signor Martinelli was the obvious choice as concert chairman, and he is a very sweet man as well as a brilliant singer, but his English is not really equal to the task of finding volunteers for Tuesday night. I'm doing a little crusading on his behalf. I know that there are always talented people on a *Mauretania* crossing.'

Jack had already shaken his head and smiled. 'No, no. I'm not one of them. I'm sorry, but I don't think I can help you, Miss Masters.'

'Nor me,' said Paul. 'I'm completely unmusical. Tone deaf, in fact.'

Katherine Masters was not so easily brushed aside. 'No, music isn't a requirement. Between ourselves,' – she leaned forward to make sure she was not overheard – 'we have more violinists than we can possibly use. They bring their music with them, you know.' She put her hand on Paul's shoulder and he caught a whiff of expensive scent. 'I'm really hoping to find some jolly young men who wouldn't mind playing a part in a sketch.'

'Not me, I'm afraid,' said Paul.

'The only thing I can play is a hand of whist,' said Jack, 'and I'm not very good at that.'

'Whist?' said Miss Masters. 'I adore whist. I'll tell you what I'll do. I'll say no more about the concert if you include me in a four for whist.'

'Tonight?' said Jack.

'Why not? I've nearly finished going round.'

'Paul, do you play?'

'Just occasionally. I'm no expert.'

'Put it this way: if you have a choice of a few hands of whist tonight or doing a music hall turn on Tuesday, which will it be?'

Paul grinned. 'It's blackmail.'

'But is it a deal?'

'I guess it is.'

'Divine!' said Miss Masters. 'But we'll need a fourth.'

'That's all right,' said Jack. 'Paul was talking earlier to a young lady he knew from his college days. I expect she could be persuaded, couldn't she?'

'I couldn't say,' said Paul. 'I'll mention it.'

'Fine,' said Miss Masters. 'In half an hour, then?'

'We'd better meet in the smoking room,' said Jack. 'I believe that's where they keep the cards.' When she had moved away, he said to Paul, 'You see? I don't know what it is about ocean liners, but no man is safe. I hope you don't feel I've let you in for this.'

'Not at all. I enjoy a game of cards. I'd better go and look for Barbara.'

He found her sitting alone at the Cordells' table in the dining saloon. She was watching the dancing. Livy and her mother were one-stepping to *I'm just wild about Harry*. Barbara looked up at Paul. Her face lit up. Instead of asking her to play whist, he had an impulse to dance with her. He took her hand and squeezed it. Jack was right. She was very attractive. As they took the floor, he said, 'You know, in all the time we've known each other, I don't believe we've ever danced together.'

Barbara gave him a quick smile. 'Maybe someone told you I'm not so good at it.'

'You're doing fine.'

'I haven't had a lot of practice.'

'Your parents dance a lot. I saw them on the floor at the Savoy. They're pretty good.'

'Livy is. He does a marvellous tango. I don't know where he learned his dancing. It was before he met Mother for sure. Mother likes to dance because she has beautiful ankles, and she can twirl around and show them off, but she's not really a dancer. She isn't co-ordinated. See how her hips are out of time with the rest of her body?'

'Stop. You'll make me laugh.'

'I guess I'm being mean. I've seen too much of my mother lately.'

'I came to ask you if you would like to join a card game,' said Paul. 'Do you play whist?'

'Who with?'

'Only the guy who found my billfold and that woman in a blue dress who is trying to organize the concert. You and I could team up and win some free drinks. How about it, Barbara?'

'I'm not really a whist player.'

'You're pretty hot on mental arithmetic. It's mainly remembering which cards have been played. Come on, we could be a great team. I'm so confident that I'll underwrite any losses we make.'

'I ought to let my mother know where I am.'

'You think so?' said Paul. He performed a spin turn so that Barbara could see her mother nodding encouragement over Livy's shoulder.

Two card games were already in session in the walnut panelled alcoves in the smoking room. Jack had reserved a table. He had bought two packs of playing cards from the bar steward. They were on the table with the seals unbroken. Paul introduced him to Barbara.

'Now we're just waiting for Miss Masters,' said Jack.

'Katherine,' said Paul. 'Let's keep it as informal as we can.'

Katherine arrived a moment later noticeably refortified with scent. 'I had to get some money from my stateroom,' she explained after another round of introductions.

'Are we playing for money?' Barbara asked.

'Of course, dear. It's a very dull game otherwise,' said Katherine.

'I have some English money I could use up,' said Jack.

'I thought it was against the rules to gamble,' said Barbara.

'Is it?' said Katherine, disappointed. 'They take the pleasure out of everything if they can.'

'We could keep a score and settle up later,' Paul suggested.

'What a marvellous idea.'

'One English pound on each rubber?' said Jack.

It was agreed. Paul drew the lowest card and became the dealer. Clubs were trumps. He dealt himself a poor hand. Jack and Katherine won the first game and the second.

'I told you I was not much good,' Barbara said to Paul.

'My dear, you haven't had the cards to play,' Katherine told her. 'Whist is dreadfully boring if you don't get the cards.'

They played three rubbers and Paul and Barbara won just one game.

'We're not much opposition for you,' said Paul.

'Let's break off for some drinks for ten minutes,' said Jack. 'What can I get you, ladies?'

'Anything with ice in it,' said Katherine. 'Do you find it warm in here? I do. I'll just slip up to my cabin and freshen up.'

'Let's have a bottle of champagne between us,' said Jack. 'My treat.'

'Lovely!' said Katherine. 'What a marvellous man you are – good at cards and generous with drinks. See you shortly.' She gave Barbara a wave and hurried out.

While Jack was at the bar ordering the champagne, Paul remarked to Barbara, 'Nice people.'

'Yes, I like them. I still wish we could even the score at cards.'

He smiled. 'It's not important. We're enjoying the game.'

'We might do better if we both remembered that the second player generally plays low and the third ought to play high.'

Paul was laughing now. 'You told me you weren't a whist player.'

Barbara's cheeks reddened. 'I know the fundamentals.'

'Sure. It makes very good sense. I'll amend my play accordingly.' He might have added that it pleased him to find that Barbara had some spirit to match her bobbed hair and painted lips. He had been inclined to think of her as a sweet girl squashed to nothing by her mother.

'And shall we have an understanding that when either of us leads we are looking to our partner to return the same suit at the first opportunity?' Barbara went on solemnly.

'If we can also have an understanding that we try to finish the game in time to get some more dancing in,' said Paul.

She looked pleased. 'I'd like that.'

'Win or lose?'

'You ought to have more faith in my suggestions. Of course we're going to win.'

'Easy on the champagne, then,' cautioned Paul as Jack returned with a steward.

'Katherine not back yet?' said Jack. He told the steward, 'We'll open it ourselves when the lady returns.'

They did not have long to wait. 'So sorry to keep you,' Katherine told them. 'I felt I really had to go back and check my face after what happened. I was on my way back from D Deck where my stateroom is, and a door along the passage opened. The man stepped out, took one look at me and shot back into his cabin. From the look on his face, he might have seen a ghost.'

'I wouldn't worry about that,' said Jack. 'I expect he was just a fellow who thought you were going to ask him to appear in the concert. He didn't know that you'll settle for a game of whist instead.' He uncorked the champagne. Katherine's frightened man was not mentioned again.

Paul and Barbara picked up eleven tricks between them in the first game after play resumed. Paul was scrupulous in playing low when he was second and high when he was third. He watched whatever Barbara led and returned it when he won the lead. They won three games in succession and took the rubber.

'What's happened to you two?' asked Jack. 'Are you playing better or have we had too much champagne?'

'Someone has,' said Katherine with a trace of pique. 'You blocked my long suit in that last game. We could have picked up two more tricks.'

'I don't think we ought to have post mortems,' answered Jack. 'I'll try harder next time, partner.'

They won a game, but lost the rubber. The unease between Jack and Katherine was almost palpable. Jack started smoking. Katherine pursed her mouth in a way that made her look years older.

'It's incredible how your luck can change in cards,' said Paul as he and Barbara won another rubber and evened the score.

'You need more than luck,' said Katherine, with a glare at Jack.

'Shall we make this the deciding rubber?' Paul suggested.

'Just as you wish,' said Jack.

'If you don't mind,' said Barbara. 'It's a long time since I played whist. I find it hard to concentrate.'

'That's the champagne, my dear,' said Katherine. 'It affects us all in different ways. Are you going to deal, partner, or shall we sit here looking at each other until we reach New York?'

Paul and Barbara won the last rubber by two games to one.

'That's it, then,' said Jack. 'Congratulations. America wins. We owe you a pound apiece.'

'You stood us the champagne,' said Paul. 'We'll call it quits.'

'One should always pay one's debts,' said Katherine. 'Barbara, here's my pound.'

Jack with unexpected force, said, 'Put it away. You don't pass money across a table here. Are you crazy?'

Katherine pushed the pound note at Barbara and said, 'Take it.'

Barbara hesitated. She looked to Paul for help.

Paul took the note and said, 'Yes, I'll buy a round for you, Katherine. That's really generous.'

'Leave me out,' said Jack, still angry. 'I've had enough for tonight – of everything.' He curtly wished them goodnight and left.

Katherine's eyes had filled with tears.

Barbara took her hand. She gave Paul a look that said she was capable of looking after Katherine. She said, 'Maybe some coffee would be better than a drink, Paul.'

He went to arrange it, still unable to account for the force of Jack's outburst. Gambling was against the Cunard regulations, but everybody knew it happened. They would hardly be hauled before the captain because a pound was passed across a table.

He ordered the coffee. He was in no hurry to go back to the table. He reckoned Barbara would cope better with Katherine alone. He was about to go to the bar and order a scotch when he saw Livy at the smoking room entrance. He remembered the three hundred bucks he owed him.

'Mr Cordell.'

'Livy to you, son.' He put his hand on Paul's arm. 'How about a drink? Marje has gone to put her feet up. Her ankles were starting to swell. Too much dancing.'

'I'd like to clear my debt with you,' said Paul. He took out his billfold and handed Livy the money he owed him. It was a simple transaction that made the scene of a few minutes before seem all the more unnecessary.

'Thanks,' said Livy. 'A scotch?'

'I'd like that.'

They stood at the bar counter with their drinks. 'Nice atmosphere on the *Maury*,' said Livy. 'She's a great ship. I was travelling on liners when you were just a kid. I know them all. That was before I met Marje. Now I'm kind of retired. I only get on ships in the vacation.'

'What was your line of work?'

'Import, export. Plenty of profit if you have a nose for trade. I made mine and put it in gilt-edged. We live off the interest.'

'Smart.'

'You said it, son. Here I am at forty-six and I can take it easy for the rest of my life. No more sweat for Livingstone Cordell. I have my own apartment overlooking Central Park. I have the cutest wife in New York and a beautiful stepdaughter as a bonus. Say, what happened to Barbara? I thought she was with you.'

'She is. That is to say she's over there in the alcove. We were playing cards.'

'Where? I don't see her.'

'She has her back to us. She's with that lady in the blue dress.'

'Her? What's she doing with her?' Livy's tone had changed. He seemed to imply that Paul had ditched his stepdaughter.

It was too much to explain to Livy. 'They had something to discuss. They sent me to order coffee. I can take a hint.'

Livy put his hand on Paul's arm and pushed him firmly towards the table. 'You go right back to them, son, and break it up. When two women get together, you're sunk. Don't let it happen.'

Paul glanced at Barbara. She was deep in conversation with Katherine. Katherine was smiling.

He said, 'Okay.'

But Livy had left.

16

After dinner Johnny Finch entertained Alma and the Americans from their table. He sat in an armchair in the centre of the lounge and told motoring stories. They were very funny. They were spiced with the names of people in society. The gentlemen bought expensive motor cars to impress the ladies. Either the cars or the gentlemen always got overheated. 'In the art of seduction,' Johnny told his audience, 'the motor car is an unreliable accessory.' He told a story of the late King Edward and a car that he had hired. The owner had a soft drinks factory and was hoping for a warrant of appointment in lieu of payment. The King drove into the country with a lady friend. The car ran out of petrol. The King was not dismayed. There was a pleasant interval. Eventually the King lighted a cigar. He told the lady all was well. A reserve supply of petrol was on board. He got out. He unstrapped the can. It was full of lemonade. The manufacturer failed to get his royal warrant.

Johnny's stories drew more people to the circle. He was still holding forth at midnight. The stories got more risqué. A woman and her husband left the group. Alma was the last woman left. She waited for the next bout of laughter and got up to say goodnight.

'Leaving us so soon?' said Johnny.

'It's after midnight.'

'So it is, by George. And I was hoping to show you my Lanchester.'

Everyone laughed, including Alma.

'Perhaps later in the crossing,' said Alma.

'I'll keep you to that. Goodnight, my dear.' Johnny launched into a story about Henry Ford.

Alma made her way back to D Deck. She was slightly unsteady. She had drunk more wine than she intended. Each glass had helped to dilute her fears. She could not have faced a night in stateroom 89 without it.

The corridors were quiet. The ship was steady. Any sway was Alma's. But she had no trouble finding her way. She followed the signs to the rooms beginning with the digit 8. She counted them off to 89.

"Do Not Disturb" had been removed.

She opened her bag and fumbled for the key. She held it under the light and checked the number. She pushed it into the lock. She waited a second. She turned it and opened the door.

The light was on and there were curtains drawn across the portholes. The cabin trunk was open.

Alma took a long breath. She stepped close enough to look inside. The trunk was empty. She said aloud, 'Thank God.' She closed the stateroom door.

She looked inside the bathroom. She opened drawers and cupboards. She could not think of sleep until she knew exactly what was in that room. She saw Lydia's clothing, neatly folded. Everything looked clean and new. There was a nightdress in black satin. She would not wear it.

She took off the georgette evening gown. She cleaned off the make-up in the bathroom. She decided to take a bath. While she was in the water she felt as if the ship changed course. The cadence of the engines altered. The bath water slurped around her. It happened more than once. For a time she thought the ship had stopped. It lurched again as she reached for the towel. Her stomach heaved. She wished she had drunk less wine.

The ship seemed to settle to its usual rhythm. Alma was grateful. She put on her petticoat and got into bed. She had not put out the light. But she was less frightened than she had thought. The worst was over now. She turned her face to the wall. She was soon asleep.

17

The sound of someone in the passage wakened her. It was a steward serving tea. There was sunlight on the ceiling. Alma checked her watch. It was nearly eight o'clock. Sunday morning. She had slept at least seven hours. She stretched her limbs. She thought of Walter in his cabin. Had he slept so well?

She bathed and dressed and went to breakfast. The restaurant was busy. People were wearing lighter clothes. The ship's officers were now in white.

She went to her former table. Breakfast was a meal to be enjoyed alone. If Johnny Finch came over she would decline to join him. She did not look to see if he was there. She ate undisturbed, and well.

He was not the kind of man to disappear for long. After she left the restaurant, Alma went on the boat deck for some air. It was a glorious morning for a stroll. After a few steps she heard the familiar voice.

'Someone is out to prove that she got to bed early last night.'

He was seated in a deckchair with his feet up. He was wearing a blue guernsey and white flannels.

Alma stopped and greeted him.

'Did you really sleep so well?' he asked.

'Yes, thank you. I was very comfortable.'

'Lucky you. I was up half the night.'

She smiled. 'You shouldn't tell so many stories.'

'No, my dear, it wasn't that. It was all the excitement. Wasn't long after you went to bed. The blessed ship changed course.'

'I thought I noticed something.'

'So did we. We all went up on deck to see. There must have been fifty people up here asking what was happening. No-one seemed to know. But you can take my word, we turned about and started back to England. Then we turned again. The ship had turned full circle.'

'Whatever for?' asked Alma.

'Man overboard.'

Alma stiffened. 'What did you say?'

'Man overboard. Some poor soul had fallen off the ship. A courting couple on the boat deck were looking at the moon and saw someone fall into the water. They told the captain and he turned the ship to make a search. Regulations, I was told. They had to turn the ship and look, even if there's not much chance. So they switched the searchlights on, while the ship retraced its course. Very powerful beams, those searchlights have. We all leaned over trying to help. And would you believe it, my dear, we spotted her?'

'Her?'

'Yes. It was a woman, poor soul. They put down a boat and picked her out of the water. But she was dead already. What a horrible way to go.'

PART FOUR

His New Job

1

After breakfast there was great activity in the main lounge. A team of stewards set to work. They moved the occasional tables to the sides. They brought in one of the large tables from the dining saloon and placed it at the top end of the lounge near the grand piano. They arranged the easy chairs and sofas in rows to face the table. Meanwhile a squad of bellboys brought in upright chairs from the restaurant and positioned them in rows behind the armchairs. Two boys moved along the rows and left a hymn-book on each chair.

At a quarter to eleven the first class passengers who wished to worship took their places. All the armchairs were filled. Latecomers used the upright chairs. At five to eleven the congregation was completed by passengers from the second and third classes. Those who could not get chairs stood at the back with members of the crew. Among them was Walter, looking self-composed.

Alma, several rows ahead, felt sure he had seen her. She had turned only once to look for him. She was trying to stay calm. The recovering of Lydia's body was desperately unlucky, but it was not the end. Who was to know that it was Lydia? It was simply an unknown woman who had fallen or jumped over-board. They would check and find that no-one was missing. It would remain a mystery for ever.

Captain Rostron entered the lounge with the senior officers. They took their places at the table. The service began with a hymn. The purser read a lesson about "they that go down to the sea in ships, and occupy their business in great waters". The congregation stood while the captain said prayers. Another lesson was read and another hymn sung.

After the hymn, Captain Rostron asked everyone to be seated. He moved round the table and stood in front of it. He said, 'Ladies and gentlemen, our service is concluded. It is not my custom to address the passengers on this occasion, but something occurred last night that I feel bound to speak to you about. Some of you know that a passenger, a lady passenger, was seen to fall overboard. It was reported to me and I gave orders at once for the ship to be turned about and a search made. The passenger was recovered, but it was too late to save her life. We are not yet certain who she was, or in what circumstances this tragic incident occurred. The master-at-arms, Mr Saxon' – he indicated one of the officers, who stood up – 'is making inquiries. If you can help over the matter of identification or in any way that throws light on what happened, I would be obliged if you would speak to him. His office is situated next to the purser's. I would only add that tragedies of this sort are bound to occur from time to time on great ships making regular ocean crossings with up to two thousand passengers and eight hundred crew aboard. The appropriate action is taken by the captain, but the routine of the ship continues. I hope that this will not prevent you from enjoying your voyage on the *Mauretania*.'

Captain Rostron picked up his prayer book and left the lounge. A muttering somewhere in the congregation rapidly became a chorus in full voice. There was hardly a person in the room without some recollection of the previous night. Sounds and, strange movements had been noticed, lonely women seen on deck. Those who had watched the search gave their account of it.

Alma turned in her chair and pretended to listen to a man in the row behind who said he had heard a scream. She looked towards Walter. Their eyes met. He did not look disturbed. He made a slight movement of the head from side to side. Then he turned away and joined the other passengers making for the door. Alma understood his meaning. There was no need to be alarmed. She got up and made her way along the row towards the other door.

Marjorie Livingstone Cordell had managed to acquire an easy chair in the second row for the service. She had enjoyed the hymns, but she wasn't impressed by the captain. 'It's easy for him to tell us not to panic, they pick bodies from the water every trip. It doesn't satisfy me. I mean suppose the poor lady was pushed. Who's going to find out the facts? That little guy with a ginger moustache who stood up when the captain called his name? He doesn't inspire *me* with confidence.'

'Well, no, he doesn't. You've got a point there,' agreed the woman next to her.

'Marje, if you'll forgive the expression, you're all at sea,' said Livy from her other side. 'This is just the kind of job the master-at-arms is trained to do. He's the cop on the ship. Any trouble, he deals with it. Stowaways, smugglers, drunks.'

'Stowaways are one thing, murder is another,' said Marjorie acidly.

'Who mentioned murder, for heaven's sake?'

'I thought it might be suicide,' said the woman on Marjorie's right.

'Murder, suicide, accident – do you really think ginger moustache can tell the difference?'

'His name is Saxon, honey,' said Livy.

'I tell you one thing, Livy. If it was me or my daughter fished out of the sea, you wouldn't be so happy with him in charge. Where is Barbara? I didn't see her in here.'

'No. I guess she decided to miss the service.'

'We didn't see her at breakfast, either. Oh my God! Livy, where is she?' Marjorie stood up and looked wildly around the lounge.

'Take it easy, Marje. She could be anywhere – her stateroom, the café, the library. She could be laid out somewhere.'

Marjorie gave a cry of distress.

'On a deckchair, honey,' said Livy. 'On a deckchair.'

'We've got to find her.'

'Okay. You check the stateroom. I'll look around the other places.'

'Should we speak to the captain? They could put out a call on the public address.'

'Not before we check, Marje. Just do as I say, will you?'

2

When Captain Rostron returned to the bridge, the ship's doctor was waiting to see him.

'If you can spare a few minutes, Captain, I'd like you to look at the body in the mortuary.'

'I saw her last night, doctor. I didn't recognize her.'

'It isn't that. It's something nobody noticed last night.'

'Can't you tell me about it?'

The doctor's eyes flicked towards the other officers in range of his voice 'I think you should see for yourself, Captain.'

'Very well. Let's get it over with. I shall probably hold you responsible for ruining my lunch, doctor.'

In the narrow storeroom on the lower deck that served on occasions as a mortuary, the captain watched the doctor peel back the sheet and indicate the reason for his concern.

'I see.' The captain heaved a deep sigh. 'Bad, doctor. This is bad. Have you shown it to Mr Saxon?'

'Not yet, captain.'

'I think you had better. At once. Between ourselves, I hope he is equal to this. I really do.'

Livy Cordell found Barbara shortly before lunch. She was sitting at a table in the smoking room with Paul. They had some playing cards face upwards and seemed to be discussing them.

'Jesus, am I glad to find you!' said Livy.

'Hi, Livy,' said Barbara airily. 'You're just in time. Can you play auction bridge? Paul is trying to teach me.'

'We haven't seen you all morning. Your mother is nearly out of her mind with worry.'

Barbara shook her head gravely. '*She's* worried? Livy, how do you think I feel about a parent who panics when I miss breakfast? I'm not a child any more. I managed to live in Paris for a year without Mother holding my hand. You and I are going to have to talk to her.'

'Barbara, she had a reason to be worried. You weren't in the lounge for morning service, were you?'

'Is that it?' Barbara turned to Paul. 'I miss church. I really am a lost soul now.'

Livy ignored the sarcasm. 'What I mean is that you didn't hear the captain tell us about the dead woman.'

'Dead woman? Who died?'

'That's it. No one knows. She fell in the sea last night and she was dead when they got her out. They don't know who she is. Now do you see why Marje is in such a state over you?'

Barbara got up. 'I'd better go to her right now. Where is she?'

'She went up to check your stateroom.' As Barbara left, Livy said to Paul, 'That'll be quite some reunion. How about a beer?'

They took their glasses back to the same table. Livy said, 'So you want to teach Barbara to play bridge?'

Paul nodded. 'It's a good game. We played whist with some people last night and we were getting on quite well towards the end. They said that bridge is a better game, so I was trying to show Barbara how the bidding goes.'

'You young people ought to make a good team. Didn't you both study maths in college?'

'I don't know if that's much of an advantage,' said Paul with a smile.

'These people you were playing with – how did you come to fix up the game with them?'

'Oh, it was pure chance. I happened to be talking to the guy who handed in my billfold and this woman came around asking us to join the concert party.'

'The one who was in here talking to Barbara?'

'Right. Jack made some chance remark about whist and the lady said she wouldn't bother us any more about the concert if we agreed to make up a game of whist. So I asked Barbara to be my partner and we had quite a nice game until the other two fell out.'

'Why?'

'The usual thing. She criticised his play. He took it pretty well until the end when she put some money on the table. Gambling for cash is not allowed and he told her straight to put the money away. It was all a little foolish, but people get like that over cards. He walked out and she was on the point of tears, but Barbara calmed her down. That was when I met you at the bar.'

'I see. And this hasn't put you two off cards?'

'Why should it? We didn't quarrel. We won.'

'Barbara isn't so placid as she first appears. She can get quite forceful over a game of cards. She doesn't like to lose.'

'I discovered that,' said Paul. 'Livy, it's a positive attitude. I like it.'

3

There were no individual tables in the second class dining saloon. There were tables for four or six. At breakfast Walter had come early. He had sat at the end of a table for six. A young couple had sat at the opposite end. They were probably just married. They had not said a word to Walter.

Sunday lunch was different. The meal was served on time, at one o'clock. Everyone arrived together. Walter went to a table set for four. Three people were already seated. They were a couple with a child, a small girl with her hair in a plait that she kept flicking over the back of her chair. Walter asked if he could join them.

'Please do,' said the man in a Midlands English accent. 'We'd like some company. I'm Wilf Dutton. This is my wife Jean and that's our Sally.'

'Dew. Walter Dew.' Walter smiled and picked up the menu.

'Why is that man sitting at our table?' enquired Sally.

'It isn't ours. We share it,' said Jean, smiling shyly at Walter.

'Better than home,' said Wilf.

'I beg your pardon,' said Walter.

'I said better than home. Three roasts to choose from.'

'Yes, quite right.'

'We're emigrating. No work to be had in Leicester. Have you been to Leicester? Don't suppose you have. Me brother has a business in Rhode Island. He's a builder like me. Told us to sell up and come out there. He even sent us the tickets, second class. Not bad, eh? Should I know you, Mr Dew?'

Walter shook his head. 'I don't think so.'

'I seem to know your face. Was you ever in Leicester?'

'Wilf,' said Jean, 'don't ask personal questions.'

'Nothing personal in that,' said Wilf.

'I may have been there as a child,' said Walter. 'Certainly not recently.'

'What line are you in, Mr Dew?'

'Wilf,' said Jean in a long-suffering voice.

'Retired,' said Walter. Turning to the child, he asked, 'Is this your first trip on the ocean, Sally?'

'Sally, the gentlemen is talking to you,' said Jean.

'You don't look old enough to be retired,' said Wilf. 'What were you, a soldier?'

'Answer the question,' said Jean.

'No,' said Sally.

'Why should she?' said Walter. 'She's just like me, slightly shy at first. Have you seen the menu, Mrs Dutton?'

'If it isn't your face I know, maybe it's your name,' said Wilf. 'Walter Dew. You aren't famous, by any chance?'

'It's quite a common name.'

'A cricketer?'

'He's coming to take the order, love,' said Jean. 'What's minestrone?'

'Vegetable soup,' said Walter.

'She asked me,' said Wilf. 'I could have told her that.'

'Let's change the subject,' said Jean. 'Did you hear about the poor woman who fell overboard, Mr Dew?'

The same topic was discussed across the round, linen-covered tables in the first class and the folding tables linked in lines in the third. Passengers expounded theories through the afternoon. A steady stream of witnesses with information made statements to the master-at-arms. Then they made further statements to the people in the deckchairs outside. It was learned that Mr Saxon was asking curious questions. He was interested in other people seen on deck or in the cabin areas near midnight. He asked several witnesses if they had heard a struggle or a scream.

One of Mr Saxon's informants was a bellboy. He was very nervous. He stood rigidly to attention while he made his statement. He fixed his eyes on the lampshade over Mr Saxon's head.

When the boy had finished, Mr Saxon asked him, 'Are you sure you aren't confused? You see a lot of passengers on embarkation day. How can you be sure?'

'Don't know, sir.'

'What did you say her name was?'

'Mrs Brownhoff, sir.'

The master-at-arms looked towards one of the officers assisting him. The officer looked at the passenger list. He shook his head.

'There is no-one of that name aboard. You say she was a passenger with an embarkation card.'

'Yes, sir.'

'You showed this lady to her stateroom. Which room was it?'

The boy looked down.

'Don't you remember, lad?'

'It was a portside room, sir.'

'How do you remember that?'

'She asked me which side of the ship she was. She gave me a shilling.'

Mr Saxon glanced aside. 'That probably is reliable information.' He addressed the boy again. 'And you say you haven't seen this lady since. Do you make a point of checking up on all the passengers you have shown to their staterooms to see if they are still aboard?'

'No, sir.'

'If your Mrs Brownhoff happened to be unwell in her first day at sea, isn't it possible that she might stay in her room, and that you wouldn't see her about the ship?'

'I suppose so, sir.'

'You *suppose* so? What do you mean by that?'

'I mean no, sir. I wouldn't see her.'

'I think we're wasting valuable time,' said Mr Saxon.

The officer with the passenger list said, 'We have a Mrs Baranov in stateroom 89.'

The officer taking down the statements said, 'She isn't missing. She was at the service this morning. Dark-haired, rather pale, doesn't smile much, but attractive. Late twenties, early thirties.'

Mr Saxon asked the bellboy, 'Does that sound like the lady who gave you a shilling?'

'Yes, sir.'

'Well, it looks as if we've solved your little mystery. Did someone put you up to this?'

'No, sir.'

'Because if you were deliberately obstructing me in the performance of my duty I would see to it personally that you were not employed on the *Mauretania* or any other ship again. Get back on duty.'

The work of taking statements continued through the afternoon. It had to be got through, but Mr Saxon was uneasy. Other things needed to be done. Someone ought to check that every stateroom on the ship was occupied. He didn't trust cabin stewards. He knew their reputation, the stories of their unrestraint with unaccompanied lady passengers. It ought to be an independent check. He had insufficient time and insufficient help.

4

By teatime it was rumoured that the woman had been murdered. In the first class lounge designed in the eighteenth century style to provide an atmosphere of quiet grace, appalling theories of homicide were aired across the salmon sandwiches and silver teapots. Ladies listened open-mouthed as their companions told them what horrors lurked beneath them on the lower decks. Lascars with daggers, drunken Irish stokers, rapacious engineers, thieving emigrants skulked in the steerage waiting for the night. No-one was safe. It was a horrifying prospect. There was no escape. They were imprisoned in the ship.

The anxieties were voiced in varying degrees in all the public rooms:

'There could be a maniac at large. What action are they taking?'

'My dear, they're not taking action. They're only taking statements.'

'That's absurd. The captain ought to give us some protection.'

'You're not really frightened, are you? You've always been so brave.'

'Don't give me that soft soap. If you cared the smallest bit about my safety you would go and see the captain and demand to know what he is doing to protect us from this maniac.'

'Give him a chance, my dear. He's doing his best, I'm sure.'

On the boat deck, Alma overheard a similar conversation. The wind carried the last of it to her ears after she had passed the speakers: 'It's poor women like her that I feel sorry for. Fancy being all alone when there's a murderer at large.'

She had spent the afternoon reading in the stateroom. She had come out to get some air. At the word "murderer" a shock went through her body. She began to tremble. Had she misheard? She felt nauseous. She turned towards the sea and gripped the rail.

'I say, do you need help?' a man enquired.

'No thank you.'

'You look frightfully pale. Have you tried Mothersill's? They're very efficacious. I've got some with me if you'd like one.'

'No, it isn't that. I'm perfectly all right.'

Below, on the main deck, Wilf and Jean Dutton were walking

arm in arm. Sally was behind them with her skipping-rope. Jean kept glancing back.

'Can't you forget her for a moment?' said Wilf. 'She's not daft. She won't jump over.'

'You know why I want to keep an eye on her,' said Jean.

'Love, it was a grown woman. Men who go after woman don't bother with little girls. If anyone's at risk, it's yourself.'

'It's horrible,' said Jean. 'I wish we'd stayed in Leicester, job or no job.'

'Well, I don't. Hey, isn't that the bloke we had lunch with?'

Jean looked at the hunched figure staring at the ocean. 'Yes, that's him. Leave him, Wilf. He's not our sort. He doesn't want to mix.'

'He's no-one special. We established that. Mr Walter Dew, retired. Retired from what, I'd like to know. Why was he so cagy when I asked him? What do you reckon he did for a living, Jean? Kept a pawnshop? No, that's not his style. Something smarter. One of them lounge-lizards. Hey, that's more like it. How would you fancy a foxtrot with him?'

'Don't be so daft.'

'Well, if it isn't that, what is it? Something shady, or I'll eat my hat.'

'Good thing if you did,' said Jean. 'It's horrible. Greasy and fraying at the sides. I don't know what your brother's going to say. They don't wear things like that in America.'

'I've got it. He's the murderer. That's why he won't say much.'

'Keep your voice down, Wilf.'

'Dr Crippen himself.'

'Stupid. He was hanged before the war.'

'I know that. It's just a joke. Poor old Crippen on the boat, and . . .' Wilf stopped. 'By God, I *do* know who that is!'

5

The hour between seven and eight in the evening was when the passengers congregated in the lounge for cocktails. It was the hour when the ladies paraded their evening gowns and the rich colours of the silks and satins were seen in brilliant glimpses among the black jackets and boiled shirts of the men. At this climax of the day even the intricate workmanship of the three hundred Palestinian craftsmen who had carved the mahogany panels in the lounge did not seem too ornate for the occasion. The *Mauretania* had been conceived for just such dazzling scenes.

Barbara was in an emerald green dress in taffeta by Lanvin that she had bought in London. It would have cost her half as much in Paris, but she had not given a thought to fashion then. It was a good thing Livy was so generous with money. She had pendant ear-rings set with emeralds and she was carrying a black fan. She had found the previous night that the cigar fumes in the smoking room got quite overpowering, but she would not let that deny her another game of cards. She wanted Paul to partner her at bridge. She was sure they would be a winning combination.

'We'll have to see if Jack is interested,' Paul told her as they sipped sherry. 'We ought not to assume he is.'

'Katherine will play,' said Barbara. 'She said to me last night that bridge is a better game than whist.'

'They might not want to play together after that dust-up over the money.'

'It was just too silly,' said Barbara. 'My guess is that they will both be glad of a chance to start over again.'

'Maybe,' said Paul. 'We'll need to ask them. Have you seen either of them today?'

Over the conversation came the sound of the bugle.

'Pity,' said Paul. 'It would have been nice to catch them before dinner.'

Barbara's eyes were on the arch connecting with the smoking room. 'There's Jack. He just came in.'

They moved round a large group to meet him as he came through. He had a preoccupied look that remained on his face as Paul greeted him.

'Jack, you're just the guy we were looking for. How about

some more cards after dinner? Barbara wants to learn bridge.'

'What?' said Jack vacantly.

'Katherine says I'd like it better than whist,' said Barbara in support.

'Katherine – have you been talking to Katherine?'

'Last night after you went. She said a sea-trip is the ideal chance to learn.'

'Yes,' said Jack without a trace of enthusiasm.

'If you'd rather not, I guess we could find someone else,' said Barbara. 'It must be pretty dull playing with a beginner.'

'It isn't that,' said Jack. 'It isn't that at all.'

'Put it this way,' said Paul. 'If we talk to Katherine, and she is agreeable to a game, shall we meet in the smoking room like last night?'

Jack seemed not to hear the question. He said to Barbara, 'What else did she say last night?'

'I don't know. Nothing important. We had a coffee. She was a little unhappy, but she soon got better. It was mainly women's talk.'

'What do you mean by that?'

Barbara felt herself go pink. 'Well, I was telling her how I got to know Paul.'

'That was all?'

'Just about. She went to bed soon after. Is there anything I should have noticed?'

'No. I'm sorry. I didn't mean to be inquisitive.'

'I don't think she would want to make an issue out of one small incident in a game of cards,' said Barbara.

'Probably not,' said Jack. 'If you'll excuse me now . . .' He started moving with the general drift towards the door to the dining saloon.

Barbara started to say, 'But you still haven't told us –'

Paul touched her arm and said, 'Let's leave it for now.'

6

'Here you are!' said Johnny Finch as if he had made the most momentous discovery of the crossing. 'I haven't seen you for hours.'

'I spent the day quietly,' Alma explained.

'And no wonder at that,' said Johnny. He was standing by Alma's table in the dining saloon. He bent his head confidentially closer. 'Look here, there's a certain matter I'd rather like to ventilate with you. Would it be terribly pushy of me to invite you to my table again?'

Alma had rehearsed this speech several times. 'Mr Finch, I appreciate your kindness and I enjoyed your company at dinner yesterday evening, but I think it right to tell you that I am travelling alone by choice. So perhaps you will forgive me for declining your invitation.'

Johnny blinked. 'Oh my word, what have I said? Dear Mrs Baranov, I must have given you quite the wrong impression. The matter I mentioned is not of a personal character at all. I'm not the sort of fellow ladies often take me for. This is a matter of public interest, I assure you. It concerns the unfortunate business of the lady who was taken from the sea last night.'

Alma stiffened. Her heartbeat quickened. She needed all her strength to keep a semblance of control. She said, 'That's another matter, I agree, but it is not a very suitable topic for a conversation over dinner.'

Johnny looked disappointed. 'I can't dispute that.'

'Anyway,' added Alma, 'I don't see how it could possibly concern me.'

'Only insofar as it concerns every unaccompanied lady on this ship,' said Johnny with an air of nonchalance that did not deceive Alma. 'But as you obviously prefer not to discuss it . . ' He held out his hands in a gesture of indifference.

'Will it wait till after dinner in the lounge?'

He gave a smile. 'I'll reserve a chair for you.'

'You see,' he told her an hour later as coffee was poured for them at a table discreetly situated behind a potted palm, 'there is a certain amount of concern among the passengers about the way the inquiry into this unhappy incident is being conducted. There is a feeling that the master-at-arms – who I am sure is perfectly conscientious – is not going about the job in the most effective way. From what one hears, he is rapidly burying himself under a mass of statements, while nothing definite is being done to establish who the woman was and how she met her death. There are disquieting rumours that she was murdered.'

'So I heard,' said Alma, 'but it's only talk I expect.'

'I hope you are right,' said Johnny. 'The talk is pretty general through the ship. People are frightened, my dear. They have no confidence that Mr Saxon can protect them. Unaccompanied ladies such as yourself are entitled to protection.'

'Oh,' said Alma, trying to conceal her relief. She had read in Ethel M. Dell – or was it Elinor Glyn? – about would-be Lotharios who offered to guard the virtue of gullible females travelling alone. 'I don't feel the need of any protection, thank you.'

Johnny's wrinkles twisted into a pained expression again. 'You are missing the point, my dear. My purpose in speaking is to ask you if you wish to join the deputation.'

'Deputation?'

'Of passengers united by their concern. There are twenty or more of us already, mostly men. We need a lady to put the feminine point of view. I thought of you.'

'No,' said Alma firmly, 'not me.'

'Why not? The captain is only human. He can't eat us.'

'I don't see any point in it. What do you hope to achieve?'

'I was coming to that,' said Johnny. 'I don't know if I mentioned that this is by no means confined to the upper decks. We have chaps from the second class and the steerage just as bothered as you or I about the way this is being handled. And they have passed the word up that by sheer good fortune there is a passenger in the second class who is far better qualified to investigate a mysterious death than Saxon. Even you must have heard of him – Inspector Dew of Scotland Yard.

7

Captain Rostron put his hand on Mr Saxon's shoulder. 'It would be no discredit,' he assured his master-at-arms. 'Nobody could fault the work you've already done to solve the crime. All those statements – sure to be invaluable. It's just the fact that Inspector Dew – if this is indeed the man – is a specialist in murder.' He smiled. 'I ought to say the detection of murder. He had twenty years or more at Scotland Yard.'

'Yes, Captain,' said Mr Saxon in a voice that was not impressed.

'That ought to count for something,' said the captain. 'Murder is regarded in the police as a matter for the experts, is it not? Did you, er, come across many cases when you were a policeman in the Port of London, before you came to Cunard?'

Mr Saxon's mouth tightened. He shook his head. 'It was mainly customs offences, sir. I'm confident that I can cope with this.'

'Yes,' said Captain Rostron. 'You've made that clear. Mr Saxon, it isn't just a question of finding a murderer. It's just as important to show the passengers that we have their welfare very much in mind. This suggestion that we employ the services of Dew originated with the passengers. I can't ignore it, can I? It's a question of confidence, you see.'

'We don't even know if he *is* the Scotland Yard man,' put in Mr Saxon.

'That is one of the matters I propose to clarify. The other is whether he is willing to help. He may not be too pleased with the suggestion. He retired from Scotland Yard before the war.'

Mr Saxon looked more hopeful. 'He might prefer to act as my assistant, sir.'

The captain looked dubious. 'I don't think I can ask a man of Dew's reputation to be subordinate to you. And I think the passengers would be happier to be told that he was in control. But let's not jump to any conclusions, Mr Saxon. I simply wanted you to know the possibilities. I take it that I can rely on your cooperation whatever the outcome?'

'Yes, sir,' answered Mr Saxon flatly.

'I shall want you here to say as much if necessary, but say nothing until I ask you.' The captain reached for his jacket and put it on. 'He should be outside with the junior third officer. Be so good as to ask him to step inside, will you?'

The man who came in was tall enough to be a policeman. He was old enough to be a retired policeman. He had the heavy black moustache just familiar from the press pictures of Inspector Dew bringing Crippen and Le Neve off the ship to face their trial.

But today he looked more like the quarry than the sleuth. His eyes raced across the office as if searching for a means of escape.

Captain Rostron was on his feet and holding out his hand. 'So good of you to come and see us, Mr Dew. No point in introducing ourselves. I'm sure you know who we are, and we're pretty sure we know who you are.' The captain grinned as he spoke. He almost winked.

Walter stared glassily back.

'Let's all sit down,' suggested the captain, waving his guest towards a chair and perching himself on the edge of his great mahogany desk for informality. Saxon found a chair beside the door. 'I'm not one to beat about the bush,' said the captain. 'I haven't asked you here for cocktails, Mr Dew – if I may call you that – as interesting as that might be. As you know, we took a woman from the sea last night and she was dead, poor soul. You have heard about that?'

'Yes,' said Walter almost in a whisper.

'Mr Saxon over there took over. It's the master-at-arms who gets the job of inquiring into anything irregular while we're at sea. Mr Saxon was in the police, weren't you, Mr Saxon?'

'In the docks,' said Mr Saxon. 'Port of London.'

'He's very good with stowaways and smugglers, but suspicious deaths are something else. I'm confiding in you now, Mr Dew. I said suspicious deaths.'

Walter nodded gravely.

'Certain information has been laid before me,' Captain Rostron went on, 'information concerning you. It may be a mistake, of course. Coincidences happen. But if it isn't a mistake, you are the one man on the *Mauretania* who can help us with our inquiries.' He paused to see the effect of this.

Walter was looking down at his hands. They were shaking.

'You *are* Chief Inspector Dew, formerly of Scotland Yard?' said the captain a little less confidently.

Walter looked up. He looked at the captain. He looked at Mr Saxon. 'What is this about?'

'I thought I had explained. We need the help of an expert detective. Mr Dew, are you or are you not the same man who arrested Dr Crippen?'

He fingered his necktie. 'Well, yes.'

Captain Rostron looked across at his master-at-arms. 'That's a relief. For a moment I thought . . . Never mind.' He turned back to Walter. 'I'll be perfectly honest with you, Inspector. We believe the lady was already dead when she was put into the sea. We think she was murdered.'

'Why? said Walter, frowning.

'I think you ought to see for yourself. Make up your own mind, Inspector. That is, if you will take the case.'

'What do you mean – try to help?'

'We had rather more than that in mind. We were hoping you would agree to be in charge of the investigation.'

Walter shook his head. 'No, I couldn't do that.'

'Why not, Inspector? Mr Saxon would be only too pleased to step aside for a detective of your eminence and experience.'

Walter turned in his chair and looked at Mr Saxon, who was staring into space.

'I, em, I retired from Scotland Yard,' said Walter.

'We know that,' said the captain. 'But you're a younger man than I am, I should think.' He gave a laugh. 'I tell myself I'm not decrepit yet. You can't tell me you aren't as sharp as the day you put the cuffs on Dr Crippen.'

'I don't have the authority. I'm just a private individual.'

The captain made a sweeping gesture with his hand. 'No worries on that score. You'll have my authority. That's sufficient. Good Lord, I can christen people, marry them and bury them, so I'm damned sure I can hire a good detective to look after them.'

'Look after them?'

'To find the murderer, Inspector. You see, I have a duty to the passengers.'

'I suppose you have.'

'And I see it as my duty to ask for your cooperation.'

'I'm just a passenger on your ship,' said Walter. 'I don't have any of the things a detective needs.'

'Such as . . ?'

He moved uncomfortably in the chair. 'Well, a notebook.'

'You shall have it,' said the captain. 'Handcuffs, a magnifying glass.' He started taking things from his desk. 'A pencil, a foot rule, everything you need.'

'Criminal records,' said Walter. 'It's very difficult without criminal records.'

'I can send a wireless message to Scotland Yard,' said Captain Rostron. 'You of all people ought to remember that, Inspector.'

'Oh, yes.'

'Have we convinced you?'

'Yes,' said Walter bleakly, 'I suppose you have.'

'Good man. We're very grateful to you, aren't we, Mr Saxon?'

'Very grateful,' repeated Mr Saxon.

'Immensely,' said the captain. He got up and walked to the door. 'I expect you want to see the body now.'

8

It may have been a day to set pulses racing and nerves on edge, but it was still Sunday. At 9pm in the first class lounge every seat was taken for the *soirée*. There were to be recitals on the pianoforte and the violin. The chief attraction was unquestionably Signor Martinelli, who had consented to perform some favourite arias in the second half of the evening.

Alma had found a place at the end of a row next to a woman in a black crepe and diamanté dress who clearly had no interest in anyone other than the small man with a purple cummerbund to her left. It seemed as good a place as any to pass the evening quietly reassembling her thoughts. She had not reckoned with Johnny Finch. His voice spoke a couple of inches from her ear at the conclusion of Chopin's *Revolutionary Study*. He was in the seat behind her.

'Just thought you'd like to know that we pulled it off. The captain's a wily old character. Listened to our deputation without batting an eyelid. Anyone would think he knew that Dew was on his ship, but I'm damned sure he didn't. Thanked us for mentioning the matter and said it was under consideration. Blow me if I didn't hear twenty minutes later that Dew was called up to his office.'

Johnny's last words were overtaken by a hissing from more than one direction. The pianist was poised to begin her next piece. Alma sat through it without listening. She was trying to assimilate the inconceivable. If Johnny's assumptions were correct, Walter had been invited to investigate the murder he had himself committed. It was bizarre beyond belief. But by degrees she began to see that if he could accept the role of self-pursuer, and be convincing in it, no-one would ever guess the truth.

'The word is that the captain will be speaking to us in the interval,' said Johnny during the applause for the pianist. 'My guess is that he won't be alone. He's got the trump card now and he wants us all to take a look at it.'

After this, Alma spent the violin solo sending up prayers for Walter. The poor man could hardly have got over the shock of being called to the captain's office, and now he was about to be paraded in front of the passengers. Would he be equal to the ordeal?

The violinist was into his second piece when Alma turned to ice at the sight of the captain standing just inside the door with Walter, deathly pale, at his side. They waited for the last note. They waited for the applause. They stepped to the place where the soloist had stood.

Everyone went silent. The captain spoke: 'I shall not delay your enjoyment for long, ladies and gentlemen. Those of you who were at Morning Service today will remember that I mentioned a distressing matter, the death of a lady passenger. Some of you have been good enough since then to place information with the master-at-arms pertaining to the incident. However certain questions remain to be answered. I know that there is concern among you that the matter should be cleared up quickly, and of course I share your sentiments. I am pleased to tell you that I have accepted an offer of help from this gentleman on my left. He is a former Chief Inspector of Scotland Yard and a famous detective, indeed, outside the world of fiction I can think of no detective better known than the man who caught Crippen – Chief Inspector Dew.'

At this, there was a burst of spontaneous applause. The audience shifted in their chairs and craned their heads to look at the man who had caught Crippen. Walter's eyes bulged slightly, but he stood his ground.

The captain went on, 'In the circumstances I have asked the Chief Inspector to take over the inquiry from Mr Saxon, who of course has many other responsibilities on the ship. I don't know whether you would care to say anything at this stage, Inspector . . .'

'No,' said Walter firmly.

'In that case, I will only add that I am sure you will have the full co-operation of the passengers and crew in bringing the inquiry to a swift and satisfactory conclusion.'

'Hear, hear,' said someone, and there was more applause.

'And now there will be a fifteen-minute interval before Signor Martinelli sings for you.' Captain Rostron turned to say something to Walter and they left the lounge together.

'Didn't I tell you?' asked Johnny.

'Yes,' said Alma, beginning to breathe again.

Further towards the front, Marjorie turned to Livy and said, 'Seems like they've got a professional on the job. Who was this Crippen guy?'

'He made a lot of headlines a few years back. Some doctor living in London. He poisoned his wife and cut her into small pieces. Then he buried them in the cellar of his house and took a boat to Canada with his lover.'

'Gee,' said Marjorie, 'these English may have beautiful manners, but they do some Godawful things to each other.'

'Honey, Dr Crippen came from Coldwater, Michigan,' said Livy.

Yet there was no doubting the approval of British and Americans alike that Chief Inspector Dew was now in charge. His career was eagerly discussed over the coffee and chicken sandwiches. In his twenty-odd years as a detective, only one case of murder had remained unsolved in all those he had featured in, and that was his first, the case of Jack the Ripper, when Dew was just a junior. There was not a brighter copper anywhere. The fears accumulated through the day were scattered to the winds. The conversation was a chorus of praise for Dew and Scotland Yard and sensible Captain Rostron.

So buoyant was the mood that when Martinelli sang, he had never known a better audience. They clapped and cheered and asked for encores. It passed quite unremarked that the last aria of the evening was *Nessun Dorma* – None shall sleep.

9

When the singing was over, Alma turned down Johnny's invitation to a "nightcap or two" and made her way forward past the dining saloon and through the embarkation hall to the drawing room. In the days before the war when the smoking room had been a male preserve, the drawing room had been a refuge for the ladies. It retained an atmosphere of quiet refinement. It had fabric-covered armchairs and a soft green carpet. There were copies of *Vanity Fair* and *Vogue* on low round tables. Alma preferred it to the stateroom. She was soon in conversation with a woman from Baltimore who was escaping from a former husband who wanted a reconciliation. It was a consolation to listen to someone else's problems.

Some time towards midnight a bellboy came into the drawing room and announced that he was paging Mrs Baranov. He repeated it twice before Alma reacted to the name. He had a note for her. It said, *Lifeboat Station 3, Boat Deck, as soon as possible. W.*

Walter. He needed her. Poor man, he had suffered an enormous shock. The plan had rebounded on him. He had lost control. This was his cry for help.

She told her companion she would have to go.

'You should be careful,' the woman warned her. 'Don't take any chances.' In their conversation this was the first reference to the subject that obsessed so many others.

Alma went first to the stateroom and put on Lydia's black velvet evening cape. It would be cold outside. She pulled up the hood before she went on deck.

The breeze caught the cape and swept her forward. She pulled it closer to her body. The boat deck looked deserted. She guessed it was not the wind that had discouraged people from taking moonlit walks. She knew there was nothing to fear, but she still felt a fluttering in her stomach as she moved along the deck.

She was not sure how the lifeboat stations were numbered. She had to hope that number 3 was on this side.

Then she felt her shoulder gripped. Fingers stabbed into her flesh. She was swung round. The hood slipped off her head. She gave a cry. She was facing Walter. In the ship's light his eyes looked demoniac.

'Alma!' he said as if amazed. 'My God, you gave me such a shock. I thought . . .' He pulled her close and held her. 'Alma, forgive me. I must be mad. In that cape I thought that you were Lydia.'

'She's dead,' said Alma, shivering with fright. 'Lydia is dead.'

'Yes. I lost control. It was quite irrational.'

'It's understandable considering what you've been through,' said Alma.

He shook his head. 'Whatever it was, I frightened you. Did I hurt you?'

'Just a little.'

A strand of hair was whipping across her face. He lifted it off her brow. She thought he was about to kiss her, but he did not.

He said, 'There's no-one up here. I've been right round the deck. Let's walk a little.'

She had raised her face to meet his lips. She lowered it as if she had meant to nod. Walter had not noticed. It was salutary to recall that men without exception in romantic fiction had to be tutored in the subtle ways of women. She would persevere.

She said, 'What a fright you must have had when you were asked to see the captain.'

'Yes, I wondered why he wanted me. I should have guessed.'

'It was my fault,' said Alma. 'It was my idea to call you Walter Dew.'

'We thought of it together.'

'We never dreamed this would happen – that they would ask you to investigate Lydia's death. Darling, what you must have been through! You looked as white as chalk when the captain introduced you to the passengers. But you were marvellous – so convincing!'

'If I was white,' said Walter, 'there was a reason for it. I had just come from looking at the body.'

She gripped his arm with both her hands. 'Walter, how dreadful! I had no idea.'

'It was somewhat disturbing. You see, it wasn't Lydia.'

'What?' Alma's spine gave a twitch. 'Not Lydia?'

'I know,' said Walter in a level voice. 'It seems impossible.'

'Are you quite certain?'

'Positive.'

'People can look different after death.'

'Alma, I was not mistaken. This was another woman.'

157

She had the appalling thought that Walter's mind had gone. It had not been equal to the strain. She said as calmly and as rationally as she could, 'How is that possible, Walter?'

He gave a shrug. 'I have no idea. But it means, you see, that we are safe. As the body is not Lydia's, we are free.'

She forced herself to talk as if she accepted what he had told her. 'But there is still a difficulty, isn't there?'

'What's that?' asked Walter.

'Everyone now believes that you're Inspector Dew. They expect results.'

'In that case, I shall have to do my best to provide them,' said Walter without a trace of perturbation.

'How can you, Walter? You're not really a detective.'

'Oh, but I am.'

'No,' insisted Alma, 'Walter, you are not.'

'Let me finish please. In the eyes of everyone aboard this ship – except for you – I am Dew, and that's what counts. I have satisfied the captain. I have his authority to back me up. You heard him in the lounge this evening. I am the man who arrested Crippen. The safety of the passengers has been vouchsafed to me.'

'Yes, darling, they believe it, but you are *not* a detective. You don't know what to do. We have four more days at sea. There's a dead woman on the ship and you say she isn't Lydia. That isn't much to work with.'

'A murdered woman.'

'But if it isn't Lydia, how can that be true?'

'Because of the bruising round the neck. The woman was strangled, Alma.'

She caught her breath. How could he sound so reasonable and say these things?

'So there must be a murderer on board,' Walter went on, 'and I really have a duty to the passengers and crew to catch him. There is no-one else to do it now.'

'No,' said Alma passively. 'No-one else.'

'The first thing is to identify the victim. I've been questioning the stewards. It's very simple. They know their passengers by now. All a detective does is verify the facts. It's a matter of looking at things and asking questions. I've done it all my life.'

'You're not afraid?'

'Not now,' said Walter. 'I'm on the side of law and order.

People look up to me. I like to be a focus of attention. I wasn't happy with the role of fugitive. *That* frightened me.' He laughed. 'And there are other advantages. I've been elevated from the second class. I have a first class stateroom just along the corridor from you. 75.' He put his arm possessively around her.

She clutched the cape across her chest. She said, 'It would be dangerous to be seen together.'

'Naturally.'

'It isn't that I wouldn't help if I knew how.'

They continued to walk along the deck. The sea looked black and evil. Alma looked towards the stars. The ship's wireless masts slid across the white full moon. She said, 'I think I ought to go to bed.'

'Yes,' said Walter. 'I'll take another turn around the deck.'

He didn't kiss her. She was thankful. She didn't want to stay a moment longer.

Near her stateroom she met the woman from Baltimore. She stared wide-eyed at Alma. 'Have you been out on deck?'

'Just to get some air.'

'I don't know how you could! You could have met the murderer out there.'

In her stateroom, Alma pushed the bolt across the door and turned the key in the lock. She still felt insecure. She pushed the armchair against the door.

Later, in bed, she tried to analyse her fear. Walter had given her a shock when he had grabbed her shoulder, but that had been explained. In the cape she had looked to him like Lydia. It was a moment's aberration and she could understand it. His insistence that the body was not Lydia's could have been another delusion of his troubled mind. It was disturbing, but it did not frighten her. The root cause of her fear was something he had said: *In the eyes of everyone aboard this ship – except for you – I am Dew*... She had felt resentment in those words *except for you*. He wanted to be Dew. It was a new identity, thrilling and impressive. Crippen's captor, now the saviour of the *Mauretania*. There was only one impediment to the illusion, and that was Alma. She knew the truth, and that was why he frightened her.

10

Johnny Finch had not been introduced to Paul Westerfield II, but he was not inhibited by protocol.

'Not a bad morning,' he said when he found him taking a look at the sea from the promenade deck after breakfast on Monday. 'When that mist lifts, we'll be in for a scorcher, if I'm any judge.'

'You think so?' said Paul.

'A chance to put in some practice at deck tennis, old boy. Who knows, you might be the fellow to beat big Bill Tilden? It's a different game altogether from the sort they play at Wimbledon. Or are you more of a shuffleboard player?'

'Are you from the social committee?' asked Paul.

Johnny rocked with laughter. 'No, no, you won't catch Johnny Finch on any committee, least of all that one. I don't go in for deck games myself. Just a little flutter on the result, and that's pleasure enough for me.'

'I don't bet,' said Paul.

'No?' said Johnny with a note of scepticism. 'I could have sworn I saw you in the smoking room playing whist the other night.'

'That was a friendly game.'

'Goes without saying,' said Johnny with a wink. 'But if you should fancy a sporting bet, I hear that the ship's barber has started a book on how long it takes Inspector Dew to get his man.'

'That's enterprise,' said Paul.

'Too true,' said Johnny. 'I'm thinking of putting on a fiver. He's offering four to one against Dew making an arrest tomorrow.'

'I'm not too interested.'

'You should be, old boy. Did you hear that Dew's already had his first success? He's named the murdered woman. He was with the first class cabin stewards this morning, checking for a stateroom that had not been slept in. They found two or three, of course – knowing what people on ships get up to in the night. Eliminated all but one, and took the steward down to have a look at the body.'

'He identified her?'

'Right away. No hesitation.'

'Who was she?'

'That's the point. She was a friend of yours, old sport. She was in that four for whist. Her name is Katherine Masters.'

PART FIVE

The King in New York

1

The deckchairs on the boat deck were arranged in four rows. Seasoned travellers made a point of seeking out the chief deck steward as soon as possible after going aboard to make a reservation. Once booked, a chair was labelled. It was secure for the rest of the crossing. The precise location of the chair was crucially important. No-one except a Spartan or a first-time passenger accepted a position on the starboard side for the crossing to New York. Even the south-facing port side was best enjoyed from under a blanket. And there were finer considerations. A front row position was essential if you wanted to be noticed or attract the notice of a steward. A discerning traveller would want to know who would be seated near him. A shipboard romance might well be engineered with a bribe to the chief deck steward.

Thanks to Marjorie's planning, the Livingstone Cordells were superbly placed in the front row on the port side in the shelter of the funnel that was never used and did not scatter soot. The seat next to Barbara was labelled *P. Westerfield II*. This morning it was not occupied.

'What's happened to that boy?' Marjorie asked her daughter. 'You two haven't fallen out again, have you?'

'No, mother. Paul has gone looking for Mr Gordon.'

'Who is that?'

'The Englishman who found his billfold. He played cards with us on Saturday evening. Paul wants to make sure that Jack knows about Katherine being the woman who was found.'

'He ought to know by now. I thought everyone on the ship has heard about it. Was he a friend of hers?'

'No, they just came together for the card game. Actually they didn't get along too well. She was a little upset by the end of the game.'

'Poor lady – what a terrible thing this is,' said Marjorie. 'You don't think she committed suicide?'

'Mother, she was strangled. All the stewards are talking about it.'

Marjorie turned to the chair on her other side. 'Did you hear that, Livy? Barbara says the lady was strangled.'

'Hm?'

'He's out to the world,' said Marjorie. 'Barbara dear, I don't think it would be wise for you to get mixed up in this.'

'I can't alter what already happened, Mother. I played cards with Katherine on the evening she was killed. I'm sure to have to answer questions about that.'

'Livy and I wouldn't want to see your name in the newspapers. If that Inspector asks you anything, keep it short, huh?'

'There isn't much that I could tell him. He'll hear it all from Paul and Jack anyway. Her murder couldn't have anything to do with the card game, so don't fret about it.'

'You can't say for sure,' said Marjorie. 'This Jack Gordon – what do you really know about him? He could be the strangler.'

'Mother, that's ridiculous.'

'Believe me, Barbara, I've had three husbands and I know a few things about men.' She checked that Livy's eyes were closed. 'They can be perfect gentlemen as far as anyone can see, but get them alone with a helpless woman and they turn into monsters. Some of them, anyhow.' She glanced at Livy again. 'Men have to be house-trained like any other animal or they go for you. It wouldn't surprise me at all if your nice English friend Mr Gordon turns out to be the murderer.'

'I guess it has to be someone unexpected,' said Barbara.

'Yeah,' said Livy without opening his eyes. 'Have you thought of Paul?'

2

The ship's doctor looked up from his notes to see his next patient.

'Inspector. Do come in. I thought you wanted treatment. What can I do for you?'

Walter hesitated. 'Actually, I would like to consult you, doctor.'

'Of course. I'm at your service. Is it about my examination of the body?'

'No. It's about my thumb. I seem to have injured it.'

'Really? Let's have a look. How did this happen?'

'This morning after breakfast I made an examination of the dead woman's stateroom.'

'Ah,' said the doctor, 'don't tell me. You wanted to see whether the body had been pushed through the porthole, so you tried to open it. You're suffering from porthole thumb, Inspector. Next to *mal de mer* it's the commonest complaint we get. You should have asked a steward to do the job. Much easier. They carry port keys for the purpose. Does this hurt?'

'A little.'

'Can you straighten it?'

'I think so.'

'Very good. It's only a sprain. I'll give you a fingerstall if you like, but it wouldn't aid the healing. So you think the murderer pushed the body through the porthole. Perhaps you should be looking for another fellow with an injured thumb.'

'No,' said Walter, 'it's not so simple. Some of the portholes were already open when we came on board. I particularly noticed that.'

'That's Scotland Yard training,' said the doctor admiringly. 'Far be it from me to presume to tell you your job, Inspector. Did you find anything of interest in the stateroom?'

'Very little. Plenty of clothes. A few bottles of scent.'

'No jewellery?'

'No,' said Walter. 'No jewellery.' He groomed his moustache with his good hand.

'It is a point,' said the doctor. 'If her jewellery had been stolen, would that provide you with a motive?'

'I suppose it might.'

'The reason I mentioned jewellery was that when the captain

asked me to examine the body, I found the mark of a ring on the third finger of the left hand.'

'Perhaps it came off in the water.'

'The wedding finger, Inspector,' said the doctor with significance.

'She was not married,' said Walter. 'I've seen her passport. She was definitely Miss Katherine Masters.'

'I assure you I wasn't mistaken. I'll show you if you like.'

'No, no. That won't be necessary,' said Walter. A smile dawned slowly on his face. 'Perhaps it was an engagement ring.'

'That's possible, I suppose,' conceded the doctor, but he sounded sceptical. 'It is my opinion that Miss Masters was not without experience of men, Inspector.'

'You don't say,' said Walter. 'Did you meet this lady?'

The doctor was beginning to be puzzled by the Inspector's train of thought. 'No, I did not. I made an intimate examination for evidence of assault.'

'Oh. I understand you now.'

'My opinion is that she had not been sexually assaulted.'

'Quite right,' said Walter. 'We can do without another motive for the crime.'

'I was going to add that the evidence suggests that she was married.'

'Or should have been,' said Walter. 'One ought to make allowance for the war.'

'The war?'

'It changed the world, doctor. The end of innocence.'

'True.'

'I don't defend it.'

'Good Lord, no,' said the doctor not wishing to be controversial. 'Inspector, there is something else I ought to bring to your attention.'

'About my injury?'

'No, no. Another matter. It may not be significant, but I think I ought to tell you. As you know, we placed Miss Masters' body in the storeroom designated as a mortuary, below the passenger accommodation in the lower orlop.'

'Yes.'

'The room is locked, and we keep the key up here with the keys to the medical rooms and cupboards. I have an orderly in charge of them. On Sunday we were very busy here with the usual things – seasickness and sore thumbs. I had two nurses and the orderly on duty with me. At some stage of the evening a passenger – a man – came into the office outside and told the orderly that he needed the key to the storeroom where the body is. He said something about being asked to help with the identification.'

'Did he get the key?'

'Yes, he did. My orderly that evening was a young fellow by the name of Topley. This is his first crossing. He's keen to please, but none too bright. He handed over the key, and he says he can't remember what the fellow looked like. I only found this out because at the end of the evening the key wasn't on its usual hook. Topley went down to look for it and found it in the lock.'

'The passenger didn't bring it back after he borrowed it?' said Walter. 'That's a bit off.'

The doctor gave him a searching look. 'The point is that he went down there without anyone's authority. The captain didn't sanction it and nor did the master-at-arms. Why should a passenger do a thing like that?'

'I was about to ask the same question,' said Walter.

'You can talk to Topley if you wish. I don't think you'll get much out of him.'

'I'll save my breath,' said Walter. 'Thank you for mentioning it, however.' He looked at his injured thumb and tried to move it. 'There's some mobility returning. I don't think I'll bother with the fingerstall.'

'Aren't you going to ask me about the bruising?'

Walter turned his hand over and studied it.

'The bruising on the woman's neck,' said the doctor with a trace of petulance. 'I was the first to notice it.'

'Congratulations,' said Walter.

'She was definitely strangled, Inspector. The marks are consistent with manual strangulation.'

'Yes,' said Walter. 'Very unpleasant. And rather crude. Murder need not be so brutal. Well, it's nearly lunchtime. Thank you for your diagnosis.'

Alone in his office, the doctor pondered the secret of Inspector Dew's success. He seemed to have the gift of eliciting information without asking for it. His style of questioning was so oblique that it made you forget he was a policeman. Of course, he had retired from Scotland Yard before the war. He was either out of touch or devilishly clever. The doctor had not decided which.

3

In the sunshine on the promenade deck Alma's nervous intima-
tions of the previous night made her feel ashamed. She had been
overwrought. She needed to relax. She had under-estimated the
tension that the murder had inflicted on them both. In Walter's
case it was excusable because there were pressures on him still.
Hers had lifted. She ought to be behaving like any other
passenger. So when a steward mentioned that the *Berengaria*
had been sighted, she joined the gathering along the starboard
side to watch the great Cunarders pass each other.

She was glad she did. She felt exhilarated by the sight of the
great vessel steaming towards them, its black hull turning blue
water into foam, its white superstructure lined with waving
figures. Signals boomed across the water. Both ships stopped
within a few hundred yards of each other and a tender was set
down to exchange mail. There was more waving as the turbines
turned again and the whistles joined in salute. Alma watched
until only the steam from the *Berengaria*'s three funnels could
be seen. She had not noticed until then that Johnny was beside
her. She found that she did not mind.

'You know of course that she was launched by the Kaiser,' he
informed her. 'She was the *Imperator* until Cunard took her
over as their flagship. Spoils of war. She's still a glorious ship. It
doesn't worry me. I think there's a lot to be said for sailing under
different colours, wouldn't you agree, Mrs Baranov?'

If the blood rose to Alma's cheeks, it might not have been
noticed in the bracing wind. She gave a neutral smile.

'That's just my way of broaching the subject of the fancy dress
ball tomorrow,' said Johnny. 'You're going, of course?'

'I haven't given it a thought.'

'Nor me, until this morning. Some of these people bring their
costumes ready made, proper professional things, but I don't
care for that. I think it should be more spontaneous, don't you?'

'Well, yes, I didn't bring a costume.'

'Quite right, my dear. I can promise you, if you'd taken all the
trouble to bring your best crinoline and your wig and your box
of oranges, there would sure to be at least two other Nell
Gwynnes to ruin your enjoyment.'

Alma laughed. 'What will you come as?'

'That's the point. I haven't quite decided. I'm trying to think of something quite original. I did have one rather topical idea. How would I look as Dr Crippen?'

She tried to smile.

'Not bad, eh?' said Johnny.

'I think it would not be appreciated by everyone,' said Alma.

'Perhaps you're right. I'm too tall anyway. He was a little fellow, wasn't he? Difficult to do. People would be sure to think I was a politician. As a matter of fact, I have got a better idea, but I need some help with it. Pardon me for asking, my dear, but are you handy with a needle and thread?'

'It depends what you have in mind.'

'Nothing too elaborate. A few tucks here and there.' Johnny smiled to himself. 'By Jove, it's a winner, this one. Now we must think of something for you.'

4

After lunch Jack Gordon went to look for Inspector Dew. He found him seated in an armchair between the piano and a potted palm in the main lounge. He appeared to be asleep. Jack spoke his name and there was no response. He repeated it. He touched the Inspector's hand.

Walter jerked his hand away. He opened his eyes.

'Inspector Dew?' said Jack for the third time. 'I'm sorry to disturb you.'

'What is it?'

'My name is Gordon, Jack Gordon. Is it convenient to speak about the matter you are investigating?'

'That? Oh, yes. Can you find a chair?'

Jack collected one from the other side of the palm and positioned it opposite Walter.

'Not there,' said Walter. 'Slightly to the right. I want a clear view of the lounge.' He winked at Jack. 'Observation.'

Jack glanced over his shoulder along the Inspector's line of vision, but all he could see were two clergymen playing draughts.

'What did you wish to say, Mr Collins?'

'Gordon. I thought I'd speak to you before you came looking for me. I was with Miss Masters on the evening she was killed. I was playing cards with her in the smoking room. I was her partner at whist. It's obvious that you will want a statement from me.'

'And very public-spirited of you to volunteer it, Mr Collins.'

'It's Gordon, actually, Inspector.'

'I heard the first time, Mr Collins. No offence, but I make a practice of addressing witnesses by their surnames. Tell me about this game of whist. Who were your opponents?'

'A young American couple. His name is Westerfield, I think.'

Walter took out a pencil and notebook. 'I'd better make a note of it. I'm hopeless with names. I usually leave this to the nurse.'

Jack gave an uneasy laugh. 'Yes.'

'And the name of Mr Westerfield's partner?'

'That's difficult. She's called Barbara. I didn't catch the surname.'

'Not to worry, Mr Collins. I'll find it out in my own way. I'm more concerned about Miss Masters at the moment. You were friends, I gather?'

'No. We hadn't met before Saturday evening. The whole game was got up after dinner. I found myself sitting in here with Mr Westerfield. While we were talking, Miss Masters came round asking people if they wanted to help with the ship's concert. Neither of us was too enthusiastic, but we agreed to play a few rubbers of whist instead. She was quite keen on the idea. Paul – Mr Westerfield – went off to ask Barbara if she would be his partner.'

'And was it an agreeable game?'

'For most of it, yes.' Jack folded his arms and unfolded them. 'Well, you're going to hear about this from somebody, so I'd better tell you. There was a sort of misunderstanding at the end. Paul and Barbara won the deciding rubber. Miss Masters and I didn't play all that well together after the first few hands. She criticised my play. It nettled me. At the end she took out a banknote to pay the others their winnings. I don't know how familiar you are with what goes on between card-players on ships, Inspector, but no-one puts money across the table in a public room. I was quite sharp with her. I told her in a few short words that it wasn't done. Then I left them. I think she was about to burst into tears, and I can't stand that.' He gave a shrug. 'There it is. I'm sure you appreciate how badly I feel about it.'

'I wouldn't take it too much to heart,' Walter advised him. 'It's not as if she committed suicide. I can tell you confidentially that she was strangled.'

'I heard a rumour to that effect,' said Jack. He leaned forward in his chair. His lips had suddenly gone pale and his eyes fixed on Walter with extraordinary intensity. 'You must find the devil who did it, Inspector. He must hang for it.'

Walter nodded. He eased a finger gently round his collar.

'You will catch him?' said Jack.

'God willing,' answered Walter.

'I don't know how you begin to account for a vicious crime like this.'

Walter sat unmoving like the sphinx.

'There was no reason for it,' Jack continued. 'It was senseless. You're dealing with a maniac.'

'Who do you think?' asked Walter interestedly.

Jack blinked. 'I've no idea. I just want to see him caught.'

'You were sitting opposite Miss Masters during the game,' said Walter, 'so you must have seen her hands.'

'What do you mean? I don't cheat.'

'Not the cards, Mr Collins. I mean her hands. Literally, her hands. Do you remember whether she was wearing a ring on the third finger of her left hand?'

Jack shook his head. 'She was unmarried. You know she was a spinster.'

'She might have been engaged.'

'She was not wearing a ring.'

Walter made a note in his book. He looked up and said, 'Was there anything else, Mr Collins?'

'Yes, there is. May I have your notebook and pencil?'

Walter's eyes widened, but he handed the book and pencil to Jack.

Jack wrote in his name. He said, 'Just for the record, Inspector.' He handed it back. 'Don't hesitate to ask me if you need any help.'

'Thank you,' said Walter. 'Thank you very much.'

He waited for Jack to leave the lounge. Then he got up and went to ask a steward to point out Paul Westerfield.

Paul was on the boat deck. He was playing in the first round of the deck tennis tournament. This involved throwing a rubber ring over a badminton net. The court had been marked in chalk on the deck. Paul's opponent was a middle-aged Englishman who compensated for his inferior agility by cunning use of the macaroni shot, which caused the ring to wobble distractingly in mid-air. It was also possible that the presence of Walter on the sideline in his bowler hat contributed to Paul's loss of concentration. He lost the deciding game conclusively. He shook the winner's hand. A young woman handed him his sweater.

Walter said, 'Mr Westerfield, if you are not exhausted . . .'

'No, sir,' said Paul. 'It was more of a tactical match than a test of endurance. You know my name, then. This is Miss Barbara Cordell, who I guess is also on your list.'

'Oh, yes,' said Walter.

'Would you like to talk to us together?'

'Together? I hadn't considered it.'

'We have no secrets from each other.'

Barbara said, 'I believe the Inspector wants to talk to you alone, Paul.'

175

'No,' said Walter. 'This will save time.'

'Fine,' said Paul. 'Shall we go to the Verandah Café? I'm pretty thirsty just now.'

The table they chose was beside a trellis screen. As the front of the café was open to the wind, Walter asked Barbara whether she minded sitting in a draught.

'It's nice while the sun is out,' she told him, 'and I have my cardigan with me if I get cold. Aren't you going to take off your hat, Inspector?'

Walter took a look round the café. 'I couldn't decide whether we were inside or out,' he explained as he placed the bowler on the seat beside him.

'Does it matter?' asked Paul.

'One likes to do the proper thing,' answered Walter confidentially. 'Perhaps I'm a little out of date. It's a few years since I last crossed the Atlantic.'

'We heard about that,' said Paul. 'Well, who hasn't? It's passed into maritime history now.'

Walter drew back slightly in his seat. He said guardedly, 'Yes, but how did you know about me?'

Paul exchanged a glance with Barbara. This could only be the English sense of humour at work. He said, 'I guess you're quoting Dr Crippen now.'

'Ah,' responded Walter with more enthusiasm.

'I can remember seeing a picture in the *New York Times* of you and Crippen stepping off the gangplank when you got back to England, and you were wearing the hat. I can't say that I recall which ship it was.'

'The same one, in fact,' said Walter.

'The *Mauretania*?'

'The hat,' said Walter, picking it up. 'The same hat. Now, if I could trouble you with more recent recollections, what can you tell me about the lady who was killed on Sunday night?'

'Katherine? Not a lot, Inspector. We only met her that evening. She asked us if we would like to play whist.'

Barbara interrupted. 'She didn't ask me. If you remember, Paul, you invited me to join the game after it was arranged.'

'Yes,' said Paul. 'Is that important? Well, if you want the whole story, I was having a coffee and a brandy in the lounge after dinner with an English guy by the name of Jack Gordon. Katherine – Miss Masters – came up to us and asked us if we

176

could do anything in the concert. She was recruiting on behalf of Mr Martinelli, the concert chairman, whose English is not so good. She wanted people to play parts in a sketch. Jack made some kind of humorous remark to the effect that the only thing he could play was whist. Katherine took him up on it, and that was how we fixed the game.'

'I was still in the dining saloon with my parents,' said Barbara. 'Paul came in and asked me to join the game.'

'We knew each other at college,' added Paul.

'And we happened to be staying at the same hotels in Paris and London,' said Barbara.

Walter produced a notebook. 'I'd better get some of this down. Would you care to order? I think the steward is coming.'

'Sure,' said Paul. 'What's yours, Inspector?'

Walter frowned.

'What will you have to drink?'

'Oh. Tea, if you please.'

'Milk and sugar?'

'No sugar. It causes cavities. Now, Miss Cordell, how do you spell your surname?'

'B–A–R–' began Barbara.

'No, your surname, my dear,' broke in Walter. 'Cordell.'

'That isn't really my surname at all,' said Barbara. 'It's Barlinski.'

Walter looked as if he was not prepared to believe it.

'Livingstone Cordell is my stepfather,' Barbara explained. 'He is my mother's third husband. She divorced Daddy when I was seven years old. It's too much to keep explaining, so when people call me Cordell I don't usually correct them. Shall I spell Barlinski for you?'

Walter pushed the pencil and notebook across the table. 'Perhaps you would write it down instead.'

'Shall I write Paul's name as well?'

Walter looked like a man who has been caught once too often. He nodded. When Barbara handed back the notebook he studied it closely.

'Did you want to hear about the card game?' asked Paul.

'Not really. I had an account of it from Mr, er,' Walter checked his notebook – 'Gordon. Tell me about him.'

'He's nice,' said Barbara. 'He found Paul's billfold and handed it to the purser.'

'My wallet,' Paul explained. 'I lost it some time after we came aboard. There was plenty of money inside – more than a grand.'

'A thousand bucks,' said Barbara.

'Dollars,' said Paul.

Walter was crossing out words in his notebook.

'I'm not short of money,' Paul went on, 'but losing that billfold was a drag.'

'He had to borrow from Livy,' said Barbara.

'Livy?'

'Livingstone,' said Paul. 'Her father.'

'Stepfather,' said Barbara.

'Does it matter?' said Paul. 'You don't want to hear about my problem with the billfold, do you?' he asked Walter. 'The point is that Jack Gordon found it and handed it in. He saved the situation, that's all.'

'*He* did?' said Barbara, affronted. 'Hold on. How about giving some credit to Livy? He gave *you* plenty. Without his help, where would Poppy be now?'

'Poppy?' repeated Walter with a note of desperation in his voice.

'A friend of ours,' said Paul.

'Ours?' said Barbara sarcastically.

'An English girl we both met in London.'

'She had blonde hair and a figure out here and a dress that wasn't designed to hide it,' said Barbara. 'She came to Southampton to see Paul off. Through some obscure circumstance she didn't go ashore when the bell was rung. She was taken all the way to France. In all the excitement Paul mislaid his billfold. Livy loaned him enough to pay Poppy's fare back to England.'

'You can forget about Poppy,' Paul told Walter. 'She has nothing to do with your investigation. You asked about Jack. He's okay. He got a little upset when Katherine took out some money at the end of the game, but you couldn't blame him. She'd said a few mean things about his play but he let them pass.'

'Cards seem to bring out the worst in people,' Walter observed.

'As individuals they were both very likeable,' said Barbara. 'I had quite a long talk with Katherine after Jack had left the table and Paul was getting some coffee. She had no animosity towards

Jack. She was annoyed with herself for upsetting him. We agreed between ourselves to persuade the two men to have another game the next evening.'

'You didn't tell me that,' said Paul.

'Why should I have done? It was just something I agreed with Katherine. I told you she offered to teach me to play bridge.'

'What else did you two agree?' asked Paul.

'A few things about men in general.'

'And after that?' said Walter quickly.

'Paul came back with the coffee, and pretty soon after, Katherine left us to go to her stateroom. It must have been around midnight then.'

'We went into the dancing and had a couple of slow waltzes and then went off to our own rooms,' said Paul. 'The first we heard about anyone being killed was Sunday morning before lunch.'

'I still can't understand it,' said Barbara. 'She was just a lonely woman who didn't know anyone else on the ship.'

'Yes,' said Walter. 'It baffles me.'

'That's not quite correct,' said Paul. 'She must have known some other people to have got on the concert committee. And don't let's forget that she was going around asking for volunteers.'

'It's not really enough to get her murdered,' said Barbara.

'It must have scared someone. Remember what she said when she came back from putting scent on herself?'

'Oh, yes,' said Barbara. 'I forgot that.' She turned to Walter. 'Midway through the game we broke off for a drink. Katherine went back to her stateroom to freshen up. She told us when she came back that a man had stepped out into the corridor, taken one look at her and stepped back into the room as if he had seen a ghost. She was so surprised at the incident that she went back to her room to check her face again.'

'Jack suggested it must have been some guy who was terrified of being asked to appear in the concert,' said Paul. 'Well, why else would he behave so suspiciously?'

Walter gave a nervous cough. 'I'm sure I couldn't say.'

5

After dinner Alma went to her stateroom to do some sewing. She was glad to have something positive to do. Johnny had provided her with needle and thread and even a thimble. It was amazing how many materials and "props" came to hand when the passengers really applied themselves to creating fancy dress. In one stroll along the boat deck that afternoon she had seen pieces of rope being teased into wigs and beards, hats fashioned from table napkins and togas from Company bedspreads. With less ingenuity Alma had decided to go as a nurse. She hoped that this would enable her to participate without drawing too much attention to herself.

There was a knock. She got up, prepared to send Johnny away. She thought she had made it clear that she would give him his fitting in the morning. It would be most improper to receive a visit from a gentleman in the evening, whatever the pretext.

She opened the door a fraction. It was Walter. He said nothing. He expected to be admitted. She hesitated, trying to suppress her unease from the previous night.

Walter looked more tired than threatening. She stepped back and admitted him. They did not embrace.

He went towards the armchair.

'Not there,' she told him. There was a needle and thread sticking into one of the arms.

'What are you making?' he asked as he went to the upright chair.

'Fancy dress. I'm trying to behave like any other passenger.'

'Good.'

'It's easier for me. Nobody is watching me. I keep wondering how you are managing. It must be a terrible strain trying to convince them that you are a detective.'

'I am a little weary,' said Walter, 'but they accept me as Dew.'

'How do you know which questions to ask?'

'Oddly enough, I haven't asked many. People just talk to me. I try to make reasonably interested responses. I take down their names in my notebook to the best of my ability. They all treat me with awe so far. I wonder how long it can last.'

'We're supposed to be reaching New York on Thursday morning,' said Alma. 'Three more nights.'

'I don't mind the nights. I have the impression that people will start expecting me to reach some conclusions soon. I promised to speak to the captain later this evening.'

'Is there anything you can tell him?'

'Practically nothing. A faint suspicion of something – not murder, unfortunately.'

'What's that, Walter?'

'I talked to the people who were playing whist with the victim on the evening she was murdered. There was a rather smooth-tongued fellow, English, with light-coloured hair plastered back from his forehead. And a young American couple, probably very rich. While I was listening to them I found my thoughts harking back to my days in the music halls. I told you the kind of thing I used to do, didn't I?'

'Mind-reading. Walter, how brilliant! You read their minds!'

He shook his head. 'Nothing so impressive as that. What I mean is that I was reminded of the way we obtained our volunteers from the audience.'

'Yes, you told me. You called them plants.'

'Yes. It's no more than a sort of intuition, but I can't help feeling that Gordon – the unctuous Englishman – planted himself on the young Americans.'

'To cheat them at cards?'

'Ultimately. You see, Westerfield– the American – mislaid his wallet and Gordon picked it up and handed it to the purser. Naturally, Westerfield went to thank him. There was a bond of confidence between them. While they were having a drink Katherine Masters came by, apparently seeking volunteers for the concert. Instead, a game of cards was got up. On the face of it, a perfectly spontaneous arrangement.'

'But you suspect that she was in collusion with Gordon?'

'It crossed my mind. It would be a neat confidence trick. Gordon said not a word to me about the wallet being found.'

'Is that significant?'

'It is if the wallet was lifted from Westerfield's pocket and put somewhere for Gordon to pick up.'

'Who would have done that?'

'A girl called Poppy who came aboard with Westerfield.'

'It sounds a very elaborate fraud, Walter. Did they win a lot of money?'

'They lost.'

Alma shook her head sympathetically. 'It rather knocks your theory on the head, doesn't it?'

'No. As you say, it's elaborate. If there's anything in it at all, they wouldn't be aiming at one evening's cards. They would go through the week raising the stakes, and make their killing on the last night.'

'So they may have deliberately lost.'

'Yes. In fact, they appear to have played quite well for a few hands and then gone all to pieces. She was critical of his play and he reduced her to tears at the end of the evening.'

'Do you think it was stage-managed?'

'It certainly seems to have convinced the Americans.'

'But what was the point?'

'To reassure them that Gordon and Miss Masters didn't know each other, couldn't play very well together and could easily be beaten. The American girl was left comforting Miss Masters and promising to play bridge the next night.'

'It does begin to sound plausible,' commented Alma. 'You really are a detective.'

Walter's face lit up. 'Do you think so?'

'But it doesn't explain why Miss Masters was murdered.'

'No.'

'And now that she is dead it will be very difficult to prove.'

Walter nodded glumly.

'Unless . . .' said Alma.

'What?'

'You could find out for certain whether she was on the concert committee.'

Giovanni Martinelli was in the barber's shop having a manicure and an animated conversation in Italian with the barber. They stopped abruptly when Walter entered.

'Signor Martinelli?' said Walter.

The great tenor raised his eyebrows.

'Forgive me for interrupting. My name is Dew, Inspector Dew, inquiring into the unfortunate death of Miss Katherine Masters. There is one small point that you may be in a position to clarify. I was informed that on the evening of her death Miss Masters was seen to approach certain guests to ask them on your behalf as chairman of the concert committee whether they were willing to participate in the ship's concert. I merely wish to confirm that she was so engaged and was an accredited member of your committee.'

Martinelli said nothing. He simply stared at Walter.

'I am merely verifying statements from other witnesses. It is simply a formality.' Walter took out his notebook and pencil to reinforce the point.

Martinelli's face softened into a broad smile. *'Si.'*

He took the notebook and pencil from Walter, wrote something and handed them back.

He had written *G. Martinelli, Mauretania, 1921.*

The edginess apparent between Paul and Barbara in their conversation with Walter persisted into the evening. There was dancing after dinner in the dining saloon and Paul joined the Livingstone Cordells at their table. He took the seat across the table from Barbara. He could have moved closer to her when Livy took Marjorie on the floor for a tango, but he did not. He could have talked to Barbara, but he gave his attention to the dancing. Barbara began to wonder why he had joined them at all. When the tango ended and Marjorie came back, she said, 'Aren't you young people dancing at all this evening? You shouldn't let the older generation show you up.'

Barbara said, 'Paul had a very exhausting game of deck tennis today, Mother.'

Paul ignored the taunt. He said to Marjorie, 'When you and Livy go on the floor it makes the rest of us look so wooden.'

'Flatterer,' said Marjorie with a ripple of pleasure that set her sequins shimmering. 'In that case, Livy and I will sit the next one out and give you two a chance to cut a rug.'

It was a waltz. They circled the floor solemnly to *I'm Forever Blowing Bubbles*. Paul was an adequate dancer, usually able to distract his partner from any imperfections in the movement with amusing conversation. This evening he was unwilling or unable to amuse Barbara. Towards the end of it, she said, 'I'm sorry.'

'Why?'

'Because my mother inflicted this on you.'

'She didn't. I asked you myself, didn't I?'

She nodded. A touch on the drums heralded the end of the dance.

'You make a beautiful couple,' said Marjorie when they got back to the table.

They sat out the next two dances and then had an old-fashioned St Bernard waltz too intricate for any dialogue to take place. When it was over, Paul said, 'I think I'll get an early night. I'm not much company for you.'

Barbara said, 'It's not easy with my parents at the table.'

'I'm not getting at them. They're nice people.'

'We could go for a walk on the deck.'

'It's too cold. The wind is getting up.'

'Too bad,' said Barbara. 'I wouldn't want you to catch a chill on my account.' Immediately she had spoken the words, she wished she had not. They were not meant to carry the rebuke that they did. They expressed her genuine frustration at the awkwardness that had crept between them. She said, 'I'm, sorry. Please don't go to bed.'

'Paul's eyes registered bewilderment. He said quietly, 'Barbara, let's draw a line under today, huh? Maybe we can both be in a better frame of mind tomorrow. Goodnight.'

She went back to the table alone. She excused Paul's absence to her parents by saying he had not been feeling well. Her mother gave her a sharp look and said young men were more vulnerable than many women realised. Livy went to get them drinks and came back with the information that Paul was in the smoking room bar. 'I guess he needs a couple of whiskys to make his head better,' he told Barbara. 'Come on, you haven't danced with me yet.'

She was thankful for Livy's thoughtfulness. He quite often took the edge off Marjorie's remarks and now he was helping her to get over the feeling that Paul had abandoned her. He said, 'Don't worry about him. He cares about you. I've watched him. He's got a lot to learn about the ladies, but he's trying. Give him time.'

Barbara kissed Livy lightly on the cheek and said, 'You're very sweet to me.'

She decided to watch a couple more dances and then go to bed. Livy took Marjorie on the floor for a foxtrot. Barbara watched them, wondering whether Marjorie really appreciated his worth.

'All alone, then?' said a voice behind her.

She looked over her shoulder and saw Jack Gordon leaning towards her. His blond hair and white shirtfront caught the light that was over the dance floor.

'Not entirely,' said Barbara. 'My parents are dancing.'

'And why not you? Would you give me the pleasure?'

At any time previously she would have politely declined, but now she did not hesitate. She got up and took Jack's arm and stepped on to the floor. She felt the confidence of his dancing at once. He guided her without strain and with a sense of rhythm that she knew enhanced her own movement.

'I didn't know you liked dancing,' she told him.

He smiled. 'I'd be a fool not to like it when it gives me the chance to put my arm around such a beautiful girl.'

She rated this as one of the fastest remarks that she had heard from a man, and warning signals buzzed in her head, but she was still glad he had said it. She said, 'I haven't seen you on the floor before.'

'I haven't seen you alone before.'

She tried to steer him onto a less personal course. At the rate he was going it was certain to end in embarrassment. 'I believe bad weather is forecast for tomorrow.'

'I don't particularly care about tomorrow.'

'You would if you were as nervous as I am about the prospect.'

'Don't give in to it, Barbara. I know a very good remedy for seasickness.'

'Yes, Mother has some tablets in her room.'

'I don't mean tablets. This is much more pleasant to take. A glass of brandy every two hours. Would you like one now to lay the foundation?'

She practically gasped at the speed of his technique. 'We're in the middle of a dance.'

'We can wait to the end.'

'It's most generous of you to offer me a drink, but I'd rather not.'

'Why?'

'There's someone outside I would rather not be seen by. I don't know exactly where he is, but I heard he was drinking.'

'Someone I know?'

'I'd rather not say.'

'I'll collect the brandy and bring it in here.'

'I was sitting with my parents.'

'Couldn't you go to another table?'

His persistence was beginning to trouble her. What had started as a timely boost to her confidence was rapidly losing its charm. 'Jack, I don't want the brandy, thank you. Can't we just enjoy this dance?'

'Forget the brandy, then. Enjoy the dance. We'll slip out when it's over and find somewhere quieter.'

'No. I want to stay here.'

'What are you afraid of? I won't hurt you.'

The music stopped. Barbara said, 'Goodnight,' and turned

smartly aside to meet Livy and her mother as they left the floor.

'Who was that?' asked Marjorie. 'He looks like a charmer.'

'Just help me to get away from him,' murmured Barbara. But Jack was already on his way out.

After the last waltz the three of them returned to their state-rooms on D deck. Barbara's was three doors farther along the corridor than her parents'. She kissed them goodnight and moved on. She took her key from her bag and turned it in the lock. As she opened the door she was conscious of somebody standing behind her. He was so close that she could feel his breath on the back of her neck. She had a thought that it might be Paul, wanting to apologise for their friction earlier. She turned.

Jack stood a foot from her. He said in a low voice, 'You forced me. It needn't have been like this.'

She drew her breath to scream as he moved towards her.

8

'Card-sharpers?' said Captain Rostron.

'That is one theory I am working on,' said Walter guardedly.

They were in the captain's stateroom. His personal steward had brought them a decanter of scotch and a soda siphon and two crystal glasses. Walter was smoking a cigar.

'I won't say you're wrong, Inspector,' said the captain, 'but we keep a pretty close eye on that sort of thing. I don't mind admitting it was getting out of hand before the war, but we've tightened up a lot – I'm speaking of the Cunard fleet now – and I'm glad to say that there isn't much of it going on now. Of course, you can't stop people from playing cards, so it's still difficult to detect, but that's what the master-at-arms and his staff are paid to do. Mr Saxon may not be a Sherlock Holmes when it comes to murder, but he knows his card-sharpers, I assure you.'

'I don't doubt it,' said Walter.

'My chief purser has a very good memory for faces. He always tips me off when professional gamblers come aboard. They're quite well known, most of them. They spend their lives crossing the ocean – like me.'

'So you think it is unlikely that Mr Gordon and Miss Masters were involved in card-sharping?'

'I won't say it's impossible. I'm as sure as I can be that they haven't gambled on the *Mauretania* before, but there are dozens of other ships making the Atlantic crossing, as you know. I can ask Mr Saxon to make a few inquiries if you wish.'

'Not at this stage, thank you,' said Walter. 'I would prefer to work alone.'

'The best card-sharpers rarely appear in the smoke-room,' said the captain. 'The games are played behind locked doors in the staterooms. The "pigeons", as they call their victims, are allowed to win vast amounts of money. It is all recovered, of course, and much more, in one last game that is usually played after we dock, on the boat train, or in some New York hotel. We may have suspicions, but by then it's out of our control. These parasites are very artful, Inspector.'

Walter gave a nod and blew a perfect smoke ring. Captain Rostron wondered whether the Inspector was holding something back. He was certainly not saying much.

'If they *were* card-sharpers,' the captain ventured, 'why should one of them be murdered?'

'Walter drew on the cigar, exhaled, and said with great significance, 'Exactly.'

'I suppose it's possible that one of their former victims may have recognized them and decided to take revenge,' the captain went on, 'but murder is an extreme form of revenge.'

'Extreme,' agreed Walter.

'A man would have to be very desperate to resort to that, or very callous.'

'Either,' said Walter.

'Yes,' said the captain.

'Indeed,' said Walter.

There was silence between them. It was a long time since Captain Rostron had come across anyone so unforthcoming as Inspector Dew. It was beginning to antagonise him. The man clearly had a lot more going on in his head than he was prepared to discuss. The only way to prise it out was by direct questions.

'Well, Inspector, have you decided why Miss Masters was murdered?'

'No.'

'Do you have any suspects yet?'

'Suspects?' repeated Walter. He reached for his glass and took a sip of whisky. 'No.'

'I see. The case is proving difficult?'

Walter considered the question. 'No.'

'I asked to see you in the hope that you would have some ideas about the murder, but all we seem to have discussed is whether the victim may have been a card-sharper. Let's suppose for the sake of argument that she was. Where will you go from here?'

'To bed,' said Walter. 'To sleep on it.'

The captain sighed heavily.

Walter cleared his throat. 'I was about to observe . . .'

'Yes?'

'That this is a very good whisky, captain.'

'Oh. I'm glad you like it. I hope you enjoy your sleep. Make the most of it. There are squalls ahead.'

189

That night Alma slept badly. She dreamed that she was being pursued by Walter. He was wearing his long overcoat and bowler hat. He was no longer Walter Baranov. He had become Inspector Dew, and she was Ethel Le Neve. He was hunting her through every section of the ship, around the decks, through companionways, into the second class and the third and the galleys and the holds and the bilges. Each time she found a place to hide, he came towards it and she fled in terror. Everyone was hostile, pointing at her, telling Walter which way she had gone. At last he trapped her in a passageway deep in the part of the ship where no passengers ventured. As he came towards her his eyes were gleaming like a madman's and his hands were spread like talons. She reached out to protect herself and her hand came into contact with a doorknob. She turned it and a door opened and she threw herself inside and slammed it shut. She was in a brick-lined cavernous place filled with motionless figures. It was the Chamber of Horrors. Suddenly one of the figures moved, a woman in a long black cloak. Her face was pallid and there were strips of seaweed in her hair. It was Lydia. She took Alma's arm and guided her across the stone-paved floor past the effigies of infamous killers, Burke and Hare, William Palmer, Dr Pritchard and Neill Cream. There was one figure standing alone. A plaque in front of it said *H. H. Crippen*. Alma looked at the face and screamed. It was Johnny Finch. They had executed Johnny, sweet-natured, innocent Johnny.

The master-at-arms, Mr Saxon, led Walter down another iron stairway and along a passage lit with bare electric light bulbs. Their shoe-leather clattered on the grating with a sound that offended the ear after the carpeted corridors upstairs. Yet Mr Saxon walked with a spring and a swagger suggestive of a millionaire on his way through the most exclusive section of the first class. This morning Mr Saxon felt like a millionaire. He had arrested the strangler.

'I decided not to disturb your sleep,' he told Walter with his words resounding from the sheet-metal on either side. 'There was no need for it, no need at all. You've had an exhausting time, Inspector, taxing your brain and drawing on all your experience at the Yard to dissect the motives of this crime. You deserved your rest. Why trouble you when we had the fellow safely in the cells for the night? I informed the captain, naturally. I think he was rather pleased that his own men cracked the case after all. Anyway, he agreed with me that we would tell you in the morning.'

Walter said nothing. He had already listened to Barbara's account of the incident last night. There was no doubt that the girl believed she had met the strangler. Jack Gordon had certainly forced his way into her stateroom. She was fortunate that her scream had been heard by another passenger sufficiently responsible to telephone Mr Saxon's office. And it was not in dispute that when Saxon and his assistant forced the stateroom door, Barbara was being held from behind by Gordon, who had one hand on her neck and the other over her mouth. Walter had inspected the bruising on her neck.

There was a man on duty outside the cell. Saxon instructed him to unlock the door and close it behind them. 'You and I are capable of protecting ourselves from a strangler of helpless women,' he remarked to Walter. 'They're craven cowards, men who do this sort of thing.'

Jack Gordon was still in his evening shirt and trousers. His bow tie and shoes had been removed. When he got up from the bare mattress on which they found him slumped, he had to support his trousers with his hand. His eyes were red-rimmed and his usually sleek hair drooped over his forehead.

Mr Saxon said, 'You've met Chief Inspector Dew.'

Gordon gave a nod.

Walter said, 'Sit down, please,' in the voice he used in the dental surgery. Mr Saxon placed a wooden chair in the centre of the floor for his prisoner, and retired behind it. Walter perched himself on the edge of a table.

He said to Gordon, 'I have just been talking to Miss Barbara Barlinski. I have seen the marks on her neck.'

'Marks?' repeated Jack abstractedly.

'The marks inflicted by your hand.'

Jack shook his head. 'Was I holding her that tightly?'

From behind him, Mr Saxon said, 'Don't put on that innocent voice, Gordon. I caught you in the act of strangling her.'

He twisted round abruptly and said, 'That's a lie! I was trying to stop her from screaming.'

'From breathing,' said Saxon.

'No!'

'Inspector Dew has seen the strangulation marks.'

'This is mad. I didn't strangle her.'

'You strangled the other one,' said Saxon.

'You don't know what you're talking about.'

Walter asked, 'Mr Gordon, are we to understand that you deny strangling Miss Masters?'

'I haven't strangled anyone, for God's sake.'

Mr Saxon stepped forward and said confidentially in Jack's right ear, 'We have two women, one dead, with the mark of the strangler's hands on her neck, the other fortunately, very fortunately, alive, with the mark of your hands on hers.'

'Will you listen to me? They're not the same.'

'What are you talking about?'

'The marks!' shouted Jack in desperation. 'The marks are not the same.'

'There was a pause. Mr Saxon straightened up. He smiled. He said in a voice so small that it was almost a whisper, 'How do you know?' He began to laugh. He said more loudly, 'How do you know, Gordon, how do you know, how do you know?' He was shaking with laughter and the elation of his triumph.

Jack Gordon's head sank on his chest. He covered his eyes.

'You know because you saw the marks you made,' said Mr Saxon, almost singing it. 'You saw the body.'

'Yes,' said Jack without looking up. He started to sob.

'They're all like this,' Mr Saxon commented to Walter. 'Full of self-pity when you catch them out. They don't show any pity for their victims.' He had broken out in a sweat, he was so excited. He took out a handkerchief and wiped his forehead and the ends of his ginger moustache. 'We'd better take a statement now he's admitted it.'

'Well, you won't need me, then,' said Walter. 'You've got a man outside. I can find my own way back, thank you.'

Jack Gordon suddenly looked up and said, 'I'm not the murderer. For the love of God, listen to me. I didn't strangle Katherine. She was my wife.'

Walter glanced towards Mr Saxon, who had retired to a position behind his prisoner. Disbelief was written on Mr Saxon's face. He shook his head. He winked. He tapped his forehead with his forefinger. He said, 'All right, Inspector, if you would rather leave this to me . . .'

Jack got to his feet and grasped Walter's arm. 'No, please stay and listen. You're the only chance I have.' But as he was speaking he was grabbed from behind by the master-at-arms and thrust back into the chair.

'Something you should learn,' Mr Saxon breathed in Jack's ear as he continued to force his head back with his forearm. 'Never lay a hand on a police officer. It leads to ugly scenes.'

Walter turned towards the door and said, 'Will your assistant open it if I knock?'

'I'll call him,' said Mr Saxon. He released Jack and moved towards Walter's side.

Jack blurted out, 'Inspector Dew, do you think a man would murder his own wife and throw her in the sea?'

Walter's shoulders stiffened. He put out his hand to restrain Mr Saxon from calling his assistant. He turned and said, 'It does sound very unlikely. Very well, I'd better hear what you have to say,' He went back to the table and leaned on it, facing Jack.

Mr Saxon gave vent to his exasperation with a huge sigh.

'I'm a boatman,' said Jack in a more controlled voice. 'I make my living on the ocean, playing cards. If you don't believe me, fetch the deck that is in the top drawer of the dressing table in my stateroom and let me show you how I handle them. Kate was my wife and my working partner.'

'He's lying,' said Mr Saxon. 'He's lying to save his life.'

'She had the mark of a ring on her finger,' said Walter. 'The doctor believed she may have been married.'

'Yes, she always left it behind,' said Jack. 'I can tell you where it is in our flat in Park Terrace. We passed ourselves off as strangers on the ships. People won't take on established pairs. There are too many stories of card-sharping.'

'You can't tell me about card-sharping,' said Mr Saxon petulantly. 'I know them all, and you're not one of them.'

Jack was more in possession of himself. He said in a calm voice, 'You know the unsuccessful ones.' He addressed himself to Walter again. 'Our mark was a young American, Paul Westerfield. His father is a millionaire several times over, and the boy isn't short of dollars. I used a girl to lift his wallet –'

'Poppy?' said Walter.

Jack's eyes widened. 'That's right.'

'How did you know that?' asked Mr Saxon.

'Go on,' Walter told Jack.

'I took the credit for finding it, and young Westerfield was suitably grateful. He bought me a drink, and while we were together, Kate approached us. She used the blind that she was from the concert committee. It was easy fixing up a game of whist. The boy enlisted his girlfriend Barbara as his partner, and we were away. Kate and I went into our routine. We won a few and lost a few more and got a little shirty with each other to soften up the opposition, and I went off to bed. Kate was supposed to suggest a game of bridge the next night.'

'And another game the next night,' put in Mr Saxon. 'And the night after. I know the way you devils work. Let them think they're winning a fortune and then slaughter them at the end with one game of black dog.'

Jack said in an aside to Walter, 'He seems to believe me now. Anyway, it's academic what would have happened after that evening, because someone murdered my wife. Inspector, I told you yesterday that I want you to find her killer. I came to you without being asked, didn't I? I gave you all the relevant information I could.'

'You didn't tell me she was your wife,' said Walter. 'Surely that was relevant?'

'Why, for heaven's sake? No-one knew it. Whoever killed her didn't kill her because she was married to me.'

'How can you be sure of that?' asked Mr Saxon. 'You must have swindled hundreds of gullible people in your time. It only wants one of them to be on this ship and have spotted you and your wife.'

'Do you think I haven't been through your passenger list to see who was aboard? I'm a professional. The pigeons I play cards with are hand-picked. I make a study of them. I don't forget them.'

'This is all very plausible,' said Mr Saxon, 'but tell me this: when was the last time you saw your wife?'

'Saturday evening, when I left the card game. I just told you.'

Mr Saxon gave the smile of a man who has baited a trap and seen his quarry walk into it. 'In that case, would you explain to the Inspector how it was that you saw the marks on her neck?'

Jack looked up at Walter. 'I think he knows.'

Walter's face betrayed nothing. He said, 'I think you ought to tell us.'

Jack gave a shrug. 'If you wish. On Sunday morning I heard about the woman taken from the sea. I didn't connect her with Kate. I had no reason to think anything had happened to Kate. It was only as the day went on, and I didn't see her about the ship and she didn't appear at meals, that I began to be alarmed. I went to her stateroom and got no reply. I couldn't take the risk of making my concern too public, because she may have been all right and it would have ruined our set-up. I decided the only thing to do was find a way of seeing the dead woman for myself.'

'A likely tale!' said Mr Saxon.

'It may be true,' said Walter. He asked Jack, 'How did you arrange it?'

'I went to the ship's hospital and saw the boy at the desk. He was very busy taking the names of idiots who had injured their hands trying to open portholes. I told him I was sent to collect the key to the mortuary room because I might be able to identify the body. He handed it over without a second look at me. I went below with the key.' Jack stopped and bowed his head. 'I never want to go through an experience like that again. The look of her – dreadful. I thought my legs wouldn't hold me up. I staggered out and up all those stairs to my room and just lay on my bed shaking with rage and distress.'

'And the key?' asked Walter.

'I must have left it in the lock.'

Walter looked at the master-at-arms and nodded. 'The doctor confirms it.'

Mr Saxon was still not satisfied. 'All this talk of distress would impress me more if I hadn't found you in the act of assaulting an innocent girl. Does a man whose wife has been killed behave like that? The distress didn't last very long, did it?'

Jack sprang from the chair with his fist raised, but Mr Saxon was too fast. He caught Jack by the wrist and swung him hard against the cell wall. He hit it obliquely, or his skull would have cracked. His shoulder took the force of the impact and he crashed to the floor with his trousers round his knees. Mr Saxon moved in to take a swing with his boot, but Walter put his hand on his chest and pushed him away.

'That's enough!'

'You saw him,' Mr Saxon rasped. 'He went for me.'

'Help him up,' said Walter with unusual authority.

Mr Saxon put his hands under Jack's armpits and bundled him into the chair with the warning, 'You'd better stick to whist in future.'

Jack used his left hand to drag his trousers over his knees into some semblance of dignity. His evening shirt was torn at the shoulder and the graze caused by his collision with the wall was oozing blood. He flexed his right hand to see if it still had mobility.

'I think you'd better get him a drink,' Walter suggested to Mr Saxon.

The master-at-arms went to the cell-door and shouted an order to his assistant.

Walter called out, 'If it's tea, I'll have one, too.' He turned back to Jack. 'Do you want to tell us about the girl?'

'I was coming to it. Inspector, I was deeply in love with my wife, and I won't have anyone disparage our feelings for each other.' He glared at Mr Saxon. 'Kate was a far better wife than I deserved. I didn't always treat her as well as I should have done, and I flirted a little with younger women who were not in her class. It makes me ashamed to think about it. When I knew for certain that she was dead, I just erupted with anger against the bastard who had done this thing. I don't know if it was revenge I wanted. I think it was the feeling that I owed it to Kate's memory to confront her killer. Yes, I know that isn't my job, it's yours, but this was personal. Can you imagine how you would feel if it was *your* wife who was murdered?'

Walter treated the question as rhetorical. He said, 'You were going to tell us why you attacked the girl.'

'Yes. When I left the smoking room on the night that Kate was murdered, Westerfield was just going off to buy a round of drinks. That would have left Kate alone at the table with Barbara. Did this occur to you, Inspector? What did those two women say to each other? Was there anything that Kate told Barbara that would help us to identify her killer?'

'Us?' said Walter.

'He wants you to believe he was helping us all the time,' said Mr Saxon sarcastically.

'Would you see whether the tea is ready?' said Walter as if he were addressing his nurse-receptionist.

'It seemed to me that your inquiry was getting bogged down,' Jack continued. 'I decided to ask some questions myself. I wanted to see what Barbara could tell me, so last night I picked my opportunity to ask her for a dance. She seemed pleased to be asked. Naturally I couldn't question her straight away.'

'Her account of it is that you tried to force your attentions on her.'

Jack shook his head. 'It was only flirting.'

'See?' said Mr Saxon. 'He admits it.'

'I had one dance with the girl,' said Jack. 'She was with her parents. I couldn't keep coming back for more. I needed to get her outside where I could put some serious questions to her. All right, I misjudged the situation. I thought she would respond to some gentle flattery – most girls do, in my experience. But Barbara wasn't impressed. She turned her back on me when the dance ended. I should have left it at that, but I was becoming desperate to find out whether she could tell me anything. When the evening came to an end, I followed her to her stateroom. I stopped her by the door and tried to explain why I was there, but she panicked. She started to scream. It frightened me. I pushed her into the room and slammed the door behind me. I suppose she thought I was going to attack her. I just wanted to calm her down so that I could talk to her. I put my hand over her mouth to stop the screaming, but that only frightened her more. I was still struggling with her when *he* burst in.' Jack indicated Mr Saxon, now standing just inside the cell door, teatray in hand.

Walter collected the two steaming mugs of tea and handed one to Jack. 'You can't really blame Mr Saxon for locking you up. You behaved very rashly.'

'You do believe me, Inspector?'

'I suppose I do. It seems consistent with what other people have told me.'

'Will you release me, then?'

'I think it would be prudent if I spoke to the captain and some of the people involved, don't you? It might be a shock if they saw you at liberty.'

'How is Barbara – did I really hurt her?'

'She is bearing up well.'

'I'd like to apologise to her.'

'Let's not rush things, Mr Gordon.'

'Will you speak to her yourself?'

'I think I had better.'

'Will you ask her what Kate said to her after the game of whist?'

'She has told me already.'

'She has? Is it significant?'

'Who knows?' said Walter cryptically.

'She didn't mention any man by name – anyone she had noticed on the ship?'

'Only you.'

Jack sighed. 'I suppose it was too much to hope that she would have named her killer. So all this happened for nothing.'

'You might take that point of view,' said Walter. 'Personally, I don't. It's done a lot for the morale of the passengers and crew to hear that we have a man in the cells. There's quite a carnival air on deck this morning. Everyone is much more friendly than before.'

'But I'm not the strangler!'

'It seems a pity to disappoint them. Would you like a second cup of tea?'

'I want to get out of here.'

'I can understand that,' said Walter with obvious sincerity.

'I've told you what happened. Don't you believe me?'

'Try to keep calm, Mr Gordon. You must understand that I have to consider what to do. I have a responsibility for the safety of over two thousand people. We can make things more comfortable for you, I am sure. Did they give you any breakfast?'

'I demand to see the captain.'

'You're in no position to make demands. The captain has other things on his mind now. There are warnings of squalls ahead. I'll tell you what I'll do. I'll have to verify your statement. It will take an hour or two, I'm certain. In the meantime I'd like the key of your stateroom.'

'I've got that,' said Mr Saxon.

'What do you want it for?' asked Jack. 'To see if the playing cards are in there as I told you?'

'No. To send you down a change of clothes. Those look dreadfully out of place.'

11

Marjorie had insisted that Barbara spent the morning resting in her stateroom. As it was grey outside and the wind was markedly cooler, she was not deprived too much. Moreover she was gratified by a personal visit from Captain Rostron, who expressed his deep concern about the frightening experience she had undergone. There were visits, too, from the ship's doctor and Inspector Dew. She was promised that the bruising on her neck would be gone before they reached New York. The Inspector talked about the weather.

The visitor who pleased her most arrived towards noon. He was carrying an enormous box of candies. It was Paul. Her mother showed him in, and stayed, out of decorum.

Paul was desperately worried over Barbara. It showed in the tiny creases round his eyes and the husky quality of his voice. 'I can't begin to say how wretched I feel about what happened,' he told her. 'If I hadn't been so stupid as to leave the dance early, he would never have approached you.'

'You weren't to know what he was planning.'

'I was totally taken up with my own foolheaded mood, Barbara. I won't forgive myself for that. Thank God your screams were heard. Are you really unhurt apart from the bruising?'

'Yes. It wasn't much.'

'It must have been terrifying for you. Appalling. Who would have thought that Jack Gordon would turn out to be the strangler? I took him for a typical English gentleman. It's incredible after he behaved so well over my billfold. It beats me, Barbara, it really does.'

'It was difficult for me to understand.'

'Yes, what made him choose you as his victim?'

Marjorie could not contain herself at this. She said acidly, 'For heaven's sake, how would Barbara know the answer to that?'

Paul blushed deeply. 'What I meant to say is that I can think of no possible reason why he should want to attack Barbara.'

'You can't?' said Marjorie. 'Don't you have a pair of eyes in your head?'

Now it was Barbara's turn to blush. She said, 'Mother, will you stop saying things that embarrass me? Paul has come here with the very sweetest motives and brought me these beautiful candies, and you have to spoil it by yapping at him.'

It was a significant moment in Marjorie's relationship with her daughter. For the first time, she admitted that she was at fault. 'I'm sorry – I spoke out of turn. I guess I'm a little over-wrought about what happened last night.'

'I guess we all are,' said Paul. 'Barbara, with all this happening I'm sure you won't have been thinking about tonight. It's a fancy dress ball. If you feel well enough to come, nothing would make me happier than to escort you.'

'You're quite right,' said Barbara. 'It went out of my mind. Yes, it'll do me good to think about something else. I'd love to be your partner.'

12

When Walter left the cells he was confident of finding his way up to the passenger accommodation. He was sure that he remembered the route through the lower decks that Mr Saxon had used to bring him down. It was a mystery to him exactly where he went wrong, but in a matter of a few minutes he admitted to himself that he was lost. He could not even tell fore from aft. Where he expected to find companionways there were bulkheads. Worse, this section of the ship was apparently uninhabited.

He tried a door, hoping to find stairs to the deck above. There was a spiral staircase, but it led down to what was evidently one of the main holds. It was as big as a warehouse and stacked high with boxes and crates containing stores of food. He moved through that into a second hold. It smelt so strongly of oil that he supposed he must have reached the engine-room until he saw a line of motor-cars ranged before him, roped to the deck and secured with wooden blocks under the wheels. One was a brand new Lanchester saloon. Walter liked cars. He had always wanted to own a Lanchester. He tried the driver's door and found it open. He got inside and put his hands on the steering wheel. With the steady drone of the *Mauretania*'s turbines somewhere below him, it was easy to imagine that the car was in motion, zooming through country lanes. He sounded the horn. It was a beautiful vehicle, inside and out.

Someone jerked open the door and shouted as if Walter were deaf, 'What the hell do you think you're doing?'

Walter took stock. The man was dressed in an overall. It was a very large overall, open at the chest because he was so broad that there was no possibility of the buttons meeting the holes intended for them. The gap was filled by a crop of black hair extending upwards in amazing exuberance to the top of his head, with only a nose and a pair of fierce brown eyes to indicate that this was an example of *homo sapiens*.

Walter said, 'Ah, you heard me signalling, then. Very good.'

The man in the overall said, 'Get out of that car.'

Walter obeyed. He was six foot tall himself, but he only came up to the shoulder of the overalls. He said, 'Chief Inspector Dew, late Scotland Yard.' When this seemed to make no impression he added, 'Investigations. Captain's orders. Do you happen to know who owns this vehicle?'

The man shook his head.

'It ought to be locked,' said Walter. 'It really ought to be locked.' He walked round to the back of the Lanchester and tried the handle of the luggage compartment. It opened. 'I don't like to see valuable property improperly secured.' He slammed the lid down. 'I'll have to report this. Which is the quickest way up to the bridge from here?'

The man pointed to a door and Walter nodded and went through it without another word being passed between them.

13

By noon, when the ship's whistle sent vibrations through the upper decks, there was standing room only in the smoking room, and not much of that. The announcement of the number of miles covered in the previous twenty-four hours aroused extraordinary excitement each day, not from pride in the *Mauretania*'s performance so much as interest in the outcome of the auction pool. The passengers' anticipation had been fuelled after dinner the previous evening when the auction of the twenty numbers had raised thousands of dollars, spurred on by a personable chairman and attentive smoking room stewards, who took ten per cent of the winnings.

Johnny Finch was in possession of a number, a fancied number from the centre of the range, 540 miles. He had paid almost as many dollars for it in the auction. 'I splash out once a crossing,' he confided to Alma, who had come out of curiosity to hear the announcement. 'Never won yet, but never had the nerve before now to pay a top price for a really good number. My right ear-lobe has been itching like the devil, and that's a very reliable omen.'

Alma glanced at his ear. It certainly looked more pink than the other one. 'Perhaps it has something to do with your morning walk round the promenade deck,' she suggested. 'That ear is more exposed to the sea-wind. Why don't you try going clockwise for a change?'

Johnny laughed. 'Because then I wouldn't have a lucky ear. Lydia, my dear, I never met anyone so solemn as you, and it's such enormous fun. Win or lose, I'm going to crack a bottle of fizz with you tonight and see if I can't make you laugh.'

'I'm not much of a drinker,' said Alma doubtfully.

'It shouldn't take much then,' said Johnny, with a wink, followed by a deft change of subject: 'I hear that the strangler's still at large.'

'I thought they caught someone attacking an American girl last night.'

'They did, but it was all a mistake. Inspector Dew spent the morning questioning the chap and now he's released him. It wasn't the strangler after all. I hope Dew knows what he's doing.'

'So do I.' Alma spoke from the heart, though without much

confidence. She had the petrifying suspicion that Walter had set a killer loose out of some peculiar sense of fair play. What would he do if *she* were attacked tonight?

The chairman of the auction pool was beating the mahogany table with his gavel. Something close to silence descended on the smoking room. Fingers were crossed and private prayers sent up. Syndicates clustered in whispering groups, making final checks of the numbers they held. Individual possessors of numbers, like Johnny, knew theirs by heart.

'My lords, ladies and gentlemen, the officer of the watch has just sent down from the bridge this note of the number of sea miles the *Mauretania* has travelled since mid-day yesterday. I understand that there is a certain amount of interest in the information.'

'Get on with it!' came a shout from the back.

'Five hundred and fifty!' shouted someone else, and there was pandemonium as numbers were suggested from all over the room.

The chairman knocked on the table for order. He took another look at the sheet of paper in his hand. 'The winning number is five hundred and forty –'

'By God – it's mine!' said Johnny in a gasp.

'– six,' said the chairman. 'Five hundred and forty-six.'

'Oh, no!' cried Alma in disappointment. 'Johnny, I'm sorry!' She put both her hands round one of his and squeezed it.

'Ah, well,' said Johnny philosophically, 'it seems you were right about those sea breezes on my ear.'

'Not necessarily,' said Alma.

'What do you mean?'

'There's still the prize for the best fancy dress, isn't there?'

14

After lunch the sea was choppy, if not rough. There was a distinct pitch and roll developing in the motion of the ship. Members of the crew were seen stringing lengths of rope across places where rails were not provided. The children's sports on deck were cancelled in favour of some Chaplin two-reelers in the drawing room. The screen proved so unstable that the pictures were projected onto the wall.

The fancy dress ball was not affected, except for the small number of passengers who retired to their rooms regretting ever having looked at food and drink. Coloured lanterns appeared in the dining saloon and their oscillations were agreed to add to the gaiety of the occasion. The chandeliers, by contrast, stayed immobile, their crystal pieces cunningly designed to stay rigid, confuting any movement of the ship.

Livy and Marjorie came as Antony and Cleopatra so that Marjorie could wear sandals and anklets. She had painted her toenails. Livy was wearing a bedspread and tennis shoes. He did not have the figure of an Antony, but he was happy to make any sacrifice for Marjorie. He had his flannels rolled up above the knees, ready to revert to 1921 at the earliest opportunity.

They had not been sitting for long at their table close to the dance floor when they were joined by Paul and Barbara as two Pilgrims. Through his false beard made from frayed rope Paul explained that they were hoping the judges would see the connection between their present voyage and the *Mayflower* crossing.

'They will,' said Livy. 'If it gets any rougher tonight, I'll be leading the prayer meeting.'

Barbara still looked pale from her frightening experience the previous night, and she made a convincing Pilgrim in a long brown skirt, white apron and high-buttoned jacket with a white collar and a plain scarf covering her bobbed hair.

'You feeling any better, honey?' Marjorie asked her.

'I'm fine now, Mother.'

'Inspector Dew has been talking to Barbara,' Paul added. 'It seems like it was all a misunderstanding. Jack Gordon didn't want to hurt her.'

'I heard,' said Marjorie, unconvinced.

'He only wanted to talk to me,' said Barbara.

'Do you really believe that?'

'It must be true, Mother. The Inspector has released him.'

'Yes, and it's a scandal. You have the marks on your neck still.'

'Mother, he is not the strangler. He wanted to talk to me about Katherine, the lady who was killed. She was his wife.'

'I know about that. They were card cheats. They were going to take you two for suckers. Have you thought about that? Gordon is a rat, Barbara. He shouldn't be walking free.'

'They didn't actually do anything,' said Paul. 'I guess the Inspector figures it's a waste of time to hold Jack Gordon.'

'You can ask him yourself,' said Livy. 'Looks like he's coming this way.'

Walter was not in fancy dress. He was wearing his usual dark suit and striped necktie. He looked more out of place than the people wearing outlandish fancy dress. He walked with a slight, self-conscious stoop, as if he was aware of it. He may have given a modified bow as he reached the Cordells' table, but it was hard to tell. He asked if he might join them for a few minutes.

Livy answered, 'Sure, Inspector. My wife Marje was just talking about you.'

'Livy!' said Marjorie through her teeth.

'She thought you would win the fancy dress prize,' Livy went on blithely, 'on account of the fact that you probably know more about disguise than anyone on the ship.'

Walter gave a thin smile. 'I see.'

'I thought you might be the Keystone Cop over there, or Mr Sherlock Holmes with the pipe and deerstalker and the blonde on his arm, but I guess that's too obvious.'

'I just looked in to have another word with your step-daughter,' said Walter. 'How are you feeling now, Miss em . . ?'

'Much better, thank you,' said Barbara.

'I neglected to ask you something. When you had finished your coffee with Miss Masters – or Mrs Gordon, as I ought to call her – on Saturday night, did she go directly to bed?'

Paul interrupted. 'How would she know the answer to that?'

'She *said* she was going to bed,' said Barbara.

'You didn't go in that direction with her?'

'No.'

'We went back to the dining saloon for a couple more dances before the band finished,' said Paul. 'Hey! That was a big one!'

As Paul was speaking, the ship gave a strong lurch that sent the wine glasses sliding across the table. Barbara put her arm out and stopped them from falling off.

'Okay,' said Livy, picking up a waterjug. 'There's a way to deal with this.' He poured several small amounts of water onto the tablecloth. Then he positioned the glasses on the damp patches. 'See?'

'Livy has travelled by sea before,' said Marjorie proudly. 'My God, what's that?'

Everyone turned to see what had caught her attention. It was a figure under a white sheet, that had just come down the main staircase.

'If that is meant to be a ghost, I think it's in very bad taste,' Marjorie declared. 'Really! You'd think people would have more respect after what happened on Saturday. It's horrible.'

'I don't think it's meant to be a ghost,' said Barbara. 'If you look closely, it's pointed at the top and it has things projecting from the sides like cardboard boxes.' She laughed. 'Poor man, he's finding it hard to stand up with the ship rocking like this.'

'It's pretty spectacular, whatever it is,' said Paul. 'It must be eight feet tall. Why is the lower section coloured blue, do you think?'

'That's the sea,' said Livy. 'It's meant to be an iceberg.'

'Oh, my God!' said Marjorie in a scandalised voice. 'That's even more offensive. What a thing to do on a night like this! It's given me goose-bumps all over.'

'Mother, it's only someone having fun,' said Barbara.

'Fun! I don't call that fun. How do you think Livy feels, seeing a thing like that. It's no laughing matter to a man who was on the *Titanic*, is it, my darling?'

Livy gave her a puzzled look, and said. 'I was never on the *Titanic*, Marje. It was the *Lusitania*.'

'Same thing,' said Marjorie.

'Not really,' said Livy. 'We were struck by a torpedo, not an iceberg.'

'And the sea was perfectly calm,' added Walter unexpectedly. 'I never saw such a placid sea.'

'You?' said Livy. 'You were on the *Lusitania*?'

'Yes. With my, er . . .' Walter paused as if temporarily distracted. He had gone unexpectedly pale. '. . . my father.'

'Strange,' said Paul. 'I was reading a piece about you last year in the *Saturday Evening Post*. They didn't mention it.'

'It was never made public,' said Walter resourcefully. 'I was using another name at the time.'

Across the room, Alma steered Johnny Finch to an empty table. He moved with difficulty under the sheets and with the boxes tied to his head and torso. 'Is it getting plenty of attention?' he asked her as he lowered himself carefully onto a chair.

'Yes, indeed. Everyone is looking this way. Are you comfortable?'

There was a muffled laugh from under the sheet. 'I could say I have a terrible thirst.'

'But if I get you a drink how can you possibly manage it?'

Another laugh. 'Don't worry, my dear. Johnny Finch isn't as dim as you think. I've got a flask of brandy under here.'

'I hope you can walk straight in the parade. The ship is starting to roll rather badly.'

'I'll be as firm as a rock.'

But by the time the drum-roll sounded for the parade, it looked doubtful whether anyone would be capable of staying upright for long. The ship had settled into a metronomic rise and fall, mercifully slow, but reaching more and more precipitous extremes. There was an unspoken sense of bravado among the revellers as they oohed in chorus when their stomachs told them that their side of the ship had peaked and was about to plunge again. Those with frailer constitutions had gone, leaving empty chairs that slid towards the centre unless they were wedged behind the tables.

Yet the parade mustered and moved off to a rousing regimental march, snaking between the tables so that support was to hand when it was wanted. There must have been nearly a hundred intrepid entrants for the competition, pirates arm in arm with ballerinas, cavaliers with witches, two pantomime horses and an ostrich, everyone laughingly assisting those around them to keep their footing, encouraged by the less bold spirits who provided the audience. There were a few minor slips and some collisions that added to the fun, and somehow the parade survived. Alma in her nurse's costume followed Johnny with her hands against his back, but he was right in his self-confidence. He did not falter once. Farther forward, Marjorie walked with one hand linked to Livy's arm, the other lifting the front of her Egyptian gown to mid-calf level. Paul and Barbara walked behind them holding hands and exchanging squeezes that had nothing to do with the movement of the ship.

Captain Rostron should have judged the fancy dress, but there was no objection when it was announced that he had decided not to leave the bridge. Instead the chief purser stood on the rostrum with the band and studied the variety of cóstumes passing by. Wisely no attempt was made to halt the movement. When the music stopped, the parade dispersed to listen to the results from the tables.

The winner of the ladies' section was one who came as Mlle Lenglen, the tennis champion. It did not seem to matter that she looked totally unlike the unstoppable Suzanne. She carried a racket and wore a similar dress and, as Marjorie pertinently pointed out, she had been seen dancing with Big Bill Tilden every evening and it was in the interests of Cunard to keep on the right side of its more famous passengers.

A Charlie Chaplin costume took the gentlemen's prize, mainly because its wearer had created great amusement by tottering out of line repeatedly with the pitch and roll in a passable imitation of the famous tramp. The prize for the most original fancy dress went to the ostrich.

'Original, my foot!' said Johnny from under his sheet as he started to shed the boxes that had formed the understructure of the iceberg. 'He got it from some theatrical costumiers. There's no connection at all between an ocean voyage and an ostrich. Next time I shall come as a blessed albatross. Ah, well, there's still that bottle of fizz I promised you. You don't mind waiting while I change back to something I can dance in?'

'Of course not, but I doubt if I can drink champagne,' said Alma, glancing towards the table where Walter had been sitting before the parade. She felt sure he must have noticed her in Johnny's company, and she felt uneasy at his possible reaction. It was a dilemma. She hardly dared admit to herself that she felt differently now that Walter was a murderer, that he frightened her, that she only felt safe with Johnny. Being seen with Johnny could only make her situation more dangerous than it was.

She was relieved to see that Walter had left the table.

15

He had borrowed an oilskin and gone out to the boat deck at the request of the master-at-arms. One of the crew had reported seeing Jack Gordon on the starboard side, near number 5 lifeboat. Earlier in the day, when he had been released from detention, Gordon had given an undertaking to remain in his stateroom for the rest of the day. It had been thought that his presence in any of the public areas of the ship might alarm certain passengers. And now the wretched man appeared to have broken his word. They had checked his stateroom and found it empty.

Walter cursed him as he stepped into a driving wind that sprayed his face with what felt like hail, and was actually spindrift whipped off the highest waves. He remembered Mr Saxon's advice to keep hold of the rail. He reached for it and started moving forward, watching the horizon rise to a point somewhere above the monkey island high above the bridge and then plunge out of sight below the prow. With the wind from the north-west, three-quarters of the night sky was clear. Wisps of cloud intermittently blotted out the moon, but Walter soon discerned a figure in an oilskin gripping the rail below one of the boats. Jack Gordon seemed completely absorbed in the breaking crests of the sea.

Walter got so close that he touched Jack's arm before he was noticed. He had to shout above the shrieking squalls.

'You said you would stay below.'

Jack turned his face to look at Walter. He said nothing.

'You gave your word,' shouted Walter.

Jack shrugged. 'What's the fuss? Nobody else is here.'

'You can't do this.'

'Leave me alone. Go back to the dance.'

'You're coming with me – back to your stateroom.'

'No.'

Walter showed that he was unused to dealing with open defiance. He became more conciliatory. 'This is no place to be on a night like this.'

Jack just stared at the sea.

'Why did you come up here?' shouted Walter conversationally.

'I feel safer.'

Walter laughed.

'I mean it. I'd rather be here than shut in my stateroom.'

'Why?'

'Safer to be near a lifeboat.'

'You must have been through storms before, scores of times.'

'Never felt safe,' shouted Jack. 'Leave me alone, for God's sake.'

It was clear that nothing short of physical force would get him below. He was a very frightened man.

Walter was starting to turn away, with one hand still on the rail when he was suddenly thrust back with astonishing force as if someone had kicked him viciously in the chest. He crashed helplessly against Jack's legs, almost upending him as well.

'What was that?' demanded Jack.

Walter just groaned. He seemed stunned.

'Are you all right, Inspector?'

'My shoulder.' Walter's right hand covered his left shoulder. He made no attempt to rise. He said, 'The pain!'

Jack crouched beside him. 'Let me see. You must have dislocated it, falling like that. Let me help you up.' He tried to support Walter, but he was a large man, difficult to move. 'Put your hand over my shoulder.'

Walter lifted his hand feebly. Jack succeeded in getting him into a sitting position.

'Whatever happened?'

Walter groaned again. 'I think I'm going to pass out.'

'Is this some kind of trick?'

It was not. Walter's body went limp in Jack's arms. 'Damn you!' said Jack.

He got up to go for help. At the door to the stairway leading to the embarkation hall and the purser's office was a ship's light. As he put out his hand to open the door he saw that his fingers were stained with blood.

16

When Alma opened her eyes there was sunlight on the ceiling. It was streaming through the porthole with piercing intensity. Her head ached. She turned to face the wall and saw the empty champagne bottle and the two glasses on the bedside cupboard. She closed her eyes again, pressing them hard as if to squeeze out the image. She turned over and buried her face in the pillow. But she knew that when she opened her eyes again the bottle and the glasses would still be there. Scattered across the floor would be the stark reminders of the hour after midnight, the remnants of fancy dress – velvet cloak, white head-dress made from a teatowel, white blouse with a paper red cross pinned on the front, grey skirt, black lisle stockings and lace-up shoes. She could not escape the evidence that she had done the thing that even the most passionate and romantic heroines forswore until it was sanctified and licensed. She had admitted one of the opposite sex to her room and to her bed. She had broken faith with Ethel M. Dell. And God. And Walter.

Walter. What she had done was unforgivable. She had promised herself to him and given herself to Johnny.

Worse, she knew now that she loved Johnny, that what she had felt for Walter had amounted only to – what was the word used so often and so tellingly in *The Way of an Eagle*? – infatuation. Whatever had been in her heart for Walter had gone for ever, supplanted by her overwhelming love for Johnny, that gentle, irresistible man who had taken her in his arms and told her she was the loveliest creature on God's earth. Walter had never spoken words like that. He had never whispered to her that she inflamed him with her eyes and that her skin was smoother and more white than purest porcelain.

The act of love had not been the ordeal she had imagined and expected. The initial moments of discomfort had been more than compensated by sensations that had surprised and gratified her. She had said nothing to Johnny about her inexperience, yet he had understood and been pleased and helped her tenderly over the threshold of pain into sheer joy.

But she felt an obligation to Walter that was inescapable. He had listened to her, plotted with her and been persuaded by her. Because of her he had put himself in jeopardy. He had murdered Lydia. He would not have done it without Alma's prompting.

Except for her, he would still be in England and Lydia would be alive and sailing to America. Her loyalty had to be with Walter, even if her love was with Johnny. She was weeping into the pillow.

There was a knock on the door. The steward! He had brought the morning tea.

'Wait a moment, please.' She sprang out of bed and put the bottle and the glasses in the wardrobe and scooped up the clothes and flung them in as well. She snatched out one of Lydia's negligees and wrapped it round her shoulders, slammed the wardrobe shut and got back into bed. 'You may come in now.'

'Lovely morning, madam. Is it your birthday?' He was a very young steward, certainly not twenty, perfectly efficient and friendly without too much familiarity as a rule.

'No, it isn't. Why do you ask?'

'Card for you, ma'am.' He placed the tray on the bedside cupboard where the champagne bottle had been. A square envelope that obviously contained a greetings card was propped against the milkjug. 'Did you sleep through it, then?'

'I beg your pardon,' said Alma.

'The storm, ma'am. Some passengers didn't get to sleep at all. There won't be many for breakfast.'

'I suppose not.'

'What I say, madam, is that if it was just the weather that was laying them low we wouldn't have much to worry about.'

'What do you mean, exactly?'

'Another passenger copped it last night. It was that Inspector Dew from Scotland Yard.'

'No! What happened?'

'He was shot, ma'am. He went up on deck and someone took a shot at him.'

'Oh, my God! Is he . . .'

'I couldn't say, ma'am. We was told to keep our mouths shut. Will that be all?'

'Yes.' Alma was shaking. She sank back on the pillow. Walter shot? Dead? It was beyond belief.

She sat in a state of shock for more than a minute. Who would want to kill Walter, and why? She was very afraid. But she would have to get up and find out for certain what had happened.

Without thinking much about it, she reached for the teatray and picked up the envelope and opened it. The card inside had been drawn by hand. It showed two hearts linked by an arrow. She opened it and read the message inside. It comprised two lines of an old song:

Because God made thee mine,
And I am yours.
J

Alma said aloud, 'Oh, Johnny, Johnny, Johnny.'

She did not drink the tea. She did not take her morning bath. She put on her clothes and went straight to Walter's stateroom and knocked on the door.

A nurse, a genuine nurse, opened it and looked disdainfully at Alma. 'Yes?'

'I heard that the Inspector has been shot.'

'That's right.'

'I am a friend, a personal friend. Tell me please, is he badly hurt?'

'It's not for me to say.'

'Please – is he in danger?' As she asked the question, her voice expressed the real concern she felt, but even as she was speaking, some dissident section of her brain anticipated Walter's death and freed her from her obligation to him. She would be free to marry Johnny.

'He is not in danger,' said the nurse.

A voice inside the room, not Walter's, said, 'Who is it, nurse?'

The nurse asked Alma, 'What is your name?'

She hesitated. Without knowing Walter's state of consciousness, she dared not say that she was Lydia. He had probably been given morphia. To be told that Lydia was at his door might shock him into some calamitous response.

'If you won't tell me your name, how can I give him a message?'

'There is no message,' said Alma. She turned and almost ran towards the door at the end of the passageway.

The nurse clicked her tongue, closed the door and rejoined the master-at-arms beside Walter's bed. Mr Saxon was triumphant. From his exuberance it appeared that he was unconcerned at Walter's plight. He was as cock-a-hoop as if he had fired the shot himself. 'Take your time recovering,' he said. 'Your responsibilities are over now, Inspector. It's a glorious day outside, and you're entitled to enjoy it.'

'What do you mean?' asked Walter, ready to take issue.

'Quite simply that there's nothing more for you to do when you've given me your statement. Gordon is under arrest. He hasn't written his confession yet, but he will.'

'Gordon? Jack Gordon?'

Mr Saxon smiled. 'If you hadn't released the blighter in the first place, you wouldn't be nursing a sore shoulder. How does it feel?'

Walter tried lifting his head off the pillow. He winced and fell back.

'Painful, by the look of it,' said Mr Saxon.

'Jack Gordon didn't shoot me,' said Walter.

Mr Saxon turned to the nurse. 'What did the doctor give this man?'

'I had my back to him,' said Walter. 'The bullet hit me in the front.'

'I don't suppose you remember much,' said Mr Saxon. 'It's all a blur.'

'I remember clearly. I turned away from him and I was hit from in front. I fell back against him. I was shot by someone else.'

'I doubt it.'

'What happened after I was hit?'

'Gordon dragged you to the stairs and shouted for help. He's no fool, Inspector.'

'Did you search him? Was he carrying a gun?'

'I expect he dropped it overboard.'

'The man is innocent,' said Walter. With the help of his good arm he propped himself up. 'Where is he now? I want to speak to him.'

'I'm afraid that won't be possible,' said the nurse. 'You're to remain in bed for the rest of the day. You heard the doctor's orders, sir.'

'The doctor told me this is only a flesh wound.'

'He gave you something to suppress the pain. You wouldn't be very steady on your feet.'

'I'll see Gordon here, then.'

'He's under arrest,' repeated Mr Saxon.

'Good,' said Walter. 'You must know where to find him.'

17

Alma spent a long time looking for Johnny. He was not in his deckchair, or taking his usual turn round the promenade deck or his usual double scotch in the smoking room. She found him at last on the fantail, the aftermost stretch of deck on the ship. He was leaning on the rail studying the smooth centre of the wake. He turned and took her hand.

He said, 'New York tomorrow.'

'Don't look so glum,' said Alma. 'You'll make me sad, too.'

'What will you do in America – something in the theatre?'

'No. That's finished. I'm not certain what will happen.'

'There's someone going to meet you I expect,' said Johnny.

'Well, not exactly.'

'But you won't be alone in America?'

'I hope not.'

'There is someone else,' said Johnny, 'isn't there?'

Alma stared at the foam churning from the turbines. 'I think you know the answer to that already. Johnny, when you left me after the fancy dress parade last night, you said you were going to get changed.'

'Why, yes, my dear. That's exactly what I did.'

'You didn't go up on deck?'

Johnny frowned. 'No. Why should I have done? You don't think I had something to do with Inspector Dew getting shot? Why on earth should I?' His eyes widened. 'Good Lord – he's not your friend, is he?'

'Please don't ask me any more,' said Alma. 'I was only thinking of you.'

'That does rather put the damper on my plans. I was leading up to asking you to make a decent man of me, so to speak. I'm not quite so old as I appear.'

Alma felt the blood rising in her cheeks. 'I don't think you're old.'

'It's the sort of life I've led,' said Johnny. 'Never taken care of myself.' He laughed. 'Bit of a nerve, wanting to take care of you. And I know that selling motor cars isn't exactly like the Civil Service or the Stock Exchange, but it is a job with prospects.'

Alma returned a smile. 'Is this a proposal of marriage?'

Johnny kissed her softly on the cheek. 'Lydia, it is.'

At the mention of that name, she closed her eyes. How could

she marry Johnny when he did not even know her proper name?

'What's the matter?' Johnny asked.

'I can't . . .' She felt her mouth go dry. 'I can't give you an answer yet. I want to say yes, but . . . but I must speak to somebody else. Oh, Johnny.' She rested her head against his shoulder. She was starting to cry.

18

Walter was sitting up in bed when Mr Saxon returned with Jack Gordon. The nurse had left. Jack fairly bristled with resentment as the master-at-arms pointed towards a chair.

'There's no need for you to stay, Mr Saxon,' Walter generously suggested. 'The room-search for the gun must be under way by now.'

'It's imperative that I remain,' said Mr Saxon with the air of a man who knew far more than he cared to say.

'Mr Gordon isn't going to attack me,' said Walter.

The master-at-arms drew in a long, eloquent breath.

'If you insist,' said Walter, 'you can take notes of what we say.' He took his notebook from under his pillow and held it out for Mr Saxon.

'I have my own,' said Mr Saxon haughtily.

'Just as you prefer.' Walter turned to Jack. 'Mr Gordon, I want to thank you for taking care of me last night. From what I hear, you haven't been treated with much gratitude. Did you get that, Mr Saxon, or am I going too fast?'

Mr Saxon did not look up from his notebook.

Walter continued, 'I was hoping for some help and it seems to me that you're the man most likely to give it.'

Jack looked dubious. 'I've told you everything I can.'

'Everything I asked you,' said Walter. 'Questions and answers don't always produce the information one requires. You and I both want to find the murderer of your wife. Time is getting short. After we dock tomorrow, the chance of catching him is practically nil. So I thought if the two of us could put our heads together, we might get some fresh ideas. Suppose we start by looking at the facts we have. You and your wife booked a passage on the *Mauretania* with the intention of making a lot of money playing cards with the American, Paul Westerfield.'

'I told you that already.'

'Of course,' Walter went on as if Jack's impatience had passed him by. 'You know, the thing that interests me is why you should have chosen this particular crossing and that particular passenger. I wonder whether it has any bearing on the mystery.'

'I shouldn't think so,' answered Jack. 'We chose the *Mauretania* because we hadn't worked on her before. We weren't known to the captain or the purser.'

'Your first trip on the *Mauretania*. I understand,' said Walter.

'And Westerfield was the obvious mark. A millionaire's son, sociable, a graduate in maths. I don't know what you're thinking, Inspector, but I can tell you for sure that Paul Westerfield didn't suspect us. He and the girl were perfect pigeons.'

On the other side of the room, Mr Saxon was grinding his teeth.

Jack continued, 'I suppose you're going to ask me if I can think of anyone else with a grudge against us.'

'It was on the tip of my tongue,' said Walter.

'Inspector, I've been through the ship since Sunday looking at people's faces, searching for anyone I know. I'm convinced that there isn't a man or woman on board who has played cards with me before. If you want my opinion, Kate was killed by some maniac who might as well have strangled any other woman.'

'The same maniac who shot me?'

It was a simple question, but Jack took it as a criticism of his theory. 'That's a point I hadn't thought of. Is it usual for a strangler of women to take up shooting as well?' He got no answer from Walter, so he went on, 'And how can I possibly describe last night as a similar crime? Whoever fired that shot picked his victim, didn't he? The question is why did he do it.'

'I've been thinking about that,' said Walter. 'I can only presume that he thought I was getting too close to the truth.'

Jack screwed up his face in disbelief. 'I beg your pardon.'

Walter glanced at Mr Saxon. He looked just as unconvinced.

'Well, he must have had some reason to shoot me.'

There was a moment's silence before Jack said, 'I don't wish to give offence, but I don't think you were the target. I think he was aiming at me.'

'You?' Walter's eyes opened wider. He looked slightly chagrined.

Jack nodded. 'I don't know how much you remember, Inspector. You turned away from me and caught it in the shoulder.'

'I'm aware of that,' said Walter, putting his hand to his wound.

'If you hadn't moved, it would have caught me. You fell back against me.'

'Oh.'

'It *is* more likely, isn't it?' Jack persisted. 'First Kate, and then me. Someone is out to kill me.'

Walter pondered this interpretation. 'If that really is the case, Mr Saxon probably saved your life by putting you under guard.'

From the scowl that Mr Saxon gave, this was a credit he would rather have done without.

Jack continued conveniently putting words into Walter's mouth. 'I expect you're going to say that this isn't the work of a maniac after all. I'm compelled to admit that you're right. It must be someone with a grudge against Kate and me, but who?'

'Who, indeed.'

Jack rubbed his chin.

Walter fiddled with the tassels on his bedspread.

Mr Saxon sighed intolerantly.

Jack clicked his fingers. 'Paul Westerfield. It all comes back to him. I must have been mistaken about him. He was sharper than I ever gave him credit for. What do you think, Inspector? Could he have realised we were trying to rook him?'

'You're the best judge of that,' said Walter with his flair for the neutral observation.

'Even so, murder is a very extreme reaction,' Jack went on. 'He must be unbalanced to take it so personally. He didn't say anything at the time, but I suppose if he harboured his resentment ... He gives the impression of being sane, but there's something about him ... Inspector, I think you should make inquiries into Paul Westerfield. You could find out where he was last night when you were shot.'

'There you are,' said Walter with satisfaction. 'I was sure I could rely on you to help.'

'You believe me?'

'I shall do exactly as you say.'

'Am I free to go, then?'

'I don't think we should detain you. What do you say, Mr Saxon?'

The grunt emitted by the master-at-arms could have meant anything, but it sounded less magnanimous than Walter.

'In that case ...' said Jack. He got up to leave.

'There is one other thing,' said Walter.

'Yes?'

'Would you ask the doctor to call and see me. I think I'm ready to get up.'

221

19

It was the happiest day in Marjorie Livingstone Cordell's life, or at least the happiest since she had married Livy. Barbara had told her after breakfast that Paul had asked her to marry him. At the height of that dreadful storm the previous evening those two young people had found a quiet corner of the ship and agreed to share the rest of their lives. It was very romantic. They had still been wearing their Pilgrim costumes. Marjorie could not imagine anything more charming or appropriate.

Paul had very properly told Barbara that he would ask for the permission of her parents. There was some uncertainty about whom he should approach, because Livy was not her natural father, but Marjorie had decided that this was not important. Livy could answer for them both, as this was a formality more easily settled between men. 'We'll let them feel important,' she told Barbara. 'Poor darlings, it's the only chance they get.' It was agreed that Livy would be in the smoking room at noon, and Paul would appear a minute later. They would say the necessary things and join the ladies for lunch. Livy would order a bottle of champagne.

Mother and daughter planned these excellent arrangements. When Marjorie talked to Livy he surprised her. He was not enthusiastic. 'I'd rather leave this to you, if you don't mind,' he said. 'It's not in my character to stand on ceremony. The boy can speak to you.'

'There's no reason to be nervous,' Marjorie told him. 'Good heavens, Paul has some reason to be nervous, but you haven't.'

'Really, Marje, I just want to sit here in our stateroom and read a book.'

Marjorie was shaken. 'That's a terrible admission, Livy. Barbara is our daughter. You agreed the day you married me to treat her as your own. Now she has made the great decision of her life, and you would prefer to ignore it. How could I tell her that? Put on your suit and a collar and tie and let's think of those two young people instead of ourselves.'

Livy knew better than to prolong the argument. He closed his book and started changing his clothes. He had just got into his dark suit when somebody knocked on the door.

'Are you decent?' called Marjorie as she went to open it.

'That's a matter of opinion,' grumbled Livy. 'I don't feel decent.'

Marjorie opened the door. 'Oh. Excuse me, I was expecting someone else. Livy, Inspector Dew is here.'

'Is it convenient?' asked Walter.

'Sure,' said Livy, coming forward. 'We were just going to keep an appointment, but we can give you a few minutes. Won't you come in?'

'You don't look too good, Inspector,' said Marjorie. 'We heard about the shooting last night. What a terrible thing. Where were you hit?'

'In the shoulder, ma'am.'

'What can we do for you?' asked Livy.

'I hope you can help me. It's about the young man who was at your table last night.'

'Paul?' said Marjorie. 'Is anything the matter?'

'I don't know. That is what I hope you can tell me.'

'What do you mean? Nothing has happened to him? My husband is meeting him downstairs in a few minutes. Paul wants to ask him for our daughter's hand –'

Livy cut in. 'Honey, shall we hear what the Inspector has to say?'

Walter cleared his throat. 'This is confidential, strictly confidential. How long have you known Mr Westerfield?'

'We met him in Paris two weeks ago,' said Livy. 'Barbara knows him better. They were in college together.'

'Barbara has a room at the end of the passage,' said Marjorie.

'He knows that, Marje.'

'Of course.'

'The question is,' said Walter, 'have you noticed anything strange in his behaviour?'

'What do you mean – "strange"?' asked Livy.

'Odd, peculiar, erratic.'

'You think he's some kind of nut?'

'Oh my God!' said Marjorie. 'He's about to be engaged to my daughter!'

'Is he?' said Walter. 'I must be mistaken, then. I do apologise.' He reached for the door.

'Just a minute,' said Livy. 'If there's anything against this boy we want to know about it.'

'We sure do,' said Marjorie.

'There's almost certainly nothing in it,' Walter tried to assure them. 'In fact, you can clear him of all suspicion if you know

223

where he was after the fancy dress parade last night.'

'He was *in* the parade,' said Marjorie. 'Don't you remember? Paul and Barbara came as Pilgrims.'

'Honey, he said *after* the parade,' said Livy.

'After it? Why, that was when the two of them went off on their own and he proposed to her.'

'We've only got Barbara's word for that,' said Livy.

'Oh, no!'

'What else have you got against the boy?' Livy asked Walter.

'Nothing definite at all. It was probably coincidence that he was playing cards with the lady who was murdered on the night she died.'

'So was my daughter Barbara,' said Marjorie, close to tears. 'You don't think she had anything to do with it?'

'Take it easy, Marje,' said Livy. 'Listen, Inspector, I was in the smoking room on Saturday evening. I talked to Paul. He was buying coffee for the lady and Barbara was at the table being kind to her. Is that the action of people with murder in their minds? I think you're making a mistake. No disrespect, of course.' He put an appeasing hand on Walter's shoulder.

Walter gave a yelp of pain.

'Shucks, I forgot,' said Livy as he jerked the hand away. 'Inspector, I'm sorry. Would you like to sit down?'

'No, it's all right. I was about to leave.'

Marjorie came across the room, her face quivering with emotion. 'But you can't leave yet. You haven't told us why you think Paul is strange.'

'Forget it, Marje,' murmured Livy.

'How can I forget it when you're about to give my only daughter to a crazy?' Marjorie sobbed.

'You blame me now?' said Livy, his voice pitched high with disbelief.

'You don't care about Barbara,' Marjorie declared as her anxiety turned to malediction. 'You don't even care about me. It's self, self, self with you, Livy Cordell, and I should have seen it years back. All you ever do is talk about the old days and make smart-ass remarks at my expense. Well, I've had enough of it.'

'Do you think *I* enjoy it?' retorted Livy.

Walter said, 'I must go.'

'No you don't' said Marjorie, reaching out to grab his arm –

fortunately his good one. 'I want the truth from you, Inspector. I've spent four years of my life married to a phony, and I don't intend to let my daughter wreck her life as well.'

'Did you call me a phony?' Livy demanded.

'Would you rather I called you a small-time crook who chucked it up to trap an innocent lady into marriage and live off her personal fortune?'

'If that's what you think of our marriage, let's forget it.'

'I will – don't you worry your head about that,' said Marjorie. The things she had said had done her good. She had triumphed over her distress. She turned to Walter and almost prodded him with her finger. 'Now for you. I want it straight, Inspector. What evidence do you have that Paul Westerfield is crazy?'

'None whatsoever,' said Walter, reaching for the door again. 'It was only an hypothesis. I wanted to test it on someone who knows the young man.'

'What did you say?'

'You'd better get out of here, Inspector,' said Livy. He opened the door and pushed him through it.

When it was closed, Marjorie found the words that had temporarily eluded her. 'Did you hear that? It was hypothetical. There's nothing wrong with Paul. Is that what he said?'

'Something like that,' said Livy.

'Why didn't he say so in the first place? What kind of people does he think we are?'

'After what you said, he doesn't need to think. He knows,' said Livy acidly.

'Honey, I didn't mean those things,' said Marjorie, her eyes welling with tears. 'What got into me? How could I have been so hurtful?' She opened her arms to embrace Livy, but he stood his ground.

'Wash your face,' he said. 'It's a mess.'

'Are you angry with me? I don't blame you, Livy.'

'I'm going to meet that boy.'

'Oh, Lord help us, yes. He must be waiting in the smoking room. You won't tell him about this?'

'I don't shoot off my mouth like some people I know.'

Marjorie sniffed tearfully. 'I guess I asked for that. Livy, how can we drink champagne with those two young people in love when something like this has happened? It's going to be just awful. They're going to look at us and think that's what they

225

could become. Won't you kiss and make up before we see them?'

Livy shook his head. 'Let's face it, Marje. You and I are finished. I'm doing this for Barbara's sake, not yours. See you at lunch.' He left the room.

Marjorie closed her eyes and moaned.

20

The last social event on the *Mauretania* was traditionally the concert. It was held in the main lounge, and almost everyone in the first class attended. Captain Rostron had a place reserved in the centre of the front row. For this evening the ship's band was elevated into an orchestra and they played the captain to his seat with a chorus from *HMS Pinafore* –

Then give three cheers, and one cheer more,
For the hardy Captain of the Pinafore.

The air of gaiety certainly owed something to a feeling of relief that this was the last evening at sea and no-one else had been strangled. If there was disappointment that Inspector Dew had not arrested anyone, it was generally agreed that his presence on the ship had discouraged any more fatalities. There had even been discussion in the concert committee of the possibility of including a second Gilbert and Sullivan chorus in the preliminaries –

When constabulary duty's to be done,
A policeman's lot is not a happy one.

But it was felt that any reference to Walter ought to be omitted out of respect to the victim of the strangler.

The entire programme after the interval was given to Signor Martinelli. Before the tenor appeared, Captain Rostron addressed the audience. He expressed the wish that they had enjoyed the crossing in spite of the unhappy incident at its outset. He paid tribute to Inspector Dew's unstinting efforts to investigate the crime and guarantee the safety of the passengers and crew. There was applause at this, and Walter standing at the back, gave a small bow in thanks. The injury to his shoulder was not mentioned.

At the conclusion of the concert, Paul Westerfield remarked to his fiancée Barbara, 'I didn't see your parents here tonight.'

'No', said Barbara. 'I haven't talked to them since lunch.'

'You don't have to tell me that,' said Paul, giving her hand a squeeze. 'I've been with you all but twenty minutes.'

She smiled back at him. 'Maybe they were tired. They seemed a little strained at lunch.'

'They were sad to be giving up their lovely daughter.'

'I don't think that's the way they look at it,' said Barbara.

The smoking room soon filled with its usual clientele and

others taking a last drink with friends made on the voyage. The talk was of New York and Quarantine and customs. Trunks still waited to be packed, but it was hard to leave the *bonhomie* for such depressing tasks.

Jack Gordon was still treated with suspicion by other passengers. He stayed close to Walter.

'Did you speak to the Cordells?' he asked as he handed Walter a scotch and soda from the bar.

'I did,' said Walter. 'It was unfortunate.' He told Jack about Barbara's engagement to Paul. 'They were not pleased to listen to our theory of insanity. I wish I hadn't mentioned it. I think young Westerfield is innocent.'

'I'm sure of it,' said Jack.

Walter raised his eyebrows.

Jack explained, 'While you were with the parents, I talked to Paul and Barbara. I asked them where they were last night when you were shot. He was proposing to her in the writing room. A steward switched on the light and saw them kissing. They were in their Pilgrim costumes. He switched off again and left them there. I've checked it with him. They have an alibi.'

'I wish I had known before I saw the parents.'

'A man in your occupation can't spare people's feelings, Inspector.'

'I suppose not.'

'You didn't spare me when you considered me a suspect.'

'I didn't know you were the victim's husband. You behaved suspiciously,' said Walter.

'You mean going down to the mortuary room to look at her?'

'Yes. But on reflection I admire you for it.'

'Why is that?'

'Because you managed to find the place. I've been down there myself. It's like a maze below decks. I lost my way coming back from the cells. I don't know how you found the mortuary room without assistance. You told me yourself that this is your first trip on the *Mauretania*.'

Jack said casually, 'It's no mystery. The Maury had a sister ship.'

'Do you mean the *Lusitania*?'

'Yes. They were built the same year. The design was practically identical.'

'And you were on the *Lusitania*?'

228

'I served on her, Inspector. I was known as Jack Hamilton then. I was a cabin steward. That was how I got to know my way about the lower decks. Two years of fetching and carrying would teach anyone the short cuts, believe you me. It was damned hard work.' Jack gave a satisfied smile. 'I used to watch the first class passengers reclining on their deckchairs and rack my brains to find a way of joining them. Then another steward told me about the boatmen in the smoking room, the professional card players who made a tidy living out of fleecing the millionaires. I watched them work, and I thought this is for me.' He gave a shrug. 'Now you know the story of my life.'

'And very interesting it is,' said Walter. 'I suppose you must have stopped working for Cunard some time before the *Lusitania* was torpedoed in the war.'

'No,' said Jack. 'I was aboard her and so was Kate. She was a stewardess, Katherine Barton. We were lucky to survive. We were among the last to leave the ship. We were in the water nearly an hour.'

'You were safer like that,' said Walter, shaking his head and sighing. 'Plenty of people died in the scramble for the lifeboats.'

Jack stared at Walter. 'Were you on the *Lusitania*?'

'Yes – with my father. We were first class passengers. I suppose every survivor has his story to tell. Father had his leg in plaster. We were the last to leave the dining saloon and I've always thought it saved our lives. Most of the lifeboats were smashed to bits. We waited on deck until the water reached us and we drifted clear before the end.'

'Kate and I almost went down with the ship,' said Jack. 'After the torpedo struck, we were ordered to make sure all the suites and staterooms on B Deck were vacated. The passengers were out all right, but Kate disturbed a thief in the act of emptying a jewel-case. The bastard hit her with the damned thing and knocked her out. He slammed the door and left her there to die. He passed me in the passageway, didn't say a word. I went back to see why Kate hadn't caught up with me and found her bleeding and out to the world. Somehow I brought her round and took her up on deck. That's *my* story, Inspector. The nice thing was that six weeks later Kate married me.'

'Did you ever find out what happened to the thief?'

'No. I don't know whether he survived. I wouldn't know him if I met him again. Hardly got a look at his face. He was a short,

229

stocky fellow in a dark suit. I was close to panic by then. I still get dreams about it, the ship listing unbelievably, and Kate unconscious in my arms and the dread that any minute the water will be flooding in.'

'That will be why you wouldn't stay below decks in the storm last night.'

Jack nodded. 'I'm not one of those who swore never to set foot on a ship again, or I wouldn't have chosen this way of life. But I'm going to make sure that if there ever is a next time, I'm not trapped below deck.'

'Understandably,' said Walter. 'It must have been a vile experience. You mentioned that you wouldn't recognize the thief if he survived, but I wonder if your wife got a better look at him.'

'She did, Inspector. She always said she'd know the blighter if she saw him again.'

'Did she indeed? That's interesting.'

'Why?'

'If he were on this ship, it would give him a reason for murdering her.'

'By God, you're right.'

'I wouldn't go so far as that,' Walter said, as if he regretted having mentioned the possibility. 'It's just another theory.'

It's the only one that fits the facts,' said Jack with a voice that needed no convincing. 'He came aboard at Southampton and had the shock of his life when he saw Kate. I expect he thought she had drowned when the *Lusitania* sank. He knew she was sure to recognize him in five days at sea, so he decided to murder her. He assumed she was travelling alone, so if he threw her in the sea, there would be nothing to connect him with her disappearance. He was a thief, so he would have no trouble breaking into her stateroom. He strangled her and put her through the porthole. Then things started to go wrong.'

'The body was recovered from the sea,' said Walter.

'That was the first thing. The second was the news that you were on the ship, a famous Scotland Yard detective. And the third was me – Kate's husband. He didn't know she was married until he heard the rumours and saw me talking to you. Perhaps he remembered my face. Whatever it was, he convinced himself that I would tell you what had happened on the *Lusitania*, and you – the man who caught Crippen – would lose no time arresting him. He was desperate, so he tried a desperate remedy.'

'He shot me,' said Walter.

'Yes. Whether he aimed at you or at me is immaterial.'

'I can't agree with that,' said Walter stiffly.

'I mean that from his point of view the result would be the same,' said Jack with a slight betrayal of impatience. 'It would stop me from telling you about the *Lusitania*. But it didn't. You're in possession of the facts now. What will you do next, Inspector?'

Walter looked into his drink as if the answer might be there. He said, 'There's my packing to be done.'

Jack's jaw gaped open. He said, 'We've got to find this man. He murdered my wife. He nearly murdered you.'

'Yes. But I doubt if he'll try anything else. And he can't get away. I'll see him in the morning.'

'Do you know who he is?' Jack asked in something like a gasp.

'I think I do,' said Walter with a modest smile.

'Aren't you going to tell me?'

'It's better if I don't. But thank you for your help.'

21

Alma looked at herself in the mirror and reached for the rouge. Her face looked spectral. She dreaded what was to come. She was waiting for Walter. She had slipped a note under his door asking him to come and see her. She was going to tell him that she had been mistaken. She did not love him. It had been infatuation.

Already she wished there was some way to retrieve the note before he found it. She was afraid of him. She should never have chosen to tell him here, in the stateroom where Lydia had died. Only the strength of her love for Johnny kept her from running away. She would rather die than lose her chance of marrying Johnny.

Yet she was tormented by guilt. In her mind she had been over and over the events that had entangled her life with Walter's and each time she could reach only one conclusion. If Walter had never met her, he would not have dreamed of murdering his wife. He would still be somewhere in England trying to find a way of continuing to work as a dentist. He was not and never had been the exquisitely glamorous figure her imagination had made him. He was decent and dependable and dull, dull, dull. There was not a spark of animation in him. It was depressingly obvious to Alma now that she had been bewitched not by Walter, but an idea. She had fallen in love with the prospect of running away with a man who had murdered his wife and abandoned everything – job, home and country – to be with her for the rest of his life. And now she did not want him. He was still dull beyond belief.

Somewhere she had read that almost all murderers were boring and pathetic individuals. She had not believed it. Surely Ethel Le Neve had not believed it. But what if Crippen had never been caught? What if Ethel had faced the rest of her life with him?

The murder had not made Walter glamorous. It had changed him in one way only: he was dangerous now. Dull and dangerous. A man who has murdered once and got away with it can never be ignored.

The knock came, startling her. She was wearing a silk blouse, and it was alive with fear. She took a deep breath and went to the door.

He stood with the note in his hand and his eyebrows raised questioningly.

Alma tried to summon a smile. She stepped aside to admit him, and closed the door. She said, 'Walter, I know we agreed not to meet unless there was some over-riding reason.'

'But there is a reason?'

She nodded. 'Please sit down. I had to find a way of talking to you before tomorrow. I don't know how to start. You've had so much more to face then we anticipated.'

He shrugged dismissively. 'It hasn't been so bad. It's occupied my mind.'

'But you were shot. Are you still in pain?'

'I wouldn't call it pain. Discomfort if you like.'

'I blame myself for what has happened,' Alma told him. 'I've had more opportunity than you to think things over.'

'Blame yourself for what?'

'Everything. Lydia's death.'

'We agreed to that together.'

'If you had not met me, you would never have considered it. You would never have set foot on this ship, never have done what you did in this God-forsaken room, never have been forced to pose as a policeman.'

Walter blinked in surprise. 'That's been no hardship. I've enjoyed it immensely.'

'Enjoyed it?'

'I've never been treated so well. I thought it would be difficult at first, but it wasn't. I didn't need to ask clever questions or discover hidden clues. Being a detective is just a matter of getting other people to talk. I'm a good listener – Lydia made sure of that. Well, if you let them talk they tell you everything and give you the credit for arriving at the truth.'

Alma thought she understood. She said, 'Yes, you must have been clever to have taken them in.'

'Taken them in?' repeated Walter as if the words were offensive.

'Convinced them that you knew what you were doing – that you were solving the mystery.'

'My dear, I have solved it. I know who committed the murder and I know why. That's what I'm saying. I'm a very good detective.'

'Walter, that's impossible.'

He leaned back in the chair with folded arms and said, 'You'll see.'

She looked at him, wondering whether his mind had snapped. He seemed to have been taken over by the identity of Dew. He believed he was the great detective. He believed he had solved the crime.

Was it conceivable that he was so far in the grip of this delusion that he intended naming himself as Lydia's murderer? And herself as his accessory? Was that to be the ultimate achievement of the false Inspector Dew?

Alma started talking with all the urgency and the conviction of a prisoner pleading for life. 'Walter, listen to me, please. I have no right to say this now. It shames me, but I have to tell you.' She took hold of one of his hands and crouched beside his chair looking earnestly into his eyes. 'I have changed. When I used to come to you in the surgery I idolized you. I had never spoken to a man so confident, so strong, so handsome. I must tell you that I was very inexperienced. The only men I had known outside my family were in books, romantic stories of the sort you find in lending libraries. You were just like one of those godlike creatures to me, with your sophisticated ways and your foreign-sounding name. And like every one of them at the beginning of a book, you seemed unattainable.'

'But we overcame that,' said Walter with an indulgent smile.

'Yes.' Alma swallowed hard. 'I convinced myself that it was the way to everlasting happiness. I was completely selfish. I believed I loved you, and nothing, not even your lawful wife, should be allowed to stand in our way. It was an obsession. All the girlish dreams, frustrations, fantasies that had stayed with me right through the war were focused on you. Walter, I'm twenty-eight, almost an old maid, and I conducted myself no better than a schoolgirl.'

'There's no need to be ashamed of that,' said Walter.

'There is – because I deluded myself and you. These few days at sea have brought me to my senses. How can I tell you this without hurting you?'

'You don't love me?' said Walter in a level voice.

Alma lowered her eyes.

'You don't want to live with me in America?'

She bowed her head.

'There is someone else?'

234

'Yes.' She started to sob.

He stroked her hair. He said, 'Thank you for telling me. To be honest, it's rather a relief. You see, I was feeling guilty over you. I took advantage of your feelings for me. Alone, I would never have plucked up the courage to do what I have. I faced it with your help. Like you, I have learned from the experience. Now I can stand alone.'

He was calm and in control. He meant what he had said. She leaned forward and kissed him lightly on the cheek. She said, 'What happened in this room will be our secret. I'll take it to my grave.'

Walter thanked her and stood up. He said, 'There are some trunks of Lydia's in the hold. When we are in America, would you take them? If they were unclaimed, there might be questions.'

'Of course I will,' said Alma. As he reached the door, she added, on an impulse, 'It was a perfect murder.'

'Almost,' said Walter. 'Good luck with Mr Finch.'

Alma was alone again.

22

Before 7am on Wednesday, the morning the *Mauretania* was due to dock in New York harbour, there was a meeting in the captain's quarters. Walter had been summoned by his cabin steward. In the room where he had first been asked to investigate the murder, he saw, besides the captain, the master-at-arms, Paul Westerfield II, his fiancée Barbara and, her face stained with tears, Marjorie Livingstone Cordell. The captain nodded towards a chair and Walter sat down. He was opposite Mr Saxon, who was giving him a withering look.

'Inspector, I'll be brief,' said Captain Rostron. 'Another passenger has disappeared. This lady's husband, Mr Livingstone Cordell, has not been seen since yesterday afternoon. He did not return to his stateroom last night. Mrs Cordell reported the matter at 0300 hours this morning and a search has been conducted by the master-at-arms and his staff. They are experienced at searching the ship. They know the places to look for stowaways. After more than three hours they have found no sign of Mr Cordell. For obvious reasons, I decided that you ought to be brought in at this stage.'

Walter nodded sagely.

'He's dead,' said Marjorie. 'Livy is dead. I know it.'

Barbara turned to her and said in a calm voice, 'Mother, you have no reason to say such things. He probably got into a card game in someone else's stateroom. People lose track of time when they have a good game going. He'll walk in for breakfast asking what the panic is about.'

'There's no panic,' Mr Saxon said aggressively.

Paul cleared his throat. 'I think we should put Inspector Dew more fully in the picture.' He said to Walter, 'Yesterday I asked Livy to allow me to marry Barbara. He seemed a little far away in his thoughts, but he gave his consent, and we all had a pleasant lunch with champagne to celebrate.'

'Did he drink much?' enquired Mr Saxon.

'Not that I recall. Maybe a glass and a half. He was quiet, but then he often is. When he does speak, it's generally a humorous aside. But I have to admit that he wasn't on his usual form.'

'He kept looking around the restaurant as if something was bothering him,' said Barbara.

Marjorie gave a tearful sniff. 'I might as well tell you all,

236

because I know the Inspector will drag it out of me if I don't. Before lunch – just after you came to see us in our room, Inspector – Livy and I had the first cross words in our marriage. We had three years of perfect bliss and then this happened – on the very day that these dear young people should have made us so happy. It was awful having to make a charade of being cheerful over lunch when we had just come from tearing each other to pieces.'

Barbara put her hand out to Marjorie and said, 'Mother, I had no idea. What was it about?'

'It doesn't matter, dear. Some dumb things I said to the Inspector. I was in a very nervous state.'

'Why?'

'Don't ask me now. It's not important – is it, Inspector?' Marjorie glanced imploringly at Walter.

He shook his head in support.

Captain Rostron had sensed something of significance in this. He decided it should not be brushed aside. He asked Walter, 'Is this right, Inspector? You interviewed Mr and Mrs Livingstone Cordell yesterday?'

'Quite correct, Captain.'

Everyone waited for Walter to amplify his statement. He did not.

The captain persisted. 'So there was some connection with your inquiry into the death of Katherine Masters?'

'I wouldn't go so far as to say that.'

Marjorie closed her eyes as if she were offering up a prayer.

'But you must have had a reason for going to see them, Inspector,' insisted the captain.

'Yes, indeed.'

'The shooting,' blurted out Mr Saxon. 'You saw them about the shooting.'

'That was it,' said Walter quickly. 'The gun. I was looking for the gun.'

Marjorie opened her eyes and said, 'Yes, that was what it was about. Livy's gun.'

'Your husband has a gun?' said the captain.

'Mother, what are you saying?' asked Barbara, shocked.

'Oh, God help me!' muttered Marjorie.

'And you suspected this, Inspector?' said the captain.

'More or less,' answered Walter evenly.

237

'I don't know how,' said Mr Saxon.

'Experience,' said Walter crushingly.

'But you didn't dispossess him of it?'

'No need,' said Walter. 'It wasn't there.'

'I guess he threw it in the sea,' said Marjorie. 'He was so careful over everything. My poor Livy. He tried so hard to bury his past, and I had to be the one who betrayed him to the Inspector.' She covered her face with her hands, while Barbara got up to comfort her.

'You didn't tell us you suspected him,' Mr Saxon said in a recriminating tone to Walter.

Captain Rostron intervened. 'Mr Saxon, it's not for you to question the way the Inspector conducts his investigation. I've no doubt that he had his reasons for acting as he did.' He turned expectantly to Walter.

'Several,' responded Walter.

Paul said, 'Would you kindly tell us what this is about?'

Walter shook his head. 'I would rather not distress the ladies.'

'It's all right,' said Marjorie dabbing at her eyes with a handkerchief. 'You have a right to know, Paul. I shall tell you myself. Yesterday the Inspector came to see Livy and me. As you know, he's been keeping close to us all for quite a while, and the strain was starting to tell. He's a great detective, Paul, and he knew the exact moment to move in. He very cleverly threw me into a panic by suggesting something totally bizarre. It was untrue, of course, and it doesn't matter now what it was, but it undermined us both. We started saying things we never meant to say. I called Livy a small-time crook. It was the one thing I should never have said, but I didn't know that at the time.'

Barbara broke in. 'Mother, this is absurd! Are you telling us Livy is a crook?'

'Honey, he used to be before we were married. He was a thief. He could open locked doors without any trouble at all. He used to travel on the ocean liners and help himself to money people left in their staterooms. Just enough to make a nice living. He would always leave plenty behind, and most of them never even noticed that any had gone.'

'Well, that beats everything,' said Paul, and there was the ghost of a smile as he shook his head slowly. 'He actually told me he'd done a lot of sea travel in his business. He said it was import-export.'

'His sense of humour,' said Marjorie. 'Inspector, would you like to tell them about the *Lusitania*?'

'As you wish,' said Walter. He repeated the story he had heard from Jack Gordon, with Livy now cast in the role of the thief who had knocked Katherine unconscious and shut her in the stateroom in the sinking ship.

'I knew nothing of this until yesterday after lunch,' said Marjorie. 'He told me the whole story. How he was amazed and horror-stricken to see the stewardess aboard this ship on the first evening out from England. He stepped out of our stateroom and she was walking towards him. He always thought she had died on the *Lusitania*, but there she was like some spectre coming to take revenge. He stepped back into the room and slammed the door. But that wasn't the worst of it.'

'He saw her playing cards with us?' said Barbara.

Marjorie nodded. 'Actually as he described it you had finished playing, and she was at the table with you, honey, deep in conversation. He asked Paul what was going on.'

'I remember,' said Paul. 'He must have thought she was telling Barbara about him – or about to. He sent me back to "break it up" – in his words.'

'He went to her stateroom and broke in,' said Marjorie, 'and waited for her.' She stopped and took in a deep breath.

Captain Rostron said gently, 'There's no need to go on, Mrs Cordell.'

Clearly the captain spoke for everyone. In the silence of the next few seconds the mental picture of Livy with his hands on Katherine's throat needed no description. It was so vivid that Barbara suddenly cried out, 'No, Livy! No, no!'

Paul went to her and held her in his arms. He asked the captain, 'Do you need us any more? I'd like to take the ladies outside.'

'I understand. But we still need to find out what has happened to Mr Cordell. If you could bear with us a moment longer, I'm sure Inspector Dew would want to hear Mrs Cordell's own account of what her husband said before he disappeared.'

'It would be very helpful,' Walter confirmed.

Marjorie said hesitantly. 'It was kind of personal.'

'It may help us to find him,' said the captain gently.

'I don't think so,' said Marjorie sadly, 'but I'll tell you. When he had finished telling me about everything that happened, how he shot the Inspector and threw the gun over the side, he said he was sorry for me and Barbara and Paul. He said he wished he had told me before about what happened on the *Lusitania*, but he had thought it was something between him and his own conscience. Then he gave me a kiss and walked to the door and turned and said something that told me for certain that I would never see him again.'

'What was that, Mrs Cordell?'

A tear slid down Marjorie's cheek. 'You wouldn't understand. He said he hoped it was true about your past life flashing through your mind because he wanted another look at those sublime ankles in the elevator at the Biltmore. Then he left me.'

The captain's eyes flicked downwards and as quickly up again. 'I see. It does sound rather conclusive. Thank you, ma'am. You have been remarkably brave in the circumstances.' He nodded to Paul, who got up and escorted Marjorie and Barbara from the room.

When they had gone, Mr Saxon asked the captain, 'It looks as if he took a jump, sir. Can we call off the search?'

The captain turned to Walter with eyebrows raised.

'Were the cabins searched?' asked Walter

The master-at-arms glared back. 'Of course not. The passengers were asleep. You can't do that in the middle of the night.'

Captain Rostron said, 'But you can by day. The Inspector's right, of course. We must carry on the search. See to it, would you, Mr Saxon?' As soon as the door was closed, he commented to Walter, 'A reasonably efficient man, but you can see why he would never make a good detective. Inspector, I must go up to the bridge. We must be within sight of Ambrose Light, and the pilot will be coming aboard. I would like to see you after we dock, if that is possible.'

'Most certainly,' said Walter.

When he went out on deck, it was already cluttered with cabin trunks. He weaved a way through and saw America, a heavier band of blue above the sea. He smiled.

The ship was stopped to let the pilot tender come alongside. People crowded the rails to see the diminutive figure climb the Jacob's ladder. The ship's whistle sounded. She was under way again, past Sandy Hook and through the Lower Bay towards The Narrows.

There was another stop at the place off Staten Island known as Quarantine. Immigration officers came aboard. With them came the press.

An assistant purser came to Walter's side and asked if he would meet the reporters. He declined. He said it was quite impossible for him to make any comment whatsoever. He said he was going to his stateroom to finish packing. But even as he turned to walk away, something flashed ahead of him. Keystone had got its picture of Inspector Dew.

Manhattan sparkled across the water and the *Mauretania* boomed its notice of arrival. First-time passengers excitedly identified the Woolworth Building and the other landmarks. The Statue of Liberty was closer and it dominated them all.

On the decks the final tips were handed to the stewards and people who had shared tables or played cards together said goodbye. Gangs of seamen removed the coamings from the hatches and began erecting deck gear. As the ship eased into Pier 88, the ship's whistle emitted a last reverberating blast.

Alma clung tightly to Johnny's arm as he explained the routine of debarkation. The luggage would be taken by the long-shoremen to points along the pier identified by letters of the alphabet. As *B* for Baranov was some seventy yards from *F*, they would be separated. 'But don't be alarmed, my dear. All you have to do is check your pieces of luggage and have them seen by one of the customs inspectors. When you're clear, wait for me. I'll have to see the Lanchester unloaded, but it won't take long, I hope. Then, I think, a good lunch in the Waldorf.'

In the next hour Alma discovered one of Johnny's failings: he was over-optimistic. They had crossed the gangway and taken positions by their letters, and no luggage had been brought to them except their cabin trunks. The Lanchester had not been lifted from the hold. But she enjoyed the excitement of the scene, the creaking blocks and winches, the throb of dynamos, the shouting gangs of men.

'Are you still waiting?'

She turned to find Walter at her side.'

'I thought I'd see if I could help,' he told her.

She was grateful. He had always treated her with kindness. 'It hasn't all arrived,' she told him. 'There are those trunks of Lydia's.'

'Three,' he said. 'They're over there.'

They were in a place she had not considered, a few yards beyond the letter *B*. Walter hailed a longshoreman and got them moved next to the things Alma had brought ashore. He found a customs man to check them. As it was being done they saw the Lanchester hoisted from the number 2 hold at the forward end. It looked very fragile suspended high above the pier, but it was lowered without mishap and Johnny was there to see the tackle removed without damage to the gleaming coachwork.

'Come on,' said Walter. 'Let's take the small things over.'

'What about your own luggage?'

'It can wait a while. I've got to go aboard again to see the captain.' He picked up a suitcase and escorted Alma past the numerous stacks of baggage to where the cars had been unloaded. Johnny was inspecting the bodywork for scratches. He caught sight of Alma and came to meet them.

'This is very decent of you, Inspector.'

'Not at all,' said Walter. 'Shall I put it in the back?'

'Leave it, old man. I'll have to unlock the boot.' Johnny felt in his pocket for the key.

'No need,' said Walter. 'I think you'll find it's open.' He gripped the handle of the luggage compartment and lifted up the lid.

'What the devil . . ?' exclaimed Johnny in amazement.

Inside the boot half-hidden by a blanket, was Livy Cordell. He sat up, blinking at the sunlight. 'I guessed it would be you, Inspector,' he said resignedly to Walter.

But Walter was looking at Alma. It was difficult to tell whether his smile registered satisfaction or surprise.

23

'Inspector, I can't express sufficient thanks,' said Captain Rostron. 'It's a triumph of detection. I think it even tops the Crippen case. The world shall hear of it.'

'Thank you,' said Walter, 'but I don't want any fuss.'

The captain smiled. 'I doubt whether we can prevent it. The New York press are waiting for you. You'll get a royal welcome, and you deserve it.'

'But I don't want it, captain.' Walter nervously fingered his collar. 'I want to be left alone. Is there any way I can avoid it?'

'Well, you need not go ashore.'

Walter's eyes widened.

'I mean it,' said the captain. 'You can remain in your state-room if you wish.'

'I can't stay there for long, or I'll get taken back to England.'

'Ah,' said the captain, holding up a finger. 'I was about to come to that.'

'To what?' said Walter in alarm.

'Another whisky? I'm afraid I'm going to ask you to return with me tomorrow.'

'What?'

'Let me put it this way. I know you're not a policeman.'

Walter took a gulp of whisky.

'– since you retired, I mean,' explained the captain. 'So it's a shocking inconvenience, I'm sure, but what else can I suggest? Cordell has to be returned to England to stand trial, and as you're the man who built the case against him –'

'But he's an American,' said Walter. 'Can't he stand trial here?'

'Don't you remember your law?' said the captain with a smile. 'He committed an indictable offence aboard a British ship on the high seas. He's got to be taken back. Of course, I'll ask the police to come aboard at Southampton and take him off. No need for you to be on show again. But we *will* need you for the magistrates' court. Frankly, there's no case against Cordell without your co-operation.'

'But I made arrangements.'

'You'll be compensated generously.'

Walter stared at him in silence.

'There won't be much delay,' the captain said, still trying to soften the blow. 'This is the quick turn-round. We sail **again** tomorrow.' He put his hand on Walter's arm. 'You'll get a marvellous welcome from the police.'

PART SIX

The Immigrant

1

At midnight of the following day, the *Mauretania* was towed into the fairway of the North River and swung to face the ocean again. For this eastbound crossing she carried fewer passengers; the season of vacations in Europe was virtually at an end for 1921. The passenger list was largely composed of businessmen. In the second class appeared the name *Mr Walter Brown*.

Walter had his meals delivered to his stateroom. He took his exercise at times when he knew the deck would be deserted. He was famous now. The fascinating story of Chief Inspector Dew's unmasking of the *Mauretania* Strangler had made headlines in New York. His picture had been splashed across the front of every paper in the City.

On the captain's orders, elaborate precautions were arranged to spare Walter from inquisitive passengers and the possible intrusion of the press. His only visitor apart from cabin stewards was the doctor, who came each day to dress the injured shoulder. Walter expressed his thanks, but said he felt guilty taking up the doctor's time because as far as he could see the wound had healed.

The doctor said, 'Certainly, it's doing nicely, but we must avoid the smallest risk of infection. You'll need to be completely fit by the time we reach Southampton. You won't want a tender shoulder when the reporters mob you.'

If Walter had any doubts about the reception he could expect in England, they were buried under the mass of telegrams delivered from the wireless room. There were congratulations, invitations and lavish offers from the Fleet Street papers for exclusive interviews.

On Saturday the doctor told him, 'Have you heard? The *Daily Sketch* has found a chap in Worthing who claims you aren't Inspector Dew at all. He says *he's* the man who arrested Crippen. The things people will do to get in the papers!'

The same evening Walter had a reassuring visit from the captain. 'You're comfortable, I trust? No one has disturbed your privacy?'

'Very comfortable and very quiet, thank you, Captain.'

'Good. I expect you've heard about the fuss ashore.'

'A little.'

'Pretty daunting, I should think. Well, Inspector, someone is aware of your predicament. I've received this telegram from the Public Prosecutor's office.'

Walter examined it. *Kindly inform Inspector Dew arrangements made to disembark Cherbourg to avoid press harassment.*

He said, 'That's very considerate of them.'

'Dammit, that's the least they can do considering the inconvenience this has caused you,' said the captain. 'I expect to reach Cherbourg on Tuesday morning. Presumably they'll have a man to meet you.'

The rest of the crossing was uneventful, and in consequence seemed slow. Walter was on deck late on Monday evening when the light of Bishop Rock appeared on the horizon. Soon after midnight he saw the incandescence of the south coast of England from the port side. Then he went to bed.

In the morning it was raining. Cherbourg was scarcely visible from the breakwater where the passengers transferred to the tender that conveyed them to the inner harbour. Walter pulled up the collar of his overcoat and kept away from anyone who looked like the press. Any thoughts he may have entertained of disappearing among the teeming hundreds on the harbour were scotched at once. A figure in a uniform approached him as he stepped ashore and said in an English accent, 'Excuse me, sir, I believe I am right in saying that your name is Walter Baranov.'

Walter's facial muscles tightened, but he did not deny it. He gave a nod.

'So glad to have found you,' said the man. His uniform was not that of a police officer. It was the peaked cap, high-buttoned tunic and gaiters of a chauffeur. 'Would you come this way? There's just the formality of customs. Your luggage will be collected.'

Walter followed him across the harbour to the customs hall. They were allowed to pass immediately.

Outside, they crossed a pebbled courtyard to a black limousine.

'Where are you taking me?' Walter asked.

The chauffeur opened the rear door. 'Would you kindly step inside, sir?'

Walter inclined his head, put his foot on the running-board, and froze.

A woman was sitting inside. She said, 'Walter darling, or do I say Inspector?'

It was Lydia.

2

'The telegram was very clever, don't you think?' she asked him as they sat together at the open tables outside a bar-restaurant in Caen. 'I even took the trouble to find out the name of the Public Prosecutor, in case there was a query, but they accepted it like lambs.' She laughed. 'I dare say it gave you a bit of a turn, darling.'

'Yes,' said Walter. He was still looking pale. 'How did you find out that I was masquerading as Dew?'

'I saw your picture in the paper. It gave me quite a shock. The first time I saw it, I just turned to jelly, seeing my own sweet husband in the *Daily Mail*. Then I saw the name Inspector Dew underneath and I thought, well, everyone is supposed to have a double, and this was yours. But a couple of days later the papers were saying someone else had claimed to be Walter Dew, and if he was, then who was the mystery man in the photograph? That was when I knew for sure. I thought, heavens, what has my Walter been up to? It was obvious that you were going to be in the most awful spot when the ship reached Southampton. The press are vultures, darling, to say nothing of the police. So I sent my little telegram. And now they'll never find their mystery man.'

'I hope not. I'm grateful, Lydia.'

She held his hand tightly. 'Darling, it was the least I could do after you had been so gallant.'

'Gallant?'

Lydia giggled. 'Still the same Walter, so utterly unassuming! Sweetheart, what could be more gallant and romantic than a husband who kisses you goodbye and then secretly arranges to join you on the ocean crossing because he cannot bear to live without you? It was very touching, and dreadfully tragic that I wasn't on the ship at all.'

Walter frowned. 'But you were. I saw you go aboard. Your things were in the stateroom. I waited there for hours.'

She nipped his cheek between her thumb and finger. 'Incorrigible man. I can't think what you had in mind.' She sighed. 'And to think I missed it. Darling, this is what happened. I moved into my stateroom as you noticed, and unpacked my things. The ship moved off, but I remembered your advice about *mal de mer*, and stayed away from lunch. I sat on the bed and read a paper I had bought.'

'I saw it on the bed.'

'But did you read it, Walter? I did, and I had a fit! On the front page was the news that Charlie Chaplin was about to arrive in England! He was on the *Olympic*, two days from Southampton. And there was I crossing the other way to see him! Oh, the panic! I was in tears. I ran out on deck to see how far we had come. It was *miles*. What could I do? I just *had* to get off that ship, or my chance of getting started in films was nil. How do you think I managed it?'

Walter shook his head. 'You didn't leave the ship at Cherbourg. One young lady did, but she was the only one.'

'No, darling, your resourceful Lydia had already left by then. I went on the pilot boat. It came alongside while I was frantically wondering what to do. I simply got aboard with some people who should have got off when the bell went at Southampton. There wasn't even time to collect my luggage.'

'I know.'

Lydia squeezed his hand again. 'My poor Walter! You must have been beside yourself with worry. Did you think I'd fallen over the side? What did you do – raise the alarm?'

He said truthfully, 'I sat and waited for you. I assumed you were on the ship because your things were there.'

She rolled her eyes. 'I know what you were thinking – that I had company on the ship. Oh Walter – what kind of woman do you think I am?'

He didn't answer. He said, 'When it got to midnight I went back to my cabin in the second class.'

'Where you were registered as Inspector Dew?'

'Mr Dew. They assumed I was the Inspector.'

She shook with laughter. 'And you were too polite to deny it. Walter, you're adorable. Whatever made you use another name?'

'I intended to surprise you.'

Her face lit up. 'What a beautiful idea! Darling, I'm overwhelmed. Do you know, I can't imagine anything more romantic – and bless me if I wasn't stupid enough to spoil it, all for nothing!

'Why – didn't you see Chaplin?'

'Oh, I went to the Ritz where he is staying, and they let me in, eventually.'

'Did he remember you?'

'Of course! As if it were yesterday.'

'Did he offer to put you in a film?' Walter asked enthusiastically.

Lydia sighed. 'That's the difficulty. He would have taken me back to Hollywood like a shot, but there is the problem of my eyes.'

'Your eyes? I didn't know there was anything the matter with them.'

'There isn't, except for their colour. It seems that brown eyes show up black and it ruins the film.'

'I've never heard of that before.'

'Nor had I, but that was that. You don't think he made it up, do you?'

Walter tapped his chin as if he had thoughts of his own.

'What does it matter any more?' said Lydia, downing the last of the wine. 'It's taught me something, darling. I'm married to a man who values me. I intend to keep him close to me for ever.'

'What will we do with ourselves?' asked Walter.

'Obviously we can't go back to England until the fuss dies down. I thought we'd go to Paris – I'm completely out of clothes – and then tour France in the motor car.'

'And after that?'

'I don't know, darling. Can you think of anything?'

Walter said on an inspiration, 'How about a sea cruise?'